THE BLUE POOL MURDERS

DORSET CRIME
BOOK 7

RACHEL MCLEAN

ACKROYD
PUBLISHING

Ackroyd Publishing

ackroyd-publishing.com

CHAPTER ONE

CHRISTINA SMILED as Nick swung her hand, keeping pace with their footsteps like a pendulum. It was chilly today and she'd forgotten her gloves, but she was trying to ignore that as she felt his fingers wrapping around hers. It wasn't just the first time they'd gone for a walk together; it was the first time she'd brought him home to Dorset.

He slowed pace, forcing her to slow too, and frowned.

"What's that?" he said.

"What's what?"

"That birdsong. I'm trying to place it."

She shrugged. "No idea. D'you know birdsong?"

He swung her hand and moved off again. Christina sped up herself, anxious to keep up the pace. The brisk walking was the only thing keeping her warm.

"Not really," he said. "But I thought you might. Seeing as you live down here and that."

"Lived."

"You're here now, aren't you?"

"Only for the holidays. I'll be back in a couple of weeks. We both will."

He sniffed. Christina knew that Nick tended to travel around in the holidays, avoiding his parents' home in Edinburgh. He'd picked Bristol for uni, pretty much as far as he could get from them.

She squeezed his arm. "I'm looking forward to going back. It's dull here."

"It's lovely here."

She shivered. How could Nick think it was lovely down here in Dorset? Her whole life she'd been aching to escape. To live somewhere you could buy vapes on a Sunday morning and get a curry after 9pm on a Friday. To live somewhere where all your neighbours didn't know your business.

"It's not so lovely when you have to live here."

They turned a bend in the path and the view of the pool opened up in front of them. The Blue Pool was one of the few places around here that she liked. It was different from the landscapes across the rest of the Isle of Purbeck. Instead of miles of gorse and open views towards the coast, there were conifers on all sides and a feeling of intimacy. The pine needles on the ground muffled all sound, reminding her of the silence after snowfall. Here, she could forget she was just two miles from the home she'd been born and grown up in. The home her deathly dull sister would stay in all her life, if she had her way.

They were on the top path, on the far side of the pool from the tea room. The view of the pool had brought Nick to a halt, as she'd known it would. She allowed herself to stop alongside him and look down at the water. It was mid-blue today, not the bright shade of turquoise it reached on sunny days.

"What's that?" She pointed towards the water.

"What's what?"

"There's something in the pool."

"It's just a log or something, isn't it?" Nick seemed unbothered.

But Christina had been here enough times to know that what she was looking at wasn't a log. It was too misshapen, too thick.

She released his hand and took the side path that led steeply down towards the water.

"Are we supposed to go that way?" Nick called after her.

"It's fine." She didn't look back at him, too focused on maintaining her footing. "I've been here a thousand times."

She heard scrambling behind her, interspersed with the occasional *ouch*. She smiled. Nick would soon learn that it wasn't all perfect here in the countryside.

At the bottom of the hill, Christina paused for breath. She turned to see Nick halfway down the slope, his arms flailing and his city shoes sliding on the needles.

Don't fall, she thought. If he hurt himself, it would be hours before help made it out here.

"Stand up straight," she told him. "Act like you don't think you're about to fall over."

He looked up, wobbled, then reached out to grab a branch. "But I do."

She shook her head. In Bristol, Nick had seemed sophisticated. The older man from the city, confident and knowing.

But here... here he seemed somehow smaller.

She felt her heart dip. Was she going to have to dump him, already? Or should she wait until they got back to uni, hope that he regained his charm there?

At last he was at the bottom of the hill. He ran towards

her, propelled by momentum rather than will. He crashed into her and flung his arms around her to steady himself.

"Ow!"

"Sorry." Nick had a fist clenched into the fabric of her waterproof. He wasn't wearing a waterproof, but the same woollen coat which had seemed so cool in Bristol. It seemed silly here.

"Come on," she said. "I want to see what it is."

"Are you sure? Maybe we should call someone. That woman in the tea room looked like she knew what she was doing."

Christina frowned at him. "It'll be fine." She turned and made for the water, close to where she'd seen the shape.

As she emerged from the woods and got a clear view of the pond, she felt her breath catch.

She stopped in her tracks.

Nick carried on, striding ahead of her like he was master of the landscape rather than a boy who'd just come close to falling down a small hill.

"Nick." Christina could hear the tremor in her voice.

"Come on," he replied. "You wanted to look." His gaze was on the forest floor, his pace unbroken.

"Stop," she told him. She advanced a few steps, forcing herself to look at the object.

Nick turned to her. "You OK?" He cocked his head. "You've gone pale."

"Look at it," she told him. "Have you even looked at it?"

"Of course I've—" he turned. "Oh."

"Oh, indeed."

She could smell it now. It was like— it was like nothing she'd ever smelled before. Like blocked up drains mixed with the smell of the dead rats her cat Holly left in the shed at the bottom of her parents' garden. Like the meat processing plant on the road out to Bath mixed with the time her sister had puked all over Christina's duvet after getting drunk two Christmases ago.

"Don't go any closer," she told Nick.

"I wasn't planning to."

She took a step back. The smell was sharp, like a blade cutting into her nostrils. She felt certain it would never leave her.

"What do we do?" Nick asked. He'd taken a few steps back too, but was still staring.

Christina swallowed. She allowed herself a final look at the shape floating in the shallows of the Blue Pool.

A body. Face down in the water, and not... not exactly the shape she expected a dead body to be in. But it was a body alright.

"Maybe he's alive?" Nick suggested.

"It might not be a he," she told him. "And that smell... whoever that is, they're not alive."

"No." Nick turned to her. She saw the fear in his eyes. Was he expecting them to be next? Did he think a killer was about to emerge from the bushes and shove them into the water?

This body had been here for days. There was no chance of them being next.

She swallowed. "We call my aunt," she said. "She'll know what to do."

"Your aunt? Not 999?"

Christina nodded. "Gail. She works with the police. It's not an emergency, is it? Besides, you know what 999's like these days."

He walked towards her and put a hand on her shoulder.

"OK." His face was full of sympathy she wasn't sure she wanted to receive. "Let's call your aunt."

CHAPTER TWO

"Hey, sweetheart." Lesley leaned over Elsa's shoulder and gave her a kiss on the cheek. Elsa was at the kitchen table, her phone in one hand and a spoonful of cornflakes dripping into a bowl in the other.

"Hey," Elsa replied, her tone vague.

"You OK?" Lesley went to the coffee machine and poured herself a cup. One of the things she loved about Elsa was her ability to make fantastic coffee before Lesley was barely able to open her eyes.

"Fine."

"You don't sound it."

Elsa let her phone fall to the table. She plunged the spoon in her mouth and pulled a face. She pushed the bowl away. "Soggy."

"How long have you been sitting there letting your cornflakes turn to mush?"

Elsa looked at her watch. "Fifteen minutes. Maybe more."

"The whole time I was in the shower."

"Pretty much."

Lesley placed her coffee on the table and sat down opposite the woman she still referred to as her girlfriend, despite the fact that she would be much more than that in just five days' time.

"Talk to me, Els. Tell me what's up."

Elsa sighed. She glanced at her phone then turned it face down between them. "Another email."

"From a potential client?"

A nod.

Lesley took Elsa's hand. It was limp. "I'm sorry, love."

Elsa sniffed. "It's not your fault."

"There'll be more clients, I'm sure. You're a great lawyer, they—"

"That's the twelfth one."

Lesley leaned back. "The same thing, every time?"

Elsa pursed her lips. "They call or email telling me they need representation, we have the initial chat, then within days they tell me they've found someone else."

"The twelfth?"

A slow nod. "The twelfth."

"I don't know what to say." Lesley tried not to show her worry when Elsa talked about her fledgling business. It was barely getting off the ground. She knew that before joining Nevin, Cross and Short in Bournemouth, Elsa had been a successful lawyer in London. And she didn't want Elsa going back there.

The door to the kitchen opened: Sharon, Lesley's daughter.

"Morning." Sharon stopped in the doorway. "Oh. You had a row? Cold feet are normal, you know?"

Elsa gave a hollow laugh and turned to Sharon. "No cold

feet here. I love your mum and I have every intention of marrying her on Saturday."

Sharon put her hand to her forehead in an exaggerated gesture of relief. "Thank God for that. Cos you wouldn't believe how much work it took to convince the Goldjars to play at the reception."

Elsa patted the bench next to her and Sharon sat down. Elsa put an arm around her. "I know, love. And we appreciate it. Don't we, Lesley?"

"We do." Lesley smiled at her daughter. She loved that Sharon had thrown herself into the preparations for her wedding to Elsa. Herself, she'd rather have gone for a quiet affair at the registry office, the minimum number of witnesses and a trip down the pub afterwards. But Sharon wanted to make a thing of it, and she wasn't about to get in her daughter's way.

Sharon stood up. "OK. I need to get a shower. Don't you two go doing anything daft like calling off the wedding while I'm gone."

"We would never." Lesley grabbed Elsa's hand and squeezed it. She looked into her fiancée's eyes. The conversation that Sharon had interrupted wasn't over.

Sharon gave them each a grin in turn then hurried out of the room. Lesley felt her muscles unclench.

"So," she said, eyeing Elsa. "Do you want to talk about it?"

"I don't see what there is to talk about. My new firm is a flop before it's even started. I guess I could get a job with the CPS..."

"Don't you even think about it. Defence lawyering is in your blood. You'd hate being a prosecutor."

Elsa trailed her spoon through the cornflake mush.

"You're right. But we can't carry on living off your police salary, the three of us."

"Trevor'll be paying me maintenance, once the Child Support Agency have given him a good squeeze, and you know my DCI's salary is generous. We'll be fine." Lesley hesitated. "But this isn't really about money, is it?"

"No."

"Els, please talk to me. I'm worried about you. The fact you're losing clients, is it related to who you worked for at your old firm?"

"Arthur Kelvin, you mean. Don't beat about the bush."

"Arthur Kelvin. Could he be warning people off?"

Elsa pulled in a long breath. "That's the only thing I can think of. Now I've left the firm that represents him, he doesn't want me representing anyone else."

"Is he trying to force you to go back to work with Aurelia?"

"That'll never happen. I'll get work in London before I do that."

Lesley felt her skin go cold. "London?"

Elsa looked at her. "Don't worry, I'm not planning on moving us there. I'll commute."

"But it's a two-hour train ride."

"Not every day. I've been talking to a couple of old friends. I can do a combination of in-person and remote working."

Lesley knew it wouldn't work like that, not for a criminal defence lawyer. If Elsa was working for clients in London, she needed to be available for them in London. Often at short notice.

But they were settled in Dorset. Lesley had put down

roots. She'd built a team she could trust. And Sharon was enjoying sixth form college here.

"We'll find a way to get your firm working, love," she said.

"I'm not so sure."

"It's just twelve potential clients."

"Twelve out of a possible fifteen. I only have three clients right now. That's not enough to support a firm."

"It'll grow."

Elsa was still staring at the cornflakes. She didn't meet Lesley's eye.

"Els," Lesley said. "Is there something you're not telling me?"

Elsa's spoon stopped moving. She said nothing.

"Els? Please. You can tell me."

Elsa looked up. "If I tell you this, promise you'll hear it as my fiancée, and not as a DCI."

Lesley swallowed. "I promise."

"You sure?"

"Yes." Lesley wasn't sure if she was telling the truth. It depended on what Elsa was about to say.

"OK." Elsa paused. She pushed the bowl away. "He's been threatening me."

"Kelvin."

Elsa's gaze flicked up to Lesley's face then back to the table. "Yes."

"In what way? Why haven't you reported it?"

Elsa pushed her chair back and looked at Lesley. "I knew you'd do this."

"Do what?"

"You've immediately engaged copper mode. You want me to go to the police, to help you arrest Kelvin."

"That's not what I meant. But if you reported it, then he wouldn't—"

"That's not how it works and you know it. The man's careful. Nothing he has said to me could be used as concrete evidence. It's all inferences and hints. He knows what he's telling me, and I know what he's saying."

"Has he threatened you with physical violence?"

"Of course not. Not overtly, anyway."

"But he's insinuated..."

"Yes."

Lesley leaned across the table and put a hand on Elsa's arm. She felt it stiffen. "Elsa, you're a criminal lawyer. You're part of the system. Surely you can see that reporting him—"

Elsa stood up, sending the cornflakes crashing to the floor. "No, Lesley. I'm not going to be the one who puts her life at risk so you can hook the biggest fish in the pond."

"That's not what I—" Lesley's phone rang. "Shit. Sorry." She hit ignore.

"Answer it. It might be work."

"I don't care if it's work. I'm worried about you."

Elsa stood over her. Her fists were clenched, her face pale.

Lesley stood up. She didn't reach out, didn't want to feel Elsa push her away again. "I'm just... I worry about you. Arthur Kelvin isn't to be toyed with. If he's decided he doesn't want you around..."

"If he wanted me dead, Lesley, he would have done it months ago."

Lesley tried to swallow the lump in her throat. Her phone rang again.

Fuck off. She switched the phone off.

"I'll be fine, love." Elsa's body had relaxed. Her hand was on the table and her back was less stiff.

Another phone rang: Elsa's, on the table. She reached down and turned it around. "Why's your office ringing me?"

Lesley followed Elsa's gaze. "Maybe one of your clients..."

"I'll take it."

Lesley nodded. If this was work for Elsa, then that came first.

Elsa picked up the phone. She held Lesley's gaze as she answered the call. She frowned.

"DC Brown?"

Lesley watched her girlfriend's face. Why would Stanley be calling Elsa? If they needed a lawyer, the call came from the custody officer.

Elsa held out the phone. "It's for you."

Lesley took the phone from her. "Stanley? Everything OK?"

"Sorry, boss. I've been trying to get you on your mobile. I hope you don't mind, but I thought this number—"

"Just tell me what's so urgent."

"A body's been found, boss. At the Blue Pool."

"A body?"

Lesley watched as Elsa's eyes widened. "When?" she asked the DC.

"Just under an hour ago. The witness is a student. She's Gail Hansford's niece. She called Gail, knew it would be quicker than 999."

"Sensible girl. I'll be right there." Lesley gave Elsa an apologetic look. Elsa replied with a nod. If there was one thing that worked between them, it was that they both understood that everything stopped when there was a major crime.

"And... boss?" Stanley continued, his voice hesitant.

"Yes?"

"We think we've got an ID."

"Good. Anyone we know?"

"You could say that."

"Who, then?"

"It's him, boss. It's Arthur Kelvin."

CHAPTER THREE

"It's fucking freezing here," DC Mike Legg said. "How long did she say she'd be?"

Gail was roping off the area immediately around the body, with the help of her second in command Gavin. Their colleague Brett was back at the van, gathering up supplies. It was a fair walk down here, but she'd done worse.

"She's in Bournemouth," replied DC Stanley Brown. "So I reckon..." He pulled out his phone.

"Thirty to forty minutes," Gail said. "It'll take that long to get here from Lesley and Elsa's."

She could sense the two DCs exchanging glances behind her. Gav gave her a grin which she returned with raised eyebrows.

"Ah. Yeah, thanks," said Mike.

"You want to warm up, give us a hand with this cordon," Gail told him.

"Will do." Mike approached and took a roll of tape from her. "You got here first, then?"

"I did." She looked up, across the water and towards the

tea room where her niece Christina had been taken. She wished she was up there, comforting the poor girl, but she had a job to do. And she knew PC Hughes was with her. Roy was an experienced Family Liaison Officer and would take good care of her till Lesley arrived.

"No Dennis today?" She aimed the question at no one in particular as she placed the last stretch of tape. The landowner had closed the site so they didn't need to create a larger cordon, but she was still keen to place this smaller one around the body, and keep careless police officers from getting too close. PC Mullins was up at the entrance, turning the public away and keeping a log of anyone who came in or out.

"He's off sick again," Mike replied.

"He's been doing a bit of that lately," Gail replied.

"Yeah."

"Anything I should be worried about?"

"No idea. He calls the boss, she doesn't tell us what's up."

"You haven't been to see him?"

"This is the sarge we're talking about. He'd rather be arrested than have us turn up on his doorstep."

Gail wrinkled her nose. She could see Brett coming down the hill, carrying two pilot cases. She knew he'd have to disappear into the forest and skirt the water before he reached her. This was all going to take a long time.

The body was still where Christina had seen it in the water. Gail knew better than to move it before the pathologist got here. And with him floating out there, it was going to be impossible to erect a tent. She just hoped that Brett had brought waders as part of the kit. And that the pathologist got here quickly, so they could remove the body from the water.

Still, at least it was cold. It might make her fingers feel like they'd fallen off, but it helped preserve the body.

At last Brett arrived. He placed the two cases on the ground a distance away from the water and stretched, his fists in the small of his back.

"This is going to be fun," he said. "You sure there's no way to bring the van round here?"

"Seems not," Gail replied. "I spoke to the owner when I got here, but he said the only way was the one you took."

"Great." He huffed out a breath. "I've brought waders for the three of us. Figured it would make sense to start looking in the shallows asap."

"Good idea." Gail trudged up the slope towards him and grabbed a pair of waders. A few minutes later, she was suited up and in the water up to her thighs. The waders were made from thick latex and helped keep the cold out to some extent, but she still felt like she was taking a dip in the Arctic.

"He's watching," Gav muttered, standing behind her.

"Who?" She didn't look up.

"The manager."

Gail nodded. "Let him look. He seemed like a sensible bloke to me, won't come yomping down here."

"He won't be happy at losing business."

Gail turned to Gav. "I think we've got bigger things to worry about than that, don't you?" She pointed at the body. "You know who this is?"

Gav grimaced. "Arthur Kelvin."

"Exactly." Gail had turned the man briefly to take a look at his face and been shocked when she'd recognised him. "However he died, there's going to be consequences. And they won't be good."

CHAPTER FOUR

"I'LL PROBABLY BE LATE BACK, love. Sorry." Lesley grabbed her coat and turned back to give Elsa a kiss.

Elsa felt her shoulders dip. "We're supposed to be seeing the caterers tonight. Final approval on the menu."

Lesley's face fell. "Oh, shit. I'm sorry. Look, I'll try and get back. But if I can't, do you mind...?"

"No." It wasn't as if Elsa had anything else to do. "It's fine."

Lesley put a hand on her arm. "I'm really sorry. But you know what it's like with a murder case."

Elsa gave a tight nod. "I hope it's a straightforward one. That you get an ID quickly."

Lesley's jaw tensed. "I'll let you know when I'm going to be home. And yes, let's hope this is an easy one."

She turned away and pulled the door behind her. Elsa stood in the hall for a few moments, listening to her fiancée's car start up outside.

"Sorry, I've got to go too. Get the bus." Sharon was behind her.

"OK." Elsa turned to the girl and gave her a hug.

"I can come with you to the caterers if you'd like."

"You sure?"

Sharon nodded, her eyes bright. "It'll be fun. A posh meal on a Monday night."

Elsa allowed herself a smile. She knew she should be happier, what with getting married on Saturday. But the business worries were bothering her. "Thanks, sweetie. It'll be fun."

"Yeah." Sharon pulled the door open and was gone, leaving Elsa alone.

The flat was quiet. Elsa shuffled through to the kitchen and asked Alexa to turn on the radio. Anything to break the silence.

It was Radio 1: Sharon's choice. Elsa switched to Radio 4 and wandered through to the living area.

Her limbs heavy, she slumped onto the sofa.

She had three clients. She'd been touting for business for ten months now and all she had to show for it was three clients. The fees she'd earned hadn't even covered the startup costs, and she'd contributed nothing to the household expenses since leaving Nevin, Cross and Short. Lesley repeatedly told her it wasn't a problem, but it didn't sit well with her. After all, this was her flat and she was supposed to be the one paying the mortgage.

It would be Lesley's flat too, next week. They'd arranged for a transfer of title to coincide with the first working day after the wedding. Elsa had never shared her finances with another person before. She knew it was the right thing to do, that it made sense financially and legally. But there was something about it that daunted her.

Her phone was on the kitchen island behind her, along

with the cup of coffee that was going cold and the cornflakes that were destined for the bin.

She stood up and went to the island. She gulped down some coffee then pulled a face. Not cold, but still tepid.

She switched on the coffee machine and picked up her phone, idling through emails while she waited for her drink to brew.

He couldn't do this to her. She'd legitimately quit and there'd been nothing he could do to stop her. He was represented by the firm, not her, and as soon as she'd handed in her notice, she'd no longer been his lawyer. At the time, she'd expected it to be the biggest relief of her life.

But he still had his hooks in her. He'd found her walking on the beach three times now. Each time there'd been a veneer of friendliness, but an undercurrent of threat. It made her lie awake at night imagining possibilities. She'd bought extra locks for the flat's doors and windows, and she checked them every night before bed and every day before going out. She hated leaving Sharon alone here.

She had to do something.

She dialled from memory. The number wasn't saved in her contacts; she'd known better than to do that back when she'd represented him.

"I'm unavailable. Don't leave a message."

"It's Elsa," she said, ignoring his instructions. "We need to talk. I'm not going to let you threaten my clients anymore."

She put the phone down on the coffee table, all but screwing it into the wood.

Had she done the right thing? Using the word *threaten*, had she just put herself in more danger?

Elsa swallowed and poured a cup of coffee. It was done

now. She had to stop him somehow, or she'd never be able to rest easy.

CHAPTER FIVE

LESLEY HAD NEVER BEEN to the Blue Pool before. It was a tourist destination, or somewhere for walkers, and she was neither. The pool was privately owned, an old clay mine along a narrow lane leading off the A351 south of Wareham.

She pulled up in the car park, surveying the cars already there. Gail's van was near the entrance. A squad car was further along, PC Mullins checking people in and out. Two more cars, including Mike's Corsa.

No sign of Dennis's Astra. But he had left a message on her voicemail while she'd been in the shower that morning, letting her know in clipped tones that he wasn't well enough to make it in today.

A migraine, he'd said. She knew full well that wasn't the real problem.

She parked and headed towards the buildings that separated the car park from the old quarry and the pool. The place was quiet today, the gift shop locked and the tea rooms almost empty. PC Hughes was inside with two people: a young woman and young man. The three of them sat in silence, PC Hughes and the woman at one table and the man at another.

Lesley approached them, rubbing her hands together against the cold. It seemed no one had bothered to turn the heating on.

"PC Hughes," she said. "Can you fill me in?"

He stood up, making her roll her eyes. Hughes was old-school. But he was good with witnesses and families. He had a knack for putting people at their ease while keeping a close eye on anything untoward. Perfect for a FLO.

"Ma'am. This is Christina Thornton and Nicholas Galanis. They're both students. Christina lives in Stoborough, Nicholas is visiting her. They found the body."

Lesley gave the young people a smile. "My name's Lesley Clarke. I'm in charge of this investigation. Have any of my officers had a chat with you yet?"

The woman shook her head. Lesley looked at Hughes. "DC Legg's here, isn't he?"

"And DC Brown, Ma'am."

"So where are they?"

He gestured in the direction of the quarry. "Down by the crime scene, Ma'am. With the CSIs."

"OK. Waiting for me to tell them what to do, I suppose?"

"Not my place to speculate, Ma'am."

She sighed. If Dennis had been here, he'd have kicked things off. He lived just the other side of Wareham; he'd have made it before her. And if Tina wasn't away on maternity leave, she'd have shown some initiative and interviewed the witnesses already.

Ah, well. Lesley would have to supervise the DCs herself.

"OK. Miss Thornton and Mr Galanis, someone will be

along very soon to have a brief chat with you and take a statement. I gather from what I've been told that you were here walking and saw the body floating in the water?"

"Yes," the man said. "He was down there." He pointed.

"Which of you saw him first?"

"It was Christina." He looked at the woman. Lesley noted that he hadn't stood up or moved to the other table to be with his friend. Gail's niece.

"Christina, did you see anything else that seemed unusual? Anyone else walking through the site? Anyone in a car when you arrived?"

"No. Sorry. Just... just the man."

"OK." Lesley needed to be at the crime scene. She'd send Mike back up to question these witnesses formally. "My colleague DC Legg will be up soon, to take a formal statement. But don't worry, it won't take long and then you can get on with your day."

"Are we suspects?" the man asked.

"Suspects?" Lesley replied. "What makes you think you might be suspects?"

"Well." He licked his lips, his gaze flicking over to the woman. She wasn't looking at him. "We found it. Him."

Lesley smiled. *Bloody TV crime dramas.* "No, Mr Galanis. You aren't suspects."

His body deflated. He'd been holding in the tension, she realised. Maybe she should be suspicious.

No. This was Gail's niece and her friend. Boyfriend, maybe. Out for a walk, and they just got unlucky.

Still, she'd make sure Mike took their contact details. Just in case.

"Like I say, my colleague will be up to interview you shortly. Thanks for phoning it in."

"Aunt Gail said I did the right thing."

"You did." Lesley didn't have time to reassure Christina. "And I'm sure she'll be able to talk to you, but right now she's busy doing her job."

"I know." The young woman smiled. Lesley made a note to find out more about Gail's extended family. They'd been friends for a year and a half and the only family member she'd met had been Gail's son Tom.

She gave PC Hughes a nod. "Hang about after they're done, please. We might need a FLO for the widow."

He blanched. "Yes, Ma'am."

CHAPTER SIX

Sadie Dawes parked her car in the car park of the RSPB reserve at Arne. There were only three vehicles there besides hers: an RSPB van, a battered Ford Focus, and a shiny BMW. She'd lay money that the BMW belonged to the person she was coming to meet.

She closed the door to her car, careful not to slam it, and made for the path leading towards the shoreline. It was quiet here in January, the only visitors locals looking for somewhere tranquil to take a walk or birdwatchers hoping to spot something unusual. As the RSPB didn't allow dogs, the reserve was mercifully devoid of them.

Her phone bleeped in her pocket and she took it out. A WhatsApp message with a What3words reference: *glory.behind.fans*. She switched to Google Maps and screwed up her nose as she tried to work out which paths would take her there.

Ten minutes later she was lost. Ahead of her was a hillock topped with gorse, to her right was the harbour and to her left, some woodland. Behind her, she hoped, was the car park. Although, truth be told, the car park could just as easily have been ahead of her and she'd have been none the wiser.

No. The car park had to be behind her still. The harbour was to the right, which meant she was facing either north or west. She knew Arne well enough to remember that the areas you were allowed to walk on covered a headland that only had coastline to the east and north.

She took out her phone again and turned it in her hand. The spot was close. At the top of that mound, perhaps?

She raised a hand to shield her eyes and looked up. There was no one there. But that didn't mean he wasn't on the other side, waiting for her.

She sighed. This was all very cloak-and-dagger, given his position. She'd spoken to him in public places plenty of times before. But this was the first time he'd called her, the first time he'd asked for a meeting. Sadie's journalistic instincts, and the suspicion that he was connected to the historic murder she'd been investigating, meant she wasn't going to pass this up. Even if it did mean a morning of getting lost and ruining her favourite shoes.

She trudged up the hill, scanning the horizon for a human form as she went. There was no sign of the owner of the RSPB van or the battered Focus. The RSPB worker was probably indoors somewhere, like Sadie wished she was. And the Focus owner might be squirrelled away in a bird hide.

She stopped and turned to look back the way she'd come. There was plenty of cover. Whoever it was might be watching her, hidden from her as much as he was from the birds.

Don't be paranoid, Sadie.

She shook herself out and continued walking.

"Hello."

She started and turned to see a man behind her. Where the hell had he come from?

"What the—"

He put a finger to his lips. "It's too exposed up here. Follow me."

He turned and walked back down the hill, making her wonder why he'd dragged her up here in the first place. The bastard was determined to play his silly games with her.

Or was he trying to frighten her?

She scoffed.

It took more than a wild goose chase around Arne to scare Sadie Dawes.

He led her back down into the trees and stopped at a bench. He took a white handkerchief from his pocket and brushed invisible dirt from the bench. The incongruity forced her to stifle a laugh.

He turned to her. "After you."

Seriously? He'd made her come all the way out here, he'd crept up on her and now he was being chivalrous?

Still, Sadie knew how to keep a source happy. Do as they say, and they're more likely to open up to you.

Although this guy knew more about keeping secrets than most of her sources.

She sat down, making sure to scoot along one end of the bench so she wouldn't have to make physical contact. Superintendent Anthony Carpenter was the kind of man who made her flesh creep.

With a smile, he lowered himself onto the bench. Instead of sitting at the other end, he took a spot next to her, not quite touching but not much more than a hair's breadth away.

You're not going to intimidate me like that, mate.

She shifted so their legs were touching. Better to break

the tension than to waste time and energy worrying about his proximity.

"Why did you bring me here?" she asked him. "It's very secluded."

"I like it here." He sniffed the air then closed his eyes and took a deep breath. He turned to her, his eyes opening. They were a piercing blue. How had she not noticed that before? "I fancied a walk. I hope you don't mind."

"I've been trying to get an interview with you for months, and today you call me out of the blue and demand that I come all the way out here just so you can go for a walk?"

He smiled. "I didn't call you. I responded to one of your many messages."

"My last message was a month ago." Truth be told, she'd given up. Decided to move on to other investigations, before her attempts to get to the bottom of former DCI Tim Mackie's death drove her insane.

Carpenter leaned back. His coat was expensive, and unsuitable for the bench. He wore leather gloves and polished shoes. Mud spatters stained them. Sadie wondered if he polished them himself.

"Well, now I've got you," she said, drawing a notebook from her pocket, "I've got some questions I'd like to ask."

He shook his hand in the direction of her notebook. "This is off the record."

She bit back a laugh. "Really? You're a senior police officer and I work for the local BBC. This isn't a car park in Washington, you know."

He sniffed. "And I'd like to check your phone, make sure you aren't recording this."

She pocketed her notebook then held her phone out and closed What Three Words. "All apps closed. See?"

He nodded. "You can make as many notes as you like after I've gone."

"Fair enough." Sadie had a bloody good memory. She didn't need to take notes. "So my first question is about the investigation into DCI Mackie's death. You reopened it last May, appointed Detective Superintendent Phipps from the Hampshire force to head it up. But then a month later, Phipps went back to Hampshire and the investigation was closed. Why?"

He stared ahead, towards the distant harbour. "The Hampshire force were restructured, as I'm sure you know."

"Budget cuts."

"Phipps took early retirement. He was no longer available to lead the investigation."

"That doesn't mean you couldn't appoint someone else."

He turned to her. "Ms Dawes. You know as well as anyone about the current financial pressures on the police. The BBC has spent enough time haranguing us about it. Hampshire did not have the resources to appoint a substitute. And it was decided that investigating current cases was a better use of resources for the Dorset force."

"I don't believe you. Tim Mackie was a retired DCI. He'd only been off the force for a matter of weeks at the time of his death. If you believed his death to have been suspicious, you'd have used all the resources you could to investigate it. He was one of yours."

"Then maybe we didn't believe his death to be suspicious."

"I've seen the forensics. I know about the spot where he went off the cliff at Ballard Down. He couldn't have fallen that way, not alone. Not without being pushed."

He leaned in. Sadie resisted the urge to shrink back.

"DCI Mackie's death was not suspicious. I strongly suggest you focus on reporting things that matter. How about our work to reduce drugs-related crime across the county, or maybe a couple of school fairs?"

He stood up and strode away. She watched him for a moment.

Patronising bastard.

Sadie pulled herself up off the bench, brushed down her trousers and hurried after him. He'd taken a different path, in the direction of the sea. He was about to turn a bend and disappear from view.

She couldn't lose him. This was a one-time opportunity.

"Carpenter!" she called out as she hurried after him.

He was gone.

She came to a fork in the path. To the right, marshy ground, the path soon petering out. To the left, a stand of trees and a shallow beach.

The left turn it was. She rounded the trees and found herself on the beach. The tide was in and there was only just enough sand for her to stand on.

Where the fuck are you?

"Carpenter!"

She cast around her, searching. He'd been with her moments ago. He'd had no time to get to the other end of this beach.

He had to be in the trees.

She turned towards them just as she felt a hand on her arm. He was in front of her, his breath shallow and his face red. He had a tight hold of her arm, just above the elbow.

She shook her arm. His hold was firm.

"Let go of me. I'll report you."

"No you won't. Have you told Matt Crippins that you're meeting me here?"

She held Carpenter's gaze, forcing herself not to reveal the lie in her face. "Yes."

He smiled. "I was speaking with him not half an hour ago. He said nothing about our meeting." He dug his thumb into her arm. "And I think it's the sort of thing he would have mentioned, don't you?"

"Just because you're mates with my boss, doesn't mean you can threaten me." She took a step backward, feeling water seep into her shoe.

He stared at her for a moment. Then he dropped her arm.

"You're right. I'm so sorry. I thought you were about to fall into the water, so I grabbed you to stop you. Are you OK?"

Sadie felt her mouth drop open. She'd known Anthony Carpenter was a creep from the way his colleagues looked at him in press conferences, but this... this was beyond what she'd imagined.

"Superintendent Carpenter, how close were you to DCI Mackie?"

He took a step back. "He was a subordinate."

"Did he do something to... did he...?"

Her thoughts weren't properly formed. She'd need to do some more digging before she confronted him.

Could she talk to Matt? Could she trust him after what Carpenter had just said?

Yes. Carpenter was a liar. She shouldn't believe a word he said.

So why was she so desperate to get him to admit to covering up DCI Mackie's death? His words meant nothing.

"Thanks for your time." She turned away, hurrying along the beach and back through the trees. As she got closer to the car park she picked up pace, until she was almost running.

She fell into her car, her breath cold. She pulled down the visor and checked the mirror. Her hair was disheveled and her face pale. She lifted a hand. It was trembling.

The BMW was still there, beside her car.

She turned her key in the ignition.

Get out of here. Now.

CHAPTER SEVEN

Lesley left the tea rooms and made for the water. The woods opened out ahead of her, the trees parting and the ground dipping towards the pool. It wasn't large, but the colour was striking.

Gail was in the water, up to the middle of her thighs and wearing waders. Her colleague Gavin was with her. Mike and Stanley watched from a distance. Another CSI, the one whose name Lesley could never remember, was working on the shoreline, examining the ground.

Lesley called Gail's name. Gail looked up and waved. She gestured for Lesley to go round to the left and follow the path down to the water.

Lesley did as she was told. She was wearing hiking boots, but wasn't in the mood for tramping across rough ground.

"Gail," she said as she approached the water. "I've just been talking to your niece."

Gail stood up straight. She was next to the body, which was partially submerged and face-down.

Arthur Kelvin. Lesley felt a shiver run through her.

"Is she OK?" Gail asked.

"She's a tough young woman. Mike, you get up there and take a formal statement from her, will you? I'm not sure why you and Stanley are hanging around here like a couple of lemons."

Mike glanced at Stanley then walked towards her, making for the path. "No problem, boss. We were just waiting for—"

"Well don't, next time. You don't need me or the sarge to tell you what to do. You in particular have enough experience of this kind of thing to be able to get started without instruction."

"Of course. Sorry." He headed up the hill.

"You got some for me?" Lesley called to Gail as she approached the water's edge.

"Sorry?"

"Waders. I want to get a look at him." *Be sure it is who they say it is.*

"I'd rather limit the number of people who—"

"Gail, this is me. You know I'll be careful."

"Of course." Gail twisted her upper body, her legs not moving in the water. "Brett, give the DCI your waders."

"Sure." He started to peel them off.

Lesley grimaced at the thought of wearing gear that had been wrapped around someone else just seconds earlier, but took them from him nonetheless. She dragged them on over her trousers and waddled to the water.

"It's beautiful here," she said to Gail. "Why haven't I heard of it?"

Gail stood up again and looked at her. "I'm sorry?"

"I said why haven't I—"

"No. The other bit."

Lesley was at the body now. She glanced down at it, then back at Gail. "It's beautiful."

Gail frowned. "Have you been possessed?"

"I'm allowed to appreciate the scenery, aren't I?"

"Your nostrils *are* working, aren't they?"

Lesley looked down. The back of the man's head was intact, his dark top puffed up full of water. He stank of putrefaction. "They are. How long d'you think he's been here?"

Gail shook her head. "Not here. I reckon he was brought here overnight, but he's been dead a while."

Lesley nodded. "Do we know when anyone last came past here?"

"You'd have to ask the manager that."

"I will. Stanley, can you go up and have a chat with the man? Find out who came through here last, before Gail's niece and her mate, and when. And get him to give you the lowdown on access to the site, whether it's secured at night."

"No problem, boss."

"Good." Why hadn't he and Mike started on that already, she wondered? Not having Dennis around seemed to paralyse them.

It had been happening a lot lately. But now they had a murder on their hands. And the murder of Arthur Kelvin, no less.

"Can you turn him over?" she asked Gail.

"You don't believe it's him."

"Who made the identification?"

"I did."

Lesley raised an eyebrow. "Mike hasn't taken a look?"

"We're trying not to disturb him any more than we have to."

"No sign of a pathologist yet?"

"It's early still." Gail looked upwards. "About eight thirty?"

"You know the time just from looking at the sky?"

Gail grinned. "Nah. I checked my watch when you got here. Had you fooled for a minute, though."

"So are you going to let me look at him, or not?"

Gail gave Lesley a long look. "Are you OK?"

"Of course. Why?"

"You bit Mike's head off when you got here and now you're being arsey with me."

"I needed him to get to work."

"And me?"

Lesley scratched her chin. "We need to get to work, too."

Gail raised an eyebrow. She sniffed. "We need to be careful. There's decay."

Lesley nodded. She was already wearing forensic gloves, but she had no intention of touching the body.

"Show me."

Gail bent over the body and put the flats of her hands on the shoulders, taking care not to dig in. She wore a forensic suit under her waders. Lesley realised she should probably have done the same.

"I'll stand back," she said. "I'm not wearing a suit."

"Thanks."

Lesley shuffled back in the water. The soles of her waders had sunk in and she struggled to suck them out of the mud. She flung her arms out as she moved, working hard to ensure she didn't make contact with the body.

"You sure about this?" Gail asked.

"Let's make it quick."

"OK." Gail turned the body in the water, spinning it just

enough so that Lesley could see the face. The movement released a wave of putrefaction, making her gag.

Lesley swallowed. The man's cheek had considerable decay, and he smelt even worse now he'd been moved. He had a square jaw, hair which looked dark in the water but was greying, and a heavy build that Lesley knew had once been slim. His hair was short but his fringe long. In life, it would have flopped over his eyes.

Lesley had never met Arthur Kelvin in person. But she'd seen photos, and his face was etched in her mind.

She nodded and Gail returned him to his former position, taking great care.

"So?" Gail asked. "You believe me now?"

Lesley nodded. She gazed down at the body in the water.

Who finally decided to finish you off? And should I be grateful to them, or worried about them?

"It's him alright," she said, thinking of the conversation she and Elsa had had this morning. At least he couldn't threaten her anymore. "It's Arthur Kelvin."

CHAPTER EIGHT

"Boss!"

Lesley looked up to see a man coming down the path. He wore a tweed jacket over brown trousers and sensible shoes. He was hurrying, out of breath.

"Dennis? You're supposed to be off sick."

She exchanged looks with Gail and walked out of the water, taking her first steps carefully so as not to disturb the body.

Dennis had disappeared behind some shrubs.

"Dennis?" Lesley called. "Where are you? What are you doing here? I thought you had a migraine."

"A migraine?" Gail whispered. Lesley put a finger up to shush her.

Dennis stumbled through some bushes and staggered onto the sandy ground behind Lesley. "Sorry, boss. I would have got here earlier but..."

"You weren't expected at all."

"I heard." Dennis broke off. "Is that him?"

"That's our victim, if that's what you mean."

Dennis stepped closer to the water. Gail approached the two detectives, protecting her charge.

"No," said Dennis. "Is that... him?"

Lesley tugged at her waders. "So you *have* heard."

Dennis turned to look at her. "Kelvin. Someone got him."

"Looks like they did."

"Who?"

She laughed. "How the bloody hell should I know?"

A frown crossed Dennis's face. *Not the swear jar, not now*, Lesley thought. They'd dispensed with that over a year ago.

"The pathologist hasn't even got here yet," she told him. "I've sent Mike up to interview the people who found him, and Stanley is asking the manager about points of access."

"How long's he been here?"

"Not that long," Gail said. "There's no blood, and he'd have been seen."

"How did he... how did he die?"

"Not sure, yet," Gail said. "The pathologist hasn't—"

"You're full of questions, Dennis," Lesley interrupted. "Don't you think you should be at home, looking after yourself?"

He shook his head. "This is bigger." He looked at her. "This changes things, you know. There'll be a shift."

"Don't think I haven't considered that. There's a power vacuum in the local crime fraternity."

"It'll be filled," Dennis said, his voice low.

"It'll be filled fast."

"Do we need to worry?"

Lesley finally had the waders off. She draped them over a

rock. "I think we do. I'll talk to Carpenter, make sure resources are allocated."

"His family need to be watched."

"Darren Kelvin is in prison. The Lyme Regis case."

Dennis nodded. "But there's still the other nephew, Jake. And the widow."

Lesley thought of the Kelvin house, in Sandbanks. The luxury mansion overlooking the harbour. She'd never met Kelvin's wife, and wasn't sure Dennis had either.

"You're right." She strode towards the path. "If you're well enough to be in work, then I'd like you to take charge here. Let me know when the pathologist arrives. And make sure no one gets in. Stanley needs to tell the manager to lock all his gates."

"Or out," Dennis said. "They might still be here."

"I doubt it," Lesley told him.

"Where are you going?"

"To inform the widow. I think she should hear it from us."

"If she's still in the country," Gail said.

Lesley turned to her. "You're right. She might have fled. If someone killed her husband..."

"Who's to say it wasn't her?" Dennis suggested.

Lesley looked back towards the body. "And dump him out here? Surely she'd have done it at home."

"Not necessarily. She might have wanted it to look like someone else. Like a hit."

Lesley smiled. "Don't audition for *The Godfather* just yet, Dennis. You stay here. Unless you want to break it to the widow?"

His eyes widened. "That's your job."

"Is it?"

He nodded. "I think you should do it."

"OK." Lesley eyed Dennis. His cheeks had paled. "I'll let you know how I get on."

CHAPTER NINE

DENNIS WATCHED as the boss tramped up the path towards the tea rooms. As she approached the building, a man appeared, walking towards her. The two of them paused to speak, the DCI turning to indicate the crime scene. Dennis turned away and tried to look busy, embarrassed to be caught watching her.

He hoped the man was the pathologist. He wanted to get out of here and back to the office, as soon as possible. It felt like the forest was watching him.

The man reached the bottom of the path and placed his bag on the ground. "You must be DS Frampton. Your DCI tells me you're in charge."

Gail waded out of the water. "Gareth, I didn't know you were working this far west."

He gave a mock salute. "I've transferred. Seems they couldn't find anyone in Dorset to replace Henry Whittaker after his retirement."

Dennis watched the two of them, his mind blank. Who

was this man, and how come Gail knew him? Since when had Whittaker retired?

Had he known about Whittaker's retirement, and forgotten? Or had it happened while he'd been off sick, and no one had thought to tell him?

He swallowed. Was he so surplus to requirements now that the team didn't keep him up to date on personnel changes?

"Doctor...?" he asked, stepping forward.

The man gave him a curt nod. "Gareth Bamford. I worked with your DCI on the Lyme Regis case last year. I've transferred over from Devon."

"Ah. Well, welcome. How much has she told you?"

"Only that the body was found submerged here around an hour and a half ago, and that there's decay to his face. I gather you haven't found any evidence for cause of death yet." He turned to Gail. "Is that right?"

She nodded. "I didn't want to move him too much."

"Sensible." The doctor zipped up his forensic suit. "Have you got some waders for me?"

Gail gestured towards the waders the boss had left behind. "Gav, pass those to him, will you?"

Gavin picked the waders up and brought them to the doctor, giving Gail a pointed look as he did so.

"So, DS Frampton," the pathologist said. "Any pointers you want to give me before I go in?"

"Er..."

"It's going to be a high stakes case," Gail said, frowning at Dennis. "The victim, we believe it's Arthur Kelvin. Local organised crime boss."

"Never heard of him."

"Probably for the best."

"Any forensics yet? Any sign of how he got here?"

"This is a publicly accessible site," Gail said. "I checked the opening times when I got here, and it was open yesterday. They've got lights in the trees this time of year, and it wouldn't have closed until eight."

"So if he was here at that point, he would have been seen."

Gail gave Dennis another look. "Yes."

"OK," the pathologist said. "I'll see what I can do for you. I can already tell from the smell that he's been dead for longer than a matter of hours, though."

"Yes," Gail agreed.

The pathologist waded in to the water. Dennis took a few steps forward, but he wasn't wearing waders and didn't know how he could contribute.

What had come over him?

He'd met Kelvin a few times. Once when they'd been investigating the death of a solicitor at the firm that represented him. Another time after they'd identified Kelvin's nephew as the murderer of a former lawyer at the same firm. And then there'd been Dennis's old colleague Johnny, and the blackmail...

Nevin, Cross and Short. That firm seemed to be all tangled up with Kelvin and his operations. And the boss's girlfriend had worked for them.

Was she connected, somehow?

Don't be stupid. But...

He knew that Kelvin had some connection to DCI Mackie's death. Mackie had been poking his nose in where it wasn't wanted, getting too close to evidence that would bring Kelvin in. And instead of calling it a day after his retirement, he'd carried on as if he were still on the force.

And then he'd been killed. Of course, the coroner had said suicide, but no one believed that any more.

And now Kelvin was dead. Heaven only knew who'd take over from him. They might be worse. At least Kelvin was a known quantity.

"Sarge?"

Dennis looked up to see Stanley approaching.

"Sorry, Stanley. What can I do for you?"

"You OK, Sarge?"

"I'm fine."

"I thought you were off sick."

Dennis pulled himself straight. "Well, you heard wrong. The DCI has gone to inform the widow, and I'm in charge here. I need you to find out when this spot would last have been accessed, and to make sure no one can get in or out."

"Already done it, Sarge. The manager locked all the gates last night after the illuminations were closed for the night."

"What time would that have been?"

"Half eight, Sarge."

"And the last time anyone came down here?"

"Half an hour or so after. He says he does a circuit of the site after it closes, to make sure there are no stragglers left behind. Apparently, there was a day last summer when—"

"Thanks, Stanley."

Stanley cleared his throat. "Sarge."

Gail was in the water with the pathologist, who was bent over the body. They'd rotated him so he was face up. Dennis pulled in a breath.

Don't throw up.

"Dennis?" Gail called.

He stepped forward. He had the strongest urge to grab a

handkerchief from his pocket and place it over his nose. He resisted it.

"Yes?"

"We've got a likely cause of death."

"Yes?"

"Stab wounds," said the pathologist. "Below the rib cage, upward motion. Quite a few of them. Once we get him into the morgue, I reckon we'll find practice wounds."

"Practice wounds."

"Where the killer tries to stab him but—"

"I know what practice wounds are. But that means..."

"It means whoever stabbed him wasn't an experienced killer," Gail said.

Dennis swallowed. *Don't throw up.*

"No," he said.

CHAPTER TEN

ARTHUR KELVIN HAD LIVED in a broad two-storey house overlooking Poole Harbour in Sandbanks. Lesley parked her car on the double yellows outside and approached the high gate.

She pressed the buzzer.

"Yes?" came a voice through the intercom.

"I'm here to speak with Mrs Kelvin."

"Mrs Kelvin?"

"Yes."

She should have stopped to find out the woman's name. If Tina had been here, she'd have had that information already.

But Tina was on maternity leave. She had four months left. Lesley was missing her.

"One moment." The intercom cracked then went quiet.

Lesley waited. She took her phone out and Googled Arthur Kelvin in the hope of finding his wife's name.

There was no evidence online that he'd even had a wife.

Damn.

But the fact that whoever had just spoken to her had gone away, presumably in search of Mrs Kelvin, meant that she did exist.

The intercom crackled again. "Come in." There was a buzzing sound as the latch on a gate next to Lesley released.

She pushed it open. It was a pedestrian gate, not the wide one which spanned the driveway. She could leave her car outside, it would be fine.

She stepped through and stopped to survey the house. It was huge, at least eight windows on this side alone. The building blocked the view of the harbour, and trees surrounding it blocked much of the winter light.

The front door opened and a woman stood in the doorway. She wore a black maid's outfit and a white apron.

Jeez, Lesley thought. *What is this, Downton Abbey?*

She walked towards the woman and held up her ID. "DCI Clarke, Dorset Police. I need to speak with Mrs Kelvin in private."

"I'm sorry, Madam. May I ask which Mrs Kelvin it is you need to speak with?"

"*Which* Mrs Kelvin?" Had the man been a bigamist?

The woman nodded. "The elder Mrs Kelvin, or the younger?"

Ah. She considered. Kelvin's mother and wife, most likely.

"The younger, please." She wondered just how young this woman would turn out to be. Kelvin had been in his fifties, but in her experience, men like him tended to favour women young enough to be their daughters.

"Very well. If you'll follow me."

Lesley followed the woman into the house. They were in a wide hallway with a sofa to one side and a broad staircase to the other. Six doors led off, all closed except a set of double doors ahead of her, with a huge window beyond affording a view down to the harbour.

She smiled. So Kelvin liked to impress his visitors.

She peered past the maid, wondering if Mrs Kelvin was beyond those doors. But the maid gestured towards the sofa.

"If you don't mind taking a seat, I'll tell Mrs Kelvin that you're here."

"It's fine, I'll stand."

"Very well." The woman disappeared through one of the closed doors, pulling it shut behind her.

Lesley stood in front of the sofa, turning slowly to take in the hallway. She could hear sounds from upstairs: children?

Kelvin had grown nephews, she knew. But she wasn't aware of children. Certainly not active in his business, not to her knowledge.

The door opened and a willowy woman wearing jeans and a perfectly-fitted white shirt emerged. She gave Lesley a wary look. "DCI Clarke. I'm Amanda Kelvin. How can I help you?"

Lesley gave the woman a smile. "Is there somewhere more private where we can talk?"

Mrs Kelvin frowned. "Of course." She turned away from Lesley and opened another door, next to the double doors. As Lesley approached, she could see that the double doors led to an office. A glass-topped desk sat in the centre, angled so that the occupant of its expensive leather chair would get a view of the water.

Of course, she thought. Kelvin would take the best room in the house for himself. She wondered who'd be sitting in that chair, now he was gone.

Mrs Kelvin led her into a sitting room at the back of the

house. It had sliding doors overlooking the harbour and a set of three matching sofas, all of them huge.

So this is what organised crime buys you.

"Please, take a seat. I can ask Gerta to get you a coffee, if you'd like?"

"It's fine." Lesley waved the offer away. So far, this woman had been polite and courteous, if clearly worried. Nothing like her late husband.

Lesley gestured for the woman to sit. She took a seat with her back to the harbour and Lesley sat at right angles to her.

She leaned forward. "I'm afraid I have bad news, Mrs Kelvin."

"Amanda. I don't use Mrs Kelvin. I'm Amanda Frobisher."

Lesley hadn't been expecting that.

"Amanda. Ms Frobisher. I'm sorry to tell you that we found your husband dead this morning."

Amanda's hand went to her throat. She gasped. "Arthur?"

Do you have any other husbands?

"I'm so sorry."

Amanda nodded, her lips clamped shut. She blinked a few times, then wiped her cheek. "Arthur."

"He was found at the Blue Pool near Wareham. Can you tell me if that was somewhere he often went?"

The woman frowned at her. "Arthur? No. Arthur didn't *do* outdoors." She took a shaky breath. "I do, though. It's beautiful there." She looked at Lesley. Her eyes were welling. "How...?"

"We don't know yet. He was found in the pool though."

"Drowned?"

"Like I say, we don't know yet. As soon as we have a

cause of death, we'll let you know." Lesley looked towards the open door. "Is there anyone here who can be with you?"

Amanda's face clouded. "Oh, God."

"No?"

"His mother. The real Mrs Kelvin." Her hand, still at her throat, clenched into a fist. "She'll.... She'll be devastated."

"Would you prefer if I told her?"

Amanda shook her head. "I can do it." She squeezed her eyes shut. "*Shit.*"

"I'll send a Family Liaison Officer over, to support you while we investigate—"

Amanda laughed. Lesley stared at her.

"I'm sorry. Oh God, that's so inappropriate. But no. We can't have a Liaison Officer here." Another laugh. "Can you...?" She flattened her palm against her chest. "Sorry. Mrs Kelvin, his mother. She won't have it. Thank you, though." The widow stood up. "And thank you for telling me." She took another shaky breath and sniffed.

The grief seemed genuine enough. But her reaction to a FLO...

Not surprising really, given the kind of family it was. Still, Lesley would kill to get a FLO into this house.

"A Family Liaison Officer can help keep you informed of progress in the investigation. I've got the perfect officer in mind, DC Hughes. He's sensitive and experienced. He won't disturb your privacy."

Amanda gazed down at her. "I said no. We'll be fine as we are." Her breathing had levelled out. "Now, if you don't mind..."

Lesley stood up. "I'm sorry for your loss."

"Thank you."

"Can I ask, do you have children?"

"No."

"Oh. I thought I heard...?"

"That was Finn and Lottie. Darren's kids. Becca is living here with them while Darren's..." She flushed. "While he's away."

Lesley nodded. *Happy families.* Or maybe not.

In for a penny, in for a pound.

"Was Arthur a good husband?" she asked.

Amanda's eyes widened. "I beg your pardon?"

"Were the two of you happy together?"

"I don't see how that's any of your business."

Lesley stepped closer to the woman. She shot a glance over her shoulder, towards the open door.

"I know what kind of man he was. If you're worried for your safety, we can help."

Amanda put a hand on Lesley's chest. She gave it a small shove. "How dare you." Her voice was even.

Lesley stepped back. "It's just that, if your husband's death was suspicious, you might be worried for your own safety."

"DCI Clarke, have you seen the gates to this property?"

"I have."

"We have CCTV, monitored by the most exclusive security firm in Europe. I can assure you that I do not fear for my safety."

"You can't stay here all the time."

Amanda's face flickered. "Again, I don't see how that's any of your business. Now kindly leave."

Lesley eyed her. She had a suspicion Amanda Frobisher wasn't someone who got out much, despite her comment about liking the outdoors. Did she like it here, surrounded by expensive furniture and glass?

Or was she a prisoner in her own home?

"Thank you for your time," Lesley said. "We'll let you know when we have more information on the progress of the investigation."

"I'm sure you will."

CHAPTER ELEVEN

DENNIS WALKED DOWN towards the water, almost tripping on a tree root.

"Are you sure?" he asked.

The pathologist was wading out of the water, peeling off his gloves. "Not entirely, not yet. But his clothes have tears consistent with multiple piercings by a knife, and I can only find one actual wound."

"That could be anything. It might have happened after he went into the water. Are there any fish in there?"

The pathologist smiled. "These aren't bite marks, Sergeant."

"No." Dennis pushed his glasses up his nose. "So you think that whoever stabbed him took a few attempts to build up to it."

"That's what practice wounds normally indicate. Of course, I'll be able to tell you more once I've done the PM. And if we can find the weapon..."

"I'll make sure the guys are looking for it," Gail said. The pathologist hadn't yet been able to give any clues as to what it would be, other than sharp. A knife, of some sort.

Dennis nodded. "We need to do a thorough trawl of this site, and not just for the knife. I'll speak to the DCI, but I'm sure we'll be able to get Uniform involved."

"Good. This is a bloody big site, with plenty of hiding places."

Dennis winced at her language but said nothing.

"Sarge?"

Dennis looked past Gail to see Mike approaching from the direction of the tea rooms. He sighed.

"Mike. Before you ask, no I'm not sick, yes I'm fine and yes the DCI has put me in charge while she's gone to speak to the widow."

Mike said nothing, but gave Dennis an odd look instead.

"Don't worry about me," Dennis told him. He smiled. "How's the baby?"

Mike blinked. "He's fine. Tina's driving me nuts though."

"Be patient with her. It's not an easy time for them."

Mike gave him a look, as if trying to remember whether Dennis had children.

"When Pam had Jacob, she was quiet for weeks. These days she'd be diagnosed with post-natal depression."

"Oh, it's not that," Mike said. "She's itching to get back to work, that's all."

"Really?"

"Yeah. Wants to know the ins and outs of everything I'm working on. I tell you, she'll be solving our cases for us from home if we're not careful."

"Remote working," said Stanley.

Dennis grunted. He looked at Gail. "Anyway, I'll get that

team allocated, to help with the trawl. Anything else we should be looking for?"

"Fibres, shoe prints. The usual."

"Have we established if there's CCTV here?"

"No," said Stanley. "I asked the manager and he said they don't have it."

"Shame."

"We need to get the body safely out of the water and back to the morgue, too," said the pathologist.

"I don't want you doing that till we've searched the route you're going to take," Gail told him. "You'll disturb stuff."

"We do know what we're doing."

Gail put her hands on her hips. She was out of her waders now, and they lay on the ground next to her like two dead fish. "I know you do. But this is a bastard of a crime scene to trawl, and I want to get it right first time."

"Fair enough."

"You two can liaise over the best way to remove the body," Dennis told them. He could feel his brain emerging from the trancelike state it had been in. The job was doing him good, already, he could tell. Distracting him from the anxiety he'd been fighting off for months. "Meanwhile I'll get that team of officers to help you search."

"You sure you've got the resources?" the pathologist asked.

Dennis looked at the body, floating alone on the water. He tried to imagine what would be happening now, in the world that man inhabited. Depending on who had killed him, people would know there was a gap. They would be anxious to fill that gap.

"It's Arthur Kelvin," he said. "We'll find the resources."

CHAPTER TWELVE

LESLEY HAD MADE it to the office before the others, despite having been further away. She grabbed the board from the main office and dragged it into her own, angling it away from the window and from the glass partition.

If there was ever a crime whose investigation she wanted to keep under wraps, it was this one.

She wrote Kelvin's name at the top of the board, in the centre, then stood back to look at it.

Arthur Kelvin, dead.

The man who'd been making Elsa's life hell for the last year. The man who'd been responsible for the deaths of at least two lawyers at Elsa's old firm. The man who DCI Mackie had been investigating when he had died.

She shivered.

"Who killed you, you bastard?" she muttered, gazing at his name. "And will they be satisfied with that, or are they going to come for the rest of your family?"

Did she need to worry that whoever had killed Kelvin

would continue to threaten the people he'd had it in for? Might they be worse?

Don't think about that. Focus on the case. Evidence. Find who killed him, before they can do any more damage.

And how was she going to fit all this around her wedding preparations?

Elsa didn't have any work. She could take over. Elsa wouldn't be happy, but then Lesley was sure Elsa would want this case solved.

Elsa. She should tell her.

The outer door opened and Mike and Stanley entered. They spotted her through the partition and came into her office.

"Does no one knock anymore?" she asked.

Stanley blanched. "Sorry, boss." He backed out of the door and knocked on the glass.

Lesley smiled. "It's a bit late now, isn't it? Come in, both of you. Where's Dennis?"

"He was right behind us." Mike glanced towards the main door. "Not sure what's happened."

"I think Carpenter wanted to talk to him," Stanley said.

"Superintendent Carpenter, to you," Lesley corrected him. "What did he want him for?"

Carpenter should go through her, if he needed to speak to her team. She tugged at her sleeve, irritated.

"Wait a moment." She left her office, making for the outer door. If Dennis and the Super were talking, she wanted to be in on it.

The outer door opened just as she reached it: Dennis.

"Where were you?" she snapped.

"Sorry, boss. The Super wanted to know what resources we need."

"And he asked you?"

A shrug. "I just happened to pass him in the corridor. Sorry if I was out of line."

"What did you tell him?"

Dennis's cheeks flushed. "I... told him we need Uniform to assist the CSIs with a trawl of the site."

Lesley dug a nail into her thigh. He was right. Gail would need help, a site like that. But she didn't like him going straight to Carpenter.

"Thanks, Dennis. You should have run it past me first, though."

"I was going to, boss. But he accosted me by the lift."

Lesley smiled. "Accosted?"

"Well, not accosted exactly. But he did make it very hard for..." He straightened up. "Sorry, boss. Won't happen again."

"It's OK, Dennis. I know what Carpenter can be like when he's got the bit between his teeth. I'll have a chat with him, make sure the investigation gets everything it needs."

"I'm sure it will."

"You're right. Anyway, come on. We need to discuss what we have so far. Allocate resources. Anything you need to talk to me about, before we go in there with the DCs?"

He frowned. "Isn't it best we discuss the case between all four of us?"

"That's not what I mean. I'm worried about you. You call in sick, feigning a migraine, then you turn up at the crime scene without warning. How's your head?"

Dennis put a hand to his head, as if remembering it was supposed to be in pain. He rubbed it.

"It's fine now. Hurt terribly this morning, but it's died down. Thanks."

Lesley raised an eyebrow. "Glad to hear it. But you'll tell me if there's anything I can help you with, yes?"

"Of course." Dennis looked past her shoulder, towards the office. "They're getting impatient."

She turned to look back through the glass. Both DCs quickly looked away. Lesley chuckled.

"Come on then, Dennis. Let's get cracking."

CHAPTER THIRTEEN

GAIL HAD DECIDED to begin with a thorough search of the area immediately closest to the body. The spot where he was floating was near a kind of beach, sandy soil mixed with clay and pine needles. The three of them could cover that while they waited for Uniform to arrive and search the site properly.

Gav was at the far end of the beach, head down, facing away from her. He was stooped low, his tall frame making him look like he might topple at any moment. Brett was in the centre, covering the widest section of the beach. And Gail was at the end closest to the body. The beach tapered here to meet bushes and scrub. She had divided the area into metre squares and was cataloguing them on her tablet.

Dr Bamford, meanwhile, had retreated to his car. He was making calls, arranging for a team to collect the body and no doubt warning his own team that they'd be performing a post-mortem on Dorset's most notorious criminal. He wanted to be out of the way and, Gail imagined, he also wanted to be somewhere warm.

She heard voices behind her and straightened, squeezing a fist into the small of her back to counteract the ache that was growing there. She turned to see eight uniformed officers making their way down the hill from the tearoom. At the front was PS Dillick, who she'd worked with on these searches before.

The officers arrived at the beach and stopped, careful to stay on the path. Gail stepped forward.

"Sergeant Dillick," she said. "Good to see you. How much have you been told?"

"You've got a murder victim." He gestured towards the water. "I assume that's him out there. You've also got a tricky site and you need our help. Given that we were taken off a drugs response and told to get over here immediately, I'm assuming he's someone important. Politician? Celebrity?"

Gail eyed him. She wondered how much Lesley was telling her colleagues about this case and their victim.

"It's not my place to comment on the details of the case," she told him. It didn't do any harm for his team to have open minds while they were searching.

"Fair enough. What are we looking for?"

"First off, a knife, if we're extraordinarily lucky. Signs of a struggle. Evidence of him being carried or dragged here. Shoe or boot prints. And anything that might have been left behind. Clothing fibres, hair, blood. The usual."

"Not a problem." Dillick took a step forward. "Can I ask, is it that film star who just bought the big house at Church Knowle?"

Gail stifled a laugh. She knew nothing about any film star, but couldn't imagine anything further from the truth.

"No, Sergeant. It's not a film star. But can we keep the speculation to a minimum?"

"Sorry. Couldn't resist." He gave her a wink. "What pattern d'you want us to search in?"

"Given that a site like this is going to make it very hard to use a grid, and bearing in mind the layout of the paths, I think a spiral's best. Start at the point where the bushes meet the pool over there and work your way outwards."

"You want us to include both sides of the lake?"

"Pool. Yes. The whole site."

"Plans are here," Brett said, approaching them. He rummaged in a bag then handed a pile of papers to the sergeant. "PC Brown got them from the manager."

"You not got this electronically? It'd be much easier."

"There's a PDF," Brett said. "But it hasn't got grid references on it. I've overlaid a grid on that, so you can mark off anything you find." He looked at Gail. "Hope that's OK, with you not searching in a grid pattern?"

"It's fine," she told him. "We can still use a grid for recording, whatever search pattern we use."

"OK," said PS Dillick. "We'll make a start. Your guys are covering the beach?"

"We are. It's the closest area so it'll need the most thorough search."

"I'll make sure we search the paths leading to this spot particularly thoroughly, too."

"Thanks."

"Gail!"

Gav was near the water, standing up. He had an evidence bag in his hand.

"What is it?" she asked.

"A knife."

Gail exchanged looks with PS Dillick, who raised an eyebrow.

"Looks like you don't need us after all," he said.

"It might not be the weapon. And it's more than just the knife we want to find."

Gavin approached them, the bag in his hand. "We need to do a proper analysis," he said. "But it looks clean to me."

"How clean?" she asked.

"More than just wiped. I smelt cleaning products, before I bagged it."

"So they disinfect it, then dump it... where?"

Gav pointed. "It was partially buried. Under the bushes over there."

"Almost like they wanted us to find it."

Gav shrugged.

"OK. I'll let Lesley know. Sergeant Dillick, you carry on with your search."

CHAPTER FOURTEEN

"OK," said Lesley. "What have we got so far?"

"I've just seen an email from Gail," Mike said. "They've found a knife."

"A knife? Or *the* knife?"

"It hasn't been analysed yet. Pathology will have to compare it to the pattern of the wound."

"But they can't do that till the body's out of the water."

Mike shrugged.

"Still, that's good progress," Lesley said. "Get it up on the board, will you?"

Mike grabbed a marker and started writing.

"I don't suppose there's any forensics on it?" Dennis asked.

Mike shook his head, still writing. "Gail says it's clean. Really clean."

"How so?" Lesley asked.

"Apparently there's disinfectant on it."

"That's not nothing. We might be able to trace the brand."

"I don't think identifying which scent of Domestos it is will help us track down a killer," Dennis said.

Lesley gave him a look then turned to Mike. "Where was it?"

"Don't know."

"It can't have been far from the body," Dennis told her. "Uniform won't have had a chance to do a full search yet."

She rested her chin on her hands, gazing at the board. "Mike, get some more names up there, please."

He looked at her. "We got a suspect?"

"Not yet. But it doesn't do any harm."

"OK." He turned to the board, his hand poised with the pen. "Darren Kelvin?"

"He's in prison still," Dennis said.

"Doesn't mean he couldn't have ordered a hit," Stanley suggested.

Lesley rolled her eyes. "Can we quit with the mafia talk?" She gestured towards Mike. "Put him up there, though. And the other nephew. There *is* another one, isn't there?"

"Kyle," Dennis said.

"How come I've never come across him before?"

Dennis turned to her. "He lives in Plymouth. Organised Crime reckon he's working for his uncle, running some sort of remote operation."

"County lines," muttered Lesley, and Dennis nodded.

"*Worked* for," interjected Stanley.

"Worked for," agreed Dennis. "But from a distance."

"OK," said Lesley. "Put his name up there. I want to know if he's been to Dorset in the last few days."

Mike wrote *Kyle Kelvin* on the board.

"And the widow," Lesley said. "Amanda Frobisher."

"Frobisher?" Dennis asked her.

She raised an eyebrow. "Not all women take their husband's name."

"I know that. But if she married a man like Arthur Kelvin..."

"Maybe she doesn't want to be associated with the family firm," Mike suggested.

"Maybe she's got some balls," Lesley replied. "I met her. There's more to her than I expected. Although..."

"Although what?" Dennis asked.

Lesley shook her head, remembering her conversation with Amanda. "When I mentioned her mother-in-law, she seemed... almost scared."

Stanley snorted. "Surely if you're married to Arthur Kelvin you aren't scared of anyone."

"You haven't met Vera Kelvin," Dennis muttered.

"Vera?" Mike asked. He'd just finished writing *Amanda Frobisher* on the board. "That's her name?"

"Nothing wrong with the name," Dennis said. "Although I wouldn't say the same for the woman herself."

"You've met her?" Lesley asked.

Dennis screwed up his face. "Years ago. Decades. She and Gerard – her husband – came to a police fundraiser at the Sandbanks Hotel. Back when Henry Lampton was Chief Constable. I... tagged along."

"With DCI Mackie?" Lesley asked him, her voice low.

He nodded.

"Tell me about her."

"OK. So Gerard Kelvin, he was an old school gangster. If you'd told me he was part of the great train robbery, I'd have believed you. Thoroughly unpleasant man, but clever. Everyone was terrified of him, even when he was being sweet as sugar to their faces. Except Vera."

"She didn't take any shit?" Mike asked.

"Michael," Dennis said.

"Sorry, Sarge."

"But no," Dennis continued, "she didn't let him tell her what to do. There were some who reckoned she was the real power in that family. In those days no one would have accepted a woman at the top in that line of business, so there was a theory that she married Gerard so he could front the operation for her."

"But when he died...?" Lesley asked.

"Arthur took over."

"Not his brother or sister? Darren and Kyle's parents?"

"It was a brother, Frank. He disappeared in 1993."

"Murdered?" Mike asked.

Dennis shook his head. "No idea. Either he took himself off somewhere, or whoever killed him hid him so well he was never found."

"Hang on," said Mike. "So we've got a matriarch who's still around, a daughter-in-law who's scared of her, and two dead sons."

"I don't think this is a domestic killing, if that's what you're suggesting," Dennis replied.

"Let's save the speculation for when we've got more evidence," Lesley said. "Mike, get all those names on the board. Dennis, if you know anything more about the family tree, let's get it up there."

"What about Kelvin's own kids?" asked Stanley. "Do we know if he had any?"

"Not as far as we know," said Dennis.

"OK," said Lesley. "We have to remember that we've got practice wounds on the body. Whoever did this wasn't experienced."

"Families like the Kelvins rarely carry out the crimes themselves. They have others to do that for them," Dennis said.

"I'm not suggesting his mum or his wife took a knife to him themselves. But just that if it *is* a family thing... well, whoever did it, they might not have been comfortable with it."

Dennis turned to her. "It could be staged."

"Faked?"

A nod. "Someone with enough knowledge of how these things work might have pretended to make some practice wounds. Then plunged the knife in."

"They'd have had to be quick, if he was conscious," Mike said.

"Maybe he wasn't," Lesley replied. "We need to find out when the PM's going to happen." She blew out a breath. "OK. Stanley, I want you back at the site. Liaise with Gail, make sure I know as soon as anything's found. Mike, talk to Dr Bamford."

"Who?"

"The new pathologist."

"Sure. You want me to attend the post-mortem?"

"Please."

"What about me, boss?" Dennis asked.

Lesley eyed him. "We need to have a chat."

"A chat?" He flinched.

"I want you to fill me in on everything you know about the Kelvin family. A potted history, if you will."

"Surely Organised Crime will be better placed to do that."

"I'll be talking to them too. But something gives me the feeling you know a lot about these people."

CHAPTER FIFTEEN

Elsa sat in traffic on the A35 coming out of Christchurch. She'd been to the wedding shop for her final dress fitting.

Elsa hadn't been married before. She still entertained dreams of the fantasy wedding, the kind she saw in the magazines she secretly bought then hid from Lesley. She knew Lesley's attitude to this wedding was more practical. That Lesley had done this before, and it hadn't worked out the way she'd hoped.

Still, Elsa didn't see why that meant they had to downplay *their* wedding.

Her dress was traditional. Cream silk, cut on the bias, with just the tiniest train. Barely even a train, just a slight drag along the ground. She knew that she looked good in it. It offset her long dark hair and slim hips.

She had no idea what Lesley would be wearing. They'd agreed to keep it a secret. A surprise. But as the wedding drew closer, she found herself worrying about it.

Lesley was trying to downplay the importance of the day. She said it was the marriage that counted, not the wedding.

Would she even wear something special? Or would she just turn up in one of her work suits?

Elsa sighed, leaning on the steering wheel as she waited for the traffic to move. Should she go snooping around in Lesley's wardrobe, find out if there was a new outfit? Or would that be the top of a slippery slope that might have her checking Lesley's credit card statements in the years to come, or working out the PIN to her phone?

"Stop it, woman," she told herself, rapping the steering wheel with her knuckle. "It'll be fine." Lesley was right. The day wasn't what mattered most.

But Elsa's parents would be there. Down from London, with the emphasis, as far as they were concerned, on the *down*. The pair of them still hadn't adjusted to the fact that Elsa was marrying a woman. If that woman turned out to be what her mother called 'a scruff', it would be even worse.

Stop it.

Her parents didn't matter. She'd spent her whole life struggling under the weight of their disapproval, and that wasn't about to stop now. She should ignore it. Lesley loved her, and that was what mattered.

Not to mention Sharon. Finding a daughter like Sharon when she had given up on anything like that made up for any number of disapproving parents.

"Move, for Christ's sake," Elsa told the car in front of her.

It ignored her.

She slumped back in her seat. She had nothing to get home for, nothing she might be late for. The meeting with the hotel wasn't until seven this evening, and she had hours to kill before then. Might as well kill them in traffic as anywhere else.

Her phone buzzed. She grabbed it from the cup holder between the seats and turned it on, glancing up to check the traffic hadn't moved.

The car in front was still stationary.

A WhatsApp message. Lesley normally used text. But Sharon preferred WhatsApp.

Elsa smiled as she opened the app. She liked that Sharon sometimes contacted her instead of her mum. Elsa was more likely to pick up, for starters.

It wasn't Sharon. The number was one she didn't recognise. She read the message.

Arthur Kelvin is dead. I have information.

That was it.

She stared at the screen.

She caught movement from the corner of her eye. The car in front had moved.

At last.

She dropped the phone into the cup holder, her mind racing.

Kelvin, dead?

She glanced down at the phone. Had it been Lesley, on a number she hadn't used before? A client? A potential client?

No. The second line. *I have information.* Lesley would never have written that.

But who?

This was a dual carriageway: she couldn't pull over. And she wanted to get home. The anonymous message had given her the creeps. Especially after the 'chance' encounters she'd had with Kelvin on the beach in recent months.

She peered out of the car. Could someone be watching her?

She'd call the number, when she got home. Damn the traffic. Why did it have to start moving, just when she needed it to stay still?

CHAPTER SIXTEEN

LESLEY WAITED as Stanley and Mike filed out of the office.

"You might as well sit down, Dennis."

Dennis pulled on his fingers then took a seat.

She sat in her chair and leaned back, closing her eyes briefly. What time was it?

She looked past him at the clock. Gone eleven, and they'd barely begun the investigation. She was never going to make that meeting about the wedding food.

"OK," she said. "Let's use the board. You stay where you are, I don't want you overdoing it. I'll get a family tree up there."

He sniffed. "I wouldn't put any more than you already have up on the board."

"No? Why not?"

"It's the Kelvins."

"They're criminals, Dennis. We're investigating the murder of one of their members. We need to get all the intelligence we can."

"Yes," he said. "But I don't want what I'm about to tell you going up on the board."

She paused, marker in hand. "Why not?"

He looked out through the partition glass. "I just don't think it would be wise."

"Fair enough. I'll just put the names up."

He narrowed his eyes, then flinched as the phone on her desk rang. Lesley put down the marker and picked it up.

"DCI Clarke."

"Superintendent Carpenter would like to speak with you."

She balled a fist on the desk. "I'm in the middle of a major investigation. I'll be there in five minutes."

"He says it can't wait."

"Of course he does."

She put down the phone. "Sorry, Dennis. The Super wants me."

He nodded, not meeting her eye.

"What did you two talk about when you got back from the crime scene?"

He looked up at her. "Resources, boss. I told you."

"Hmm. OK." She handed him the marker. "Why don't you get that family tree up on the board and we can talk over the details when I get back?"

He looked at the board, his eyes wary. "Boss."

"Surely you're not scared of sticking a few names up there?"

"No." He sat where he was, making no move towards the board or the marker.

Lesley sighed. "Either way, we'll talk when I get back." She looked out into the main office to see Stanley and Mike leaving together. "Don't go anywhere."

Dennis grunted and stayed put as Lesley left the room.

"Mike," she said. "You're heading to the PM already?"

"They're moving the body in the next half hour. I thought it might be a good idea to be there for it. Then I'll head straight over to the morgue."

"They're doing the PM as soon as he gets there?"

"Seems so."

She whistled. "Wow. I wish all investigations were treated like this. Keep me posted."

"Will do." He turned to leave, Stanley holding the door for him.

Lesley looked back at Dennis. He stood in front of the board, looking at it. The marker pen was still in its holder.

"Oh, Dennis," she muttered as she left the room, making for Carpenter's office.

Moments later, she was in a chair opposite the Super, who was stationed behind his desk.

He leaned forward, steepling his chin on his hands. "So. Update me."

"I gather DS Frampton has already filled you in on some of the details."

"Don't worry about that. I want to hear it from you."

"If you don't mind, Sir, I'd prefer it if you dealt with me directly during the investigation, instead of distracting my team."

"Distracting, was I? Duly noted. Carry on."

She licked her lips. Carpenter hadn't said he would leave her team alone, but there was no more she could do.

"So far, we don't have all that much. Kelvin's body floating in the Blue Pool. What looks like a stab wound. A knife has been fou—"

"A knife? The murder weapon?"

"We don't know that yet. It hasn't been possible to compare the shape of the blade with the wound."

"When will that happen?"

"DC Legg will be at the post-mortem, which I'm expecting to take place in the next couple of hours."

"Good. Carry on."

"Uniform are searching the site now. I gather you authorised extra resources."

"I did."

"Thank you, Sir."

He nodded, giving her a patronising smile.

Lesley took in a breath. "I've spoken to his widow, too. Broken the news. She's refused an FLO."

"I'm hardly surprised by that."

"No."

"You think she might have been involved?"

"It seems unlikely. She didn't behave suspiciously, and I don't see how she would have got him to the Blue Pool."

"She might not have done the deed herself."

"Domestic murders tend to be in the moment, Sir. If she'd got someone else to carry it out, that would have been—"

"And who would she have got to do it, anyway?"

"Sir?"

"He's Arthur Kelvin, DCI Clarke. I don't imagine it would be easy to find a hired killer who'd be comfortable with being the one to finish him off, so to speak."

"No, Sir." He had a point. But someone *had* killed Kelvin.

Who, that was the question.

"The pathologist found practice wounds, which would

indicate an inexperienced killer. But DS Frampton suggested that might have been staged."

"Looks like you have a puzzle on your hands."

"We do, Sir."

"I suggest you solve it as quickly as you can, then."

She looked at him. What did he think she was going to do, sit around drinking coffee until the case solved itself?

"There are other aspects to this that you and other senior colleagues might need to consider, Sir."

"Such as?"

"Kelvin was the head of the county's largest organised crime operation."

"Allegedly."

She ignored the comment. They'd never managed to pin anything on Kelvin, but no one doubted what he was.

"He'll have left a vacuum. It might be filled from within his own family or associates. Or someone from outside might try to move in. Especially if that was why he was killed."

"You think another gang killed Kelvin so they could muscle in on his territory?"

"I don't think anything yet, Sir. Not without evidence. But it has to be considered. I think the Organised Crime unit needs to—"

"I'll take care of that, Lesley. Anything else?"

"I suggest we put surveillance on his nephews. Possibly his wife. Widow."

"You think she did it, after all?"

"I think she might lead us to whoever did."

"And his nephews. One of them's in prison, no?"

"It might be worth informing the prison. Making sure he isn't communicating with anyone on the outside."

"You want to interview him?"

"Not yet. But it might be necessary."

"Very well. I'll make the call. And we'll put a watch on his wife and on the other nephew. In Plymouth, right?"

Lesley frowned. How come Carpenter knew that, and she hadn't?

"Yes, Sir."

"I'll speak to the Devon force. They won't like it, but I'll see what I can do."

"Thank you, Sir. There are more immediate impacts on resources, too."

"It's a high priority case. You can authorise all the overtime you need. And I haven't forgotten that you're getting married on Saturday."

"That doesn't affect my abi—"

"To Kelvin's lawyer."

Lesley felt her breath catch. "Former lawyer. She left her firm so that she no longer had to work for him."

"Of course. How is Ms Short's new enterprise coming along?"

Lesley looked back at him. How much did he know?

"It's early days, Sir."

"Tell her all the best of luck with it from me," he said. "And let's hope you're able to clear up this case in time for your wedding."

"Yes, Sir."

CHAPTER SEVENTEEN

THE TRAFFIC for the rest of the journey was smooth, Elsa arriving home in ten minutes. She hurried up the stairs to the flat, phone in hand.

Once inside, she slammed the door behind her and stopped, listening.

"Hello? Lesley? Sharon? Anyone home?"

No response. Lesley would be at work for a good while yet, and Sharon wasn't due home for another couple of hours.

She was safe.

She walked through to the kitchen, trying to keep her pace steady and her breathing even. She kept glancing at the WhatsApp message as she did so.

Kelvin, dead? How? Murder?

If so, by whom? Anyone she knew?

She shivered.

Calm down, Elsa.

She flicked the coffee machine on. She needed to calm her nerves before she made the call. To do something normal.

As she flicked on the machine, she thought back to Lesley leaving the flat this morning. A call. A body.

Kelvin?

Lesley hadn't met her eye after receiving the call. Did she know something she wasn't telling her?

Stop it.

Lesley was a DCI. She headed up major investigations. And Elsa was a criminal lawyer. A criminal *defence* lawyer. It was sensible for Lesley not to share anything with her.

Still.

Maybe Lesley had a suspect in mind, someone Elsa would be representing. Or had once represented.

Elsa only had three clients now. Two of them were shoplifters. Still working their way through the courts and providing her with work, but hardly the type to be involved with murder.

The other was a property developer who'd been accused of insurance fraud. Again, nothing to do with the Kelvins.

Or so she hoped.

Just call the number, damnit. Put yourself out of your misery.

She poured a coffee and took it to the kitchen island, where she perched on a stool. She dialled.

"I wondered if I'd be hearing from you." A man's voice.

"You messaged me."

"I did. You took a while to reply. Trying to decide what to do, were you?"

"How did you get my number?"

"You've been advertising your services all over social media. You're not exactly incognito."

Elsa nodded. She'd taken the attitude that Kelvin knew

where she lived and how to get hold of her, so it was pointless trying to hide.

"Who are you? And why are you contacting me about the Kelvins?"

"Not the Kelvins. One particular Kelvin. Your former client, Arthur. Unless there are more of them you're friendly with?"

"No."

"I should hope not. Anyway, I know something about our poor departed Mr Kelvin. Something you might find useful."

"Tell me."

Silence.

"Hello?"

"I'm not just going to tell you over the phone, am I? Nowhere near as much fun. Or as lucrative."

"Lucrative?" Elsa asked. "You want money?"

"This weekend you'll be marrying the DCI who'll be in charge of the case. And you used to work for the man. I know your business is floundering, and I have access to a plum of a client for you."

"Who?"

"Again, not over the phone. I'll be wanting a commission, for referring this client. I'm a solicitor too, like you."

Elsa put her coffee cup down. If she gripped it any tighter, she'd smash it.

"Very well," she said. "You already know I've got a lot going on this weekend, so I suggest we meet today."

"Works for me. I'll see you at the Costa Coffee on Commercial Road, in half an hour."

The line went dead. Elsa held out her phone in front of her, staring at it.

Half an hour.

She didn't know who she was meeting, or whether they were dangerous.

Should she call Lesley?

No. It was fine. Just a meeting. With a lawyer. In a public place.

She downed the coffee and grabbed her keys.

CHAPTER EIGHTEEN

"Right," said Lesley as she walked back into her office. Dennis was at the board, writing names on a family tree. "What have you got for me?"

Dennis stood back and put the lid on the pen. He placed it carefully on her desk, making sure it lined up with the long edge. "I'm not comfortable with this."

She sighed. "Anything you can tell me, we'll keep verbal for now. Are you worried that someone in this office is going to tell the Kelvins what we're discussing?"

"They're the Kelvins, boss. I think there's a good chance they have someone from the police in their pay. More than one."

"And they'll be on heightened alert right now."

"They most certainly will."

"And everyone knows what we're working on."

Dennis nodded. "You don't keep something like this quiet in a nick, boss. The whole building's going to know what we're doing here. They'll be fascinated."

"Maybe that's a good thing."

"How?"

"The Super has just authorised as much overtime as we can use. I'm sure we'll be OK to rope a few extra bodies in, too."

"Bodies?"

"Detectives, Dennis. We need as many people on this case as we can get, so we can wrap it up before it comes back to bite us."

"And before your wedding."

She gave him a look. "That's got nothing to do with it, and well you know it."

"Are you planning a honeymoon?"

"You know I'm not the honeymoon type, Dennis."

"But Ms Short..."

"Neither is she. But yes, if you must know, we are going away for a few days. Scotland."

"Nice. Pam and I went there the year after we got married."

"I imagine it's changed a bit since then."

"The mountains won't have. The lochs."

"No." Elsa had hired a cabin overlooking Loch Lomond. Secluded, she'd said, amazing views. Sharon was going back to Birmingham for the week and Lesley would have Elsa to herself.

What with her work and the pressures of Elsa's new business, not to mention all the wedding planning, it had been a while since they'd spent proper time together. She was looking forward to it. More than the wedding itself, to be truthful.

"Maybe you're right, Dennis. But it's only four days. You can look after things while I'm away, if it comes to that. Or can you?"

He pursed his lips. "I can."

"Good. And if I bring in a couple more DCs, maybe another DS, it'll help you manage the workload."

"That won't be necessary."

"How about I let you pick who we bring in? You'll know who you've worked well with in the past, and who we can trust. What with Tina being off, we're short-handed anyway."

"A couple of the lads from Swanage a—"

"Not all lads, please, Dennis. There's enough of you already. At least one woman. Preferably two."

Dennis frowned, considering. "OK. How about DI Varney from Bournemouth? And two of his team, DC Vedra and DC Young."

"First names?"

"Will, Meera and Katie respectively."

"Sounds perfect. I'll speak to DI Varney's unit commander."

"We won't need them, though."

"We will, Dennis. We're going to have a lot of leads to follow on this case, and we need bodies."

"What makes you think that?"

"You've already written down the names of at least eight family members. The Super has agreed to put surveillance on three of them. Then we've got the weapon, the post-mortem, and any more forensics that Gail uncovers. And I want someone talking to Organised Crime, going through whatever intel they can give us."

"I can do that."

"You've got a trusted contact in that team?"

"DI Gough." A pause. "The DCI — the old DCI — was working with him before his retirement. Good chap."

Lesley looked at him, wondering which case Gough had worked with Mackie on. "Very well. Is there anyone on that board I need to be worrying about? We've got the mother, the wife, the nephews and the disappeared brother. Is that an aunt you've added?"

"Lydia. Gerard's sister."

"She still with us?"

"Not sure."

"She'd be how old, if she was?"

"In her eighties."

"So, unlikely to be a threat."

"No," agreed Dennis.

"OK, so that's family. What about employees, business associates?"

"That's going to make for a long list of potential suspects, boss."

Lesley slumped back in her chair. Dennis was right. With a victim like Arthur Kelvin, they couldn't start with potential suspects, or they'd be here all year. Instead, they had to focus on evidence. She could only hope that whoever had dumped him at the Blue Pool had left traces.

"OK," she said. "You have a chat with your friends in Organised Crime. Get some background. But we won't start digging too much yet. I want to see what the CSIs have got for us."

CHAPTER NINETEEN

STANLEY WRAPPED his arms around himself, trying to warm up. The wind was whistling through the conifers and sending the needles on the ground swirling around his feet. The water had even caught it, ripples and eddies whipping up like it was Swanage Bay on a breezy morning.

The body was out of the water now, thank goodness. The pathologist and one of his team had gone in and placed it on a trolley, which they'd wheeled out carefully. Gail and her team had prepared a route for them, one which was paved and had been carefully searched beforehand. No one wanted the trolley damaging any evidence.

The path they were taking out didn't seem to be the path that Kelvin had come in by, at least not according to the forensics. There'd been no sign of anyone being dragged along the ground on the route, and not much in the way of boot prints. The weather had been dry in the last week, and there wasn't much mud to capture any. And they all knew that with the public having been on the site the previous evening, anything they did find would probably be useless.

He watched as the pathology team pushed the trolley uphill towards a side path leading back to the car park. They hadn't taken the more direct route via the tea room, as there was more soft ground there for the wheels of the trolley to sink into. It wasn't long before the trolley disappeared into the trees.

Gail stretched her arms above her head and yawned.

"What time is it? I'm bloody famished."

"Half past three," Stanley told her.

"Shit. I haven't eaten since I got out of my bed at half seven." She looked around. "Where's my team when I need them?"

"You want me to fetch you something?"

She smiled at him. "D'you mind? I'll give you the money." She patted her forensic suit. "Or I would, if I could get at my pockets."

"It's fine. I'll see if I can bring down a coffee."

"Tea please, if you don't mind. And a sandwich."

"Any preference?"

She shook her head. "Anything'll do. I'm too hungry to care."

"Be right back."

Truth was, Stanley was hungry himself. He had a packed lunch back in his desk but hadn't thought to bring it out with him. He'd been so preoccupied with the case that he'd forgotten about food. But now that Gail mentioned it, he realised he was starving.

He tramped up the hill to the tea room, his legs cold and stiff. The door was locked.

He cupped his hands against the window and looked in. A woman was inside, cleaning down surfaces. He knocked on the glass.

She looked up and put a hand to her chest in surprise. She shook her head and mouthed something.

I know you're closed, he thought. *But I'm hungry*. He didn't much relish the idea of driving back to Wareham to buy something in a supermarket.

He held up his ID. The woman peered at it and approached the window.

"You part of the investigating team?" she shouted through the glass.

He nodded.

"I've been told to leave you alone."

He looked past her towards a fridge where he could see sandwiches. They would have stocked up for the day. If he knew catering, those sandwiches would be good for nothing but the bin at the end of the day.

He pointed. "We're hungry. Can I buy some food?"

She looked back at the fridge, then at him. She considered for a moment, then shrugged. She beckoned him to follow her to the door, which she opened.

"I suppose you coming up here counts as you bothering me, not the other way round. What can I get you?"

"Can I come in?"

She smiled. "Course you can. You must be frozen."

Stanley stepped inside as the woman closed the door and turned the key. It wasn't much warmer inside than out, but at least there was no wind.

"Thanks," he said. "I'll take two sandwiches and a couple of bags of crisps. And two teas, if you've got them."

"Go on then," she told him. "It's not as if I've got much to do. Any preference, on the sandwiches?"

"Whatever's going to go off first."

Her smile widened. "You're a considerate fella, aren't you?"

Stanley felt his cheeks heat up. He shrugged.

She opened the fridge. "I've got an egg and cress, and a ham. That do you?" She had a strong Dorset accent.

"Perfect. Thanks."

"You can take your pick on the crisps. They'll keep."

"Er... Salt and vinegar, and a cheese and onion please." That would cover all bases, he hoped.

"Coming right up. Sugar in the tea?"

"Oh..."

She laughed. "It's OK. I'll give you a couple of sachets. You want to invite your colleague to come up here, get out of the cold?"

"I think she's busy. I'll take away, if that's alright."

"Of course it's alright." She placed the sandwiches in a paper bag. "Horrible business. They know who it is yet?"

Stanley ignored the question. "Were you working here last night?"

"I was. Hot chocolates and coffees, daft buggers not caring about their caffeine intake after teatime. We put a dash of brandy in it for some of them, helps them get through the cold evening."

"You've got the place lit up at night."

"We have. Boss brought it in a year or so ago, gets the crowds in. Right pretty it is, too. You been to see it?"

"Sorry."

"No. Busy policeman like you. You want me to tell you if I saw anything suspicious?" She drew water from an urn and poured it into two disposable cups.

"Please."

"Well, you'll be disappointed then. But you might want to talk to Mary."

"Mary?"

"Mary's our social media person. Well, she's the boss's daughter, really, but she does a bit of social media work for the place around her shifts at Sainsbury's. She makes videos of the night-time events. Tries to get the reactions of the punters, show people how much fun it all is."

"Where will I find Mary?"

"She's got a flat in Wareham, over the Co-op. You know it?"

"I do. Thanks."

"My pleasure. Here, have your sandwiches." She handed him the paper bag and a cup holder with two teas, cocking her head and giving him another smile. She turned to pick up a card reader and he tapped his debit card against it.

She smiled as it rang through. "I'm Julie, by the way."

CHAPTER TWENTY

ELSA ARRIVED EARLY. She shivered and scanned the coffee shop. It was cold out there, and she hadn't been able to find her scarf before leaving.

There were two women with a pushchair at a table near the front, an elderly woman near the till, and a group of teenagers at the back.

No men on their own.

Good.

She ordered a flat white and took a seat close enough to the window to see through it, but not so close that she'd be seen by someone outside. She didn't want him watching her from across the street.

She put her drink down and arranged herself in her chair.

Should she take her coat off?

No. She didn't want him thinking they were going to get settled.

After five minutes by the clock behind the counter, the door opened. Elsa clenched her teeth. A man entered and she watched him. He made no sign of having noticed her. Then he turned to open the door and let a woman in behind him. He put a hand on her shoulder.

Elsa allowed herself to relax, just a little.

Calm down.

If she carried on like this, she'd be a nervous wreck by the time he got here.

If it was a he. It had been a man's voice on the phone, but maybe he'd send someone else.

She shook her head. If she was acting all cloak-and-dagger like he was, she'd turn up herself.

She pulled her phone out of her bag and forced herself to scroll through emails. She wanted to be distracted when he arrived, to avoid giving the impression she was eager to meet him.

She was halfway through the third email when she felt a shadow fall across her.

"Ms Short."

She looked up, shoving her phone into her coat pocket. A youngish man stood in front of her, early thirties maybe. He had dishevelled brown hair and pale skin with sharp red points on his cheeks. He wore a suit that looked like it had come from a mid-range chain store. He looked cold.

"That's me. Who are you?"

He smiled and took the seat opposite her. "My name's Xavier Robson."

"Xavier." She hadn't heard the name before. She wasn't about to forget a name like Xavier. "Aren't you going to get a drink?"

"It's OK," he glanced back at the till, "I've already ordered. I'm surprised you didn't see me coming in."

She said nothing. "What's all this about, Xavier?"

The young man who'd served Elsa appeared at their table. "Americano?"

Elsa nodded in the direction of her companion. He raised a hand.

"That's all mine. Thanks."

The barista placed the drink on the table and left them, not responding.

"So?" Elsa said. "You're telling me Kelvin is dead. And that you know something about it. *And* you claim to have a client for me."

He grinned, placing his coffee cup in the saucer. He wiped his mouth. "He is. I do. And yes."

"Enlighten me."

She looked around the coffee shop. There was no sign of anyone watching them. They couldn't be seen from outside. She was as confident as she could be that this wasn't one of Kelvin's 'employees'. They never travelled alone.

"I'm alone, if that's what you're wondering."

"Good. Are you going to tell me what's going on?" She checked her watch. "Because I've got a meeting to go to."

"I don't believe you."

"I beg your pardon?"

"Look, Elsa. Do you mind if I call you Elsa?"

"You might as well."

"Elsa. I know your business isn't exactly booming. I know you only have three clients. And I know why."

"You do, do you?"

"It doesn't take a legal genius to work it out."

"Go on then. Entertain me with your powers of deduction." She drank the last of her flat white.

He sat back, his hands clasped in his lap. "You used to

represent Arthur Kelvin. You'll know things about him that he won't have wanted people knowing. He wouldn't have wanted you representing someone who could use those things against him."

"I'm a professional, Mr Robson. I would never divulge confidential information about one client to another."

"Even if you were threatened? Or your fiancée or step-daughter were?"

She sighed. "So you know who I am. You know that my business is toast, or very nearly. What is it you know about Kelvin? And how did you find out he was dead before I did?"

"From the client I'm about to refer to you."

"OK. One of his associates, or a rival?"

"Neither. Or both, depending on how you look at it."

Elsa didn't know whether to be worried, or impatient. Clearly Xavier Robson enjoyed creating melodrama.

"I've finished my drink, Mr Robson. Just tell me what you came here for, and we can both leave."

"You didn't ask me what kind of lawyer I am."

She eyed him. "What kind of lawyer are you?"

He reached into the inside pocket of his jacket and brought out a business card. He placed it on the table between them.

She looked down.

Xavier Robson. Family Law.

"A divorce lawyer," she said.

"Exactly. Now do you want to know who the client is?"

"Of course."

He shook his head. "Amanda Frobisher."

"Who's Amanda Frobisher?"

"You might know her as Mrs Kelvin. His wife."

Elsa narrowed her eyes. "Hang on. You're a divorce lawyer, and—"

"Bang on. Kelvin was divorcing her, and she hired me to represent her. Now, I imagine once the police know that, there's a good chance she'll be a suspect. And she'll need a lawyer. Fancy taking the job?"

CHAPTER TWENTY-ONE

GAIL PLACED a hand on her stomach, trying to ignore the growling. *Stanley, where are you?*

She hoped he'd been able to persuade the tearoom to open up, or maybe find a snack machine somewhere. Anything, she didn't care. She just needed to fill the growing hole in her stomach if she was going to finish up here without fainting.

It was starting to get dark but they'd erected floodlights. She preferred working under electric light than daylight, anyway. It was easier to control. And she wanted to do the initial sweep of the site before leaving for the day. She knew Uniform were still out there, she could see flashlights moving in the trees. She just hoped they were being careful, not missing anything in the dark patches.

"Gail," Gav said, approaching her. "It's four o'clock. Don't you think we should call it a day?"

"I want to get the search wrapped up today. There's wildlife here, evidence could get disturbed. And if this site was locked last night, who's to say that whoever dumped the body won't come back the same way they did before and remove any evidence?"

"The police can put a watch on the place. They will do, I'd imagine."

She grunted. "No shortage of resources, when the victim's an organised crime boss. Why don't they do this for everyone, Gav? That woman whose house we had to trawl through last month, the one whose husband strangled her? The druggies who almost died after they were raided in that squat in Swanage?"

"You know that's not how it works. Besides, the quicker they solve this case, the quicker they can prevent any consequences among Kelvin's friends and family."

"Friends and family. Fellow criminals, you mean."

He shrugged. "So. Are you going to let us get home?"

Gail could see a light up hill. Stanley?

"Let me eat my sandwich, and then I'll review where we're at."

She didn't want to leave yet, but it wasn't fair on Gavin to keep him here. Brett had already gone back to the lab to work on the knife. She certainly wasn't staying on her own.

But she wouldn't *be* on her own. There would be Uniform here. They'd keep an eye on her.

The light she'd hoped was Stanley had disappeared in the opposite direction.

Shit. She needed to distract herself.

"Let me start on the patch beyond that path, then it'll be time to eat."

"OK." Gavin sighed. "I'll help."

"You do the next area along. Between the sycamore over there and that funny shaped log."

"Funny shaped log. Scientific term?"

"You know what I mean."

He grinned. "I do."

Gail headed for the next patch she was due to examine. There was an area of open ground, covered in pine needles, with a stand of trees to one side. She adjusted the floodlights to shine on it.

She stopped.

How had they not seen it?

There was a scarf snagged on a branch. It was just below eye level, and a dark colour. It would have been obscured by the greenery, invisible until the floodlights turned on it.

She grabbed an evidence bag. There was every chance this had been left there by a member of the public visiting the illuminations. But it was worth a look.

She pulled the scarf down carefully and placed it in the bag. It had a paisley pattern, green on black. No wonder she hadn't spotted it.

It was familiar. She'd seen one like this somewhere before.

Probably one of the local shops. Gail lived ten miles away in Swanage, and there was a good chance that someone visiting this site had bought it there.

Still.

She screwed up her eyes, trying to remember. Trying to picture it around someone's neck.

She opened her eyes.

It wasn't from Swanage. It had been bought in London. She'd asked the woman wearing it. She'd admired it.

She knew where she'd seen it. And who she'd seen it on.

CHAPTER TWENTY-TWO

Mike hated post-mortems. He preferred to stand as far away from the action as he could, holding his mouth firmly shut and avoiding eye contact if he could manage it.

But at least with Dr Bamford in charge, he didn't have to put up with Whittaker and his godawful music.

The post-mortem room was silent, the pathologist talking in hushed tones only when necessary, addressing his assistant who was making notes on a tablet.

Mike knew that Lesley had worked with this doctor in Devon, on the Lyme Regis case. The one where he'd finally had the chance to meet Tina's family. The one during which Tina had known she was pregnant but decided not to tell him yet.

He still felt cold when he thought about it. Tina hadn't given him a reason for her reticence, but he could make his own guesses. He was a DC, and young, and living in a pokey flat. He wasn't exactly a prospect. He could imagine how she'd baulked at the idea of having a baby with him, committing to spending her life with him.

And now look at them. No longer in the flat, they'd pooled their resources and bought a little house in Sandford. Louis had come along in November, and – this was the bit he found the hardest to believe – he had a wedding ring on his finger.

From colleagues to happy families, all in the space of a year. And he loved it.

"DC Legg?"

He blinked and looked at the pathologist, who was staring back at him.

"Yes?"

"Were you dozing off against the wall there, DC Legg?" The doctor smiled.

Mike felt himself blush. "No. Just thinking about the case."

The doctor raised an eyebrow. "I was just finishing off the examination. There are still toxicology tests to run, but I can't find any evidence of injuries other than the knife wound. And the shallower practice wounds below it."

Mike nodded. "So there's just the one wound that actually pierced his skin?"

"It's more complicated than that. The others are evenly spaced, shallow. They pierced the skin but didn't draw blood. But I'm not happy with them."

Mike stepped forward, allowing himself to look at the body. He breathed a sigh of relief. Kelvin – Kelvin! He still couldn't believe it – had been sewn up and looked almost peaceful.

"What do you mean, not happy?" he asked.

Dr Bamford beckoned him closer. "Take a look." He pointed at the wounds. There was the fatal wound below the rib cage, and six or seven smaller ones below it.

"Practice wounds," Mike said. "Like you said."

The pathologist shook his head. "They're too perfect. Equidistant, and all the same depth."

"That's not normal?"

"Not at all. Practice wounds tend to be irregular, random. Generally, the killer will build up with the knife, which means they start with one or two that are very shallow, and then get deeper as they move on. It's like they're working out how much pressure to apply."

"So you think this was faked?"

"I do. There's something else wrong with those wounds, too."

"What's that?"

The doctor gestured towards the body again. "They're post-mortem. Some of them at least should have drawn blood, but the heart had stopped and there was no blood to draw. Whoever killed your victim used one confident motion with a knife. Once the man was dead, they made these smaller wounds to make it look like a different kind of crime."

"Which means..."

"Which means your killer is someone who not only has the confidence and strength to kill a large man with one knife stroke, but also knows enough about pathology to attempt to stage a more amateur crime."

CHAPTER TWENTY-THREE

"DI Gough?"

"That's me. I assume this is about your murder case, DS Frampton."

"You've heard."

A snort came down the line. "Oh, the whole of Dorset Police has heard. You don't drag Arthur Kelvin out of the Blue Pool without it getting around."

"I imagine you were expecting my call."

"No, I wasn't."

"No?"

"Come on, Dennis. This is Arthur Kelvin. I can't tell you what we've been working on in relation to his activities, but you'll know that we've had our eye on him for some time. I was expecting your Super to ring my Super. You and me, we're a bit far down the pecking order, aren't we?"

The man had a point, Dennis thought, although it was good of him to suggest they were on the same level as each other. The DCI had asked him to call his contact in Organised Crime. Kelvin would no doubt have been the subject of an investigation, or a set of them, that went way above even the DI's level.

So why hadn't she referred it up to Superintendent Carpenter?

"Anyway," said Gough. "Now that you've got me, what is it you need to know?"

Dennis licked his lips. He was sitting at his desk in the team room, which was otherwise empty. The boss was in her office, Mike was out at the post-mortem and Stanley was still at the crime scene.

Dennis didn't envy either of them. Out in the dark and the cold, or watching Arthur Kelvin's body being cut up.

The perks of being a sergeant.

"First off," he said, "can you confirm whether there were any active investigations ongoing into Kelvin's activities at the time of his death?"

"*Ongoing*. Very formal. Yes, there were active investigations. None of them will stop. As you can imagine, Kelvin's death won't mean all the crime just stops. It just raises the stakes. The man was entangled with all number of dodgy characters from around the county and beyond, and none of them are going to let up just because he's dead."

"Do you think one of those dodgy characters, as you call them, might have killed him?"

A laugh. "Where to start, mate? Any of them could. These aren't the kind of people who have a respectful chat when they're not happy with each other."

"Anyone in particular?"

A pause, followed by a sigh. "Sadly, no. I'm sure my bosses are talking to yours. I know I'm not the only DI involved in investigating the man. But no. I can't give you any specific names. Not right now."

Dennis was surprised.

"You can't give me any names, or you're not allowed to?"

"Bit of both, really. There are investigations that even I don't know about, I'm sure. But I'm being straight with you, Dennis. I'm not aware of anyone in particular that I think you should be looking at."

"Right. Thanks."

"That doesn't mean you shouldn't be looking at any of them, though."

Dennis stood up and walked to the window, his phone at his ear. "Do you know anything about the disappearance of Frank Kelvin, DI Gough?"

"Frank Kelvin, the brother? He was last seen in 2005. Left a suicide note pinned to Swanage Pier. Nice touch. At the time, it was thought to be genuine, but no body was found."

"If he'd drowned, he might have washed out to sea."

"Exactly. And there's been no evidence of him turning up anywhere, at home or abroad, so we stopped worrying about him a long time ago."

"Right. Thanks for your time. If you do come up with anything, I'd be grateful if you could—"

"Of course I will. Assuming I'm allowed to."

Dennis turned back to the office. He paced past the desks to the far wall. In her office, Lesley raised her head and gave him a questioning look. He nodded, turned away from her, and sat at his desk.

"DI Gough?" he said, his tone low.

"Yes?"

"Am I right in thinking you worked with my former DCI before his retirement? DCI Mackie."

"Yes. Sad news, that. He was a good bloke. Horrible way to go."

Dennis sniffed. He wondered how much Gough knew about Mackie's death. Was he referring to the official suicide verdict, or the more likely explanation that Mackie had been pushed off the cliffs at Ballard Down?

"Were you investigating Kelvin at the time?" he asked.

"We were. There's a lot about that investigation that's still under wraps, but your old DCI helped us with some intelligence about one of Kelvin's nephews."

"Darren."

"No. Kyle, the one who buggered off out of the county."

"He left Dorset at that time?"

"Immediately after Mackie's death. We didn't have enough on him at the time, roped Devon Police in, of course, but they had enough nasty bastards of their own to contend with."

Dennis felt his cheek twitch. "So... do you think the Kelvins might have held a grudge against the DCI?"

"The Kelvins hold a grudge against everyone, mate. Mackie would have been no different."

The door to Lesley's office opened. Dennis straightened in his chair.

"Thanks, DI Gough. You've been helpful. And you'll give me a call if anything comes up?"

"I will, Dennis. I'll be in touch."

CHAPTER TWENTY-FOUR

"HAM AND MUSTARD, and egg and cress." Stanley held out a paper bag.

Gail peered into it. "Egg and cress, please."

He pointed. "That one."

She delved into the bag and brought out the sandwich, ripping the wrapper open.

"Slow down, boss," Gavin said. "Anyone'd think we don't feed you."

She turned to him. "I'm sorry, Gav. We didn't get you anything."

He smiled. "It's OK. Got my lunch tin in the van. I ate hours ago."

"And you didn't share with me? You sod." She gave him a mock punch, which he deflected.

Stanley sat on a rock, munching on his sandwich. Beyond the trees Gail could see lights moving: Uniform were still out there, searching.

It was too dark now.

"We should call them off," she said. "Place a guard on the place and come back at first light."

Gav groaned. "Can't I have a lie-in?"

"Really?"

"I'm joking. I'll be here soon as we can see."

"Thanks, Gav." She'd make sure he had some time off, after all this was done.

"So," Stanley said. He'd finished his sandwich and was onto the bag of crisps. "Have you found anything else? Other than the knife?"

Gail glanced at the case containing the evidence bags. The scarf was in there. She hadn't mentioned it to Gav yet.

"Not yet," she said. "But there's still time."

Why was she lying to him? It was in there, labelled up and available for anyone working on the case to examine.

But there was someone she needed to talk to before she thought about it again.

Stanley stood up. He'd balled his crisp wrapper and put it in his pocket. He slurped on his tea. "Good tea," he said. "That Julie knows what she's doing."

"Julie?" Gav asked. "Who's she?"

"Oh." Stanley blushed. "Just the woman in the tea room."

"Friendly, was she?" Gail asked.

"She made us both a cup of tea," Stanley replied. "Don't knock it."

She smiled. She didn't know much about Stanley, despite him having been in Lesley's team for almost a year now. Did he have someone at home, waiting for him? Or would he be back here in the morning, chatting Julie up?

"Thanks for your help today, Stanley," she said.

"No problem. I need to get back, though. The boss'll want a conflab before everyone goes home."

She thought of the scarf, sitting in the evidence box. She would tell Lesley about it. But not Stanley, not just yet.

CHAPTER TWENTY-FIVE

"So what did Gough have to tell you?" Lesley asked as Dennis stepped into her office.

"Not much. He didn't have any specific names he thought we should look into, and he told me that any investigations they've got going on won't stop with Kelvin dead."

"No. Did he give you any details of those investigations?"

"He couldn't. He... he suggested that if the request came from the Super to his Super, it might be more... fruitful."

She nodded. She was sure Carpenter was already talking to people. Trouble was, she couldn't be sure which people he was talking to and whether he would tell her what he found out.

"Thanks, Dennis."

The outer door opened and Mike entered. When he saw the two of them in the office, he picked up pace and came in to join them.

"Mike," she said. "How did the PM go?"

"Good."

"Bamford's a bit easier to work with than Whittaker, I imagine."

"You can say that again." He smiled.

"No classical music."

"Nope."

"So did he find anything more than that stab wound?"

"He still needs to run toxicology analysis, but there was no evidence of any other wounds."

"Signs of a struggle?" Dennis asked.

"Nothing. Fingernails intact, no scratches or bruising on his arms or anywhere else. If he was moved, it was after death. There's no bruising. Apart from that stab wound and the practice wounds below it, he's in perfect nick."

"At least it'll make the viewing with his widow easier," Dennis said.

Lesley looked at him. "That's been scheduled?"

"Tomorrow morning, so I'm told."

"Just the widow, or the mother too?"

He shrugged. "No idea."

The outer door opened again: Stanley. He gave them a little wave, shrugged off his coat, placed it on the back of his chair where it draped onto the floor, shivered ostentatiously, then joined them in the office.

"All OK?" he asked.

"Mike is just briefing us on the post-mortem," Dennis said.

"Oh. And?" Stanley looked at Mike.

"Just the stab wound. But the doc reckons those practice wounds were faked."

"He does?" Lesley said.

Mike nodded. "They're equally spaced, and all the same depth. They were done after Kelvin died, too. Should have bled but didn't. Bamford reckons whoever did it stabbed him just the once, then added those wounds after death to make it look like someone who didn't know what they were doing had killed him."

"Clever," Dennis muttered.

"Not clever enough," Lesley told him. "It didn't get past Bamford." She wondered if Whittaker would have spotted the same thing.

"So," she said. "Kelvin was killed with one stab to the abdomen, in a firm upward motion." She pointed to the board, which now had crime scene photos. There was a close-up of the wound.

"Upwards," said Dennis. "Means it was someone shorter than him?"

"Not necessarily. We don't know what position they were both in at the time."

She walked into the space between the desk and the board and motioned for Mike to follow her. Lesley was tall but Mike was about three inches taller. "Stand facing me."

Mike glanced at Dennis, who nodded, then moved to stand in front of her.

Lesley drew a hand back. She stopped. "Do we know if the killer was right or left-handed?"

"The wound goes in from right to left," Mike said. "So probably right-handed."

"Unless they faked that too," suggested Dennis.

"You'd struggle to fake that," Lesley said. "He'd need to use his strongest arm, to inflict a fatal stab in one movement."

"If it was a he," Dennis corrected her.

"Good point." She didn't know many women with the strength to overpower a man like Kelvin and stab him. But it wasn't outside the realms of possibility.

"I want the toxicology results as soon as they're in," she said. "If Kelvin was taken by surprise, he could have been drugged."

"I've asked the pathologist to send it over as soon as he has it," Mike said.

"Good."

She looked at him, then down at his chest. She took a breath and pulled her right arm back again. She lunged for him, slowing as her fist made contact just below the rib cage.

"Oof," said Mike.

"Sorry. I didn't mean to hurt you."

He shrugged. "You didn't. Just thought I should add sound effects."

Stanley stifled a laugh.

"This isn't funny," Lesley said. "Yes, I know it's Arthur Kelvin. None of us is exactly grieving his death. But there's a widow to think of."

"And the possible consequences," added Dennis. "His nephews might want revenge."

"Unless it was them that killed him." Her fist was still against Mike's chest. She pulled it away and walked to the board.

"The wound is central," she said. "To get that angle, I need to come at you from the side." She cocked her head, examining the photo, then took it down from the board. She showed it to the rest of the team.

"Maybe he was lying down," Stanley suggested.

"Or sitting," Mike added.

Lesley nodded. "I want to know exactly how Kelvin died. We know it was a single stab wound, but we don't know how it was inflicted. Mike, can you work with one of the new officers we're bringing in to establish positions, angles, that kind of thing. Ask Doctor Bamford for a 3D image."

"That'll be expensive," Dennis said.

She looked at him. "Superintendent Carpenter says we can have all the resources we need." She knew this wasn't strictly what he'd told her, but it was close enough. "So we have the budget."

"No problem," Mike said. He put his hand out for the photo. "What new officers?"

"DI Varney from Bournemouth's bringing two of his team in. You can work with one of the DCs."

"Meera Vedra. I know her."

"Fine."

Mike still had his hand outstretched. Lesley looked down at the photo.

"No," she said. "This stays on the board. You'll need to get another copy printed off."

"That and all the rest," said Stanley.

"Fair do. I'll speak to Gail."

"You do that."

CHAPTER TWENTY-SIX

SADIE KNEW BETTER than to make a phone call, when it came to talking to men like Detective Superintendent Phipps. He'd brush her off, and if he couldn't do that, he'd simply hang up.

So she'd spent the last eight weeks tracking down his new address.

The man had moved after his retirement, to a bungalow in Winchester. He'd previously lived in Lymington. She mused on the idea that a move in the opposite direction would be more typical following retirement. Maybe Phipps was trying to keep a low profile.

He certainly hadn't been easy to track down. His name wasn't in the phone book, he wasn't on social media, and there was no mention of him on the Hampshire Police website. It was as if when he'd retired, he'd ceased to exist.

She parked her car away from the streetlamps, a few doors along from his bungalow. The street was a mix of bungalows in their original state, no doubt occupied by pensioners like Phipps, and those that had been extended to within an inch of their lives. She could only imagine how big one of these places would be when converted from a single storey to a two-storey house. Certainly bigger than her room in the flat she shared with her mate Guy.

She was in the wrong job. And she was certainly working for the wrong news organisation.

Phipps emerged from his house after she'd been waiting for about twenty minutes. She'd occupied herself by listening to a true crime podcast, keeping her ears and brain occupied but her eyes free to watch. She only listened to podcasts covering crimes committed before she was born, sometimes well before she was born. Whenever she learned about anything more recent, she found herself wanting to investigate it.

Sadie watched as Phipps walked to the end of the road and turned right, towards the centre of the city. Should she follow him on foot, or crawl behind him in her car?

On foot. Following the man in her car was too creepy.

She got out of her car and hurried to the end of the road, stopping before she reached the corner.

She straightened and adjusted her stride, anxious to look like she was out for a casual stroll.

Turning the corner, she crashed straight into Phipps.

He gripped her arms above the elbows, his eyes wide and shaded with dark circles. This was a man who didn't sleep well at night, even in retirement.

"What do you want?" he barked.

She shook away from his grip. "That's assault."

He laughed. "What you've been doing is harassment. Stalking. I could have you arrested under Section 2A of the Protection from Harassment Act."

Sadie considered her options. Phipps was a former police

officer. He knew the law better than she did, and he had more powerful friends.

She brought out her business card, making him flinch. What did he think she was going to do, draw a gun?

Paranoid.

"My name's Sadie Dawes. I work for the BBC in Bournemouth."

"I've heard of you."

Good. Obscurity was the thing she dreaded most. But being on TV most evenings did make it hard for her to carry out undercover work.

"I'm looking into the death of Tim Mackie."

"DCI Mackie."

"Yes. I gather you were brought in to investigate, after the case was reopened."

"That's no secret."

She took a step back. "So what is?"

He smiled at her. "I'm retired, Miss Dawes. This isn't my job anymore." He turned away from her.

"Look," she said. "I think Mackie was murdered. And I think Detective Superintendent Carpenter has been covering it up."

He stopped walking.

She waited.

He turned to her. "That's quite an accusation."

"He threatened me, just yesterday. Told me to stop sticking my nose in where it wasn't wanted."

He looked her up and down, his eyes narrowed. "I'm going to the pub," he said. "Come with me, and maybe we can talk."

CHAPTER TWENTY-SEVEN

LESLEY YAWNED as she turned onto the Lansdowne Road into Bournemouth. She checked the dashboard clock: 6.45. She'd be in time for the meeting with the caterers. Just.

She was about to reach for the hands-free to update Elsa when her phone rang. It was Gail.

"Gail," she said. "I hope you're not still at the Blue Pool."

"I'm on my way to my mum's," Gail told her. "To pick Tim up."

"Yes." Gail's son was six years old. She wondered what it was like to juggle single parenting a small child with a career like Gail's. She'd hardly seen Sharon when the girl was small, but Terry had been at home working on his thesis, so she hadn't worried.

Maybe she should have.

"How's the search going? Did Carpenter give you the resources he promised me?"

"He did. Uniform are sixty percent of the way through the sweep."

"Have they found anything?"

A pause. "They haven't." Another pause. "But I did."

"OK. What?"

"Lesley, have you and Elsa visited the Blue Pool recently?"

Lesley looked at the phone. She frowned. "No. Why?"

"You haven't been to see the illuminations?"

"I'd never been there in my life before today. Why?" She felt her breath slowing.

"What about Elsa?" Gail asked. "I know she hasn't got much work at the moment. Does she go out for walks?"

"Along the beach, sometimes. But no. She might not have many clients yet, but touting for business is a full-time job when you're establishing a new practice."

"So to your knowledge, Elsa hasn't been at the Blue Pool lately."

"No. Gail, what's this about?"

"I think I found her scarf."

"Her scarf?"

"It was snagged in a tree. Dark green, with a paisley pattern. It was hidden until we turned the searchlights on it. It's just... I remember her wearing it when we went out for dinner last month. I asked her where she'd got it."

"Liberty. In Regent's Street."

"That's what she told me."

"Gail, what are you suggesting?"

"I'm not suggesting anything. I'm just telling you about a piece of evidence. Are you on your way home?"

Lesley felt her throat tighten. Ten to seven by her clock. She still hadn't rung Elsa. She would meet her at the hotel.

"I am."

"When you get there, can you just check for the scarf?"

"Of course. But it's a coincidence, Gail. I'm sure plenty of people have that scarf."

"I'm sure you're right. But..."

Lesley shrugged off her irritation. If Gail had presented this as evidence to the team, then it would feel less like she thought there was a basis for it. Lesley didn't like the idea of her friend trying to hide this from the others.

"I'll check, Gail. Now if you don't mind, I've got a wedding tasting to get to."

CHAPTER TWENTY-EIGHT

MIKE CLOSED the front door and felt his body slump at the sound of crying.

"Tina? I'm home."

"Mike." She opened the living room door, Louis in her arms. Tina wore a pair of jogging bottoms with a stain on the knee and a T shirt with a rip in it. She looked exhausted.

"He won't go down," she said. "It's bloody colic again."

"Surely he's too old for colic."

"He's at the prime age for it." She held Louis out. The baby reached out for Mike with his tiny hands, and Mike felt his stomach flip. No matter how hard the work of caring for his son was, he never failed to melt when he clapped eyes on the boy.

Mike bundled Louis to him. The crying didn't stop.

"Have you tried feeding him?"

"Of course I've tried feeding him. I feel like my nipples are going to melt." She leaned against the wall, then dragged herself down it, sliding to the floor and clutching her knees.

Mike stooped to get down to her level, careful not to drop the baby.

"I'll take him upstairs, love," he said. "Sing to him, or something."

She looked up at him, her eyes red. "Thanks. I just need a moment to myself. I didn't manage to get out today."

"I thought you had that singing group?"

"I did. But then he did a poonami just as we were about to leave and by the time I'd cleaned that up I was going to be fifteen minutes late. It hardly seemed worth it."

"So you didn't manage to get out at all."

She glared at him. "Going out when you've got to take all the stuff he needs and get the pushchair unfolded isn't as easy as you think."

He nodded. The pushchair was folded up under the stairs. Their house might have been larger than either of their previous flats, but the hall was little more than a corridor. There was no way they could leave an open pushchair in it.

He leaned Louis closer in to his chest and put a hand on Tina's head. Her brown curls were messed up.

"I'll take him upstairs, love. You sit down and have a cup of tea."

"That means making it."

He hesitated. "I'd do that for you, but..." he gestured down at the baby with his chin. Louis was sobbing now, the volume of his cries dropping.

"See?" Tina said. "He calms for you. Why won't he do that for me?"

Because he can sense your stress? Mike thought. But he wasn't about to suggest it. "I don't know." He placed a kiss on the top of her head and headed up the stairs.

Ten minutes later he'd managed to settle the baby and get

him into his Moses basket. He stood over it for a few minutes, humming under his breath and watching his son descend into sleep. He was so still when he slept, sometimes it scared Mike.

He crept down the stairs to find Tina in the living room, a mug of tea in her hand. She had her feet up on the coffee table but hadn't switched the TV on.

"Rough day?" he asked, sliding onto the sofa next to her.

She leaned against him. Her body was warm and soft. He relaxed into her.

"Bloody awful," she said. She sipped at the tea. "Tell me it gets easier."

"It gets easier." Truth was, Mike had no idea how it got. But if it carried on like this, surely no second children would ever be born?

"I'll choose to believe you," she said. She gulped down the last of her tea and turned to look at him. "D'you want a cup? There's nothing for tea."

He smiled. "Fish and chips?"

Her eyes brightened for a moment, reminding him of the Tina he'd known when she was working. "Fish and chips. Perfect."

He stood up. "I'll go get it."

"Thanks. I'll make you a brew while you're gone."

"I can get a bottle of wine in, on the way to the chippy."

She pulled a face. "Breastfeeding."

"Of course." He didn't like to drink when she wasn't able to. It seemed unfair. He could make up for it at the pub with Stanley, on Friday.

"I saw the news," she said, looking up at him. He raised an eyebrow. "Kelvin," she continued. "So someone finally got him."

He glanced at the TV. "It's public knowledge?"

"Local teatime news. I was trying to see if the TV would calm Louis."

Mike laughed. "The death of Arthur Kelvin would calm anyone."

"I wouldn't be so sure." Her voice had picked up, her back straightened. "He'll have left a power vacuum. And whoever killed him, there'll be people out for revenge."

"It might have been accidental."

"Really?" She put her mug down on the table. "Don't talk bollocks."

Mike leaned in and kissed her on the lips.

"What was that for?" she said. "I must stink. Louis made me spill soup down myself earlier."

"So that's what it is. I love you when you perk up like this. When your brain switches back on."

"So you don't love me when I'm being a mum."

"Come on, T. You know that's not what I mean."

She gave his knee a rub. "I'm goading you, Mike. Tell me more about the case. It's murder, right? Do you have a suspect?"

"Not yet. We've got a knife, though."

She shuffled round so she was perched on the edge of the sofa, facing him. "A murder weapon?"

Mike nodded. "Looks like it. And fake practice wounds."

Tina whistled. "So someone wanted us to think it was an amateur." She looked at him. "You reckon it was a hit?"

"The boss keeps telling us to avoid talking like we're in an episode of *The Sopranos*."

"It's Kelvin. He *was* Dorset's answer to *The Sopranos*."

"Maybe. But we're nowhere near having a suspect yet."

Tina reached over and grabbed her phone from the coffee

table. "Let's see what was going on with our beloved Mr Kelvin in the days before he died."

Mike leaned back, all thoughts of fish and chips forgotten. "Really?"

"You know this is what keeps me sane. I can't completely switch off from CID work and then expect to come back in the summer like I never left."

"You'll be fine."

"It keeps me from going mental, love. Indulge me."

He held his hands up. "OK. Tell me what you find." It occurred to him that no one on the team had thought to do this. Or maybe the boss had, while he'd been out at the post-mortem.

"OK," said Tina. "This is interesting."

"Yes?"

She peered at her phone, her forehead creased in concentration. "I'm on the government database. Court records."

"And?"

"Kelvin applied for a divorce."

"A divorce?"

Tina nodded. Her eyes were alight, nothing like the dullness he'd been greeted with when he'd arrived home.

"What's the name of his widow?" she asked.

"Amanda Frobisher."

"That's her. He applied for a divorce from her, just a week ago." She looked up. "Hasn't gone through yet, of course. And if she's still married to him, there's every chance she stands to inherit everything."

CHAPTER TWENTY-NINE

"Sorry I'm late," Lesley said as she hurried into the function room. Elsa was already there, standing in front of a table which was empty except for two place settings. Sharon stood to one side of her, and the hotel's wedding co-ordinator, Miles, on the other.

"Mum," Sharon said. "Elsa said I could come cos you were working."

Lesley looked at the table again. Two place settings. They were planning on serving the two of them a full meal.

She felt her shoulders slump. "That's a good idea, Sharon sweetheart. You do the tasting with Elsa. It'll be fun."

Elsa stepped away from the table towards Lesley. She grabbed her hand. "Hey. We can share. It'll be fine." She turned towards the wedding co-ordinator. "You can make the meal stretch to three people, can't you? Divide it up."

The man looked perturbed but caught Sharon's look of disappointment and pulled on a smile. "Of course. I'll just go and have a word." He disappeared through a set of double doors. Kitchen sounds emerged in his wake.

"There it is, then," Elsa said. She pulled on Lesley's hand. "Come and sit down while they set another place."

"This is going to cost more."

"Oh, hang the cost."

Lesley looked at her fiancée. "You're the one who's been worrying about money since you left the firm."

Elsa smiled at her. "I've got a new client."

Lesley felt her face break into a smile. "Really?" She hugged Elsa. "That's great news, sweetie. Anyone I know?"

Elsa's gaze dropped. She turned towards the table, still holding Lesley's hand. "Let's not talk about work now."

"OK." Lesley took a seat at the empty place. Sharon made to sit next to her, then stopped herself and shifted to the next place along, letting Elsa sit next to Lesley. Elsa put a hand on Lesley's knee.

Lesley looked over to a chair against the wall, where Elsa and Sharon had placed their coats. Was the scarf there?

"Let me just get rid of my coat," she said. She stood up and went to the chair, shrugging off her coat. She placed it on top of Sharon's, rifling through the items already there to check for Elsa's scarf.

There was no scarf.

"Lesley? Everything OK?"

"Fine. Did you walk, or come in the car?" Lesley took her place again.

"We walked," Sharon told her. "Bloody cold though."

Lesley flashed her a look. Sharon laughed. "You turning into Dennis, Mum? You'll be getting his swear jar out next."

Lesley rubbed her thighs under the table. Sharon was seventeen now. She had a point.

"I'm not surprised you were cold," she said, aware of the tension in her voice. "Neither of you wore a scarf."

"My coat's got a big collar," said Sharon. "I don't need one."

Lesley looked at Elsa.

"What?" Elsa said. "I lost mine. It's no big deal."

Lesley felt her throat tighten.

Stop it, she told herself.

It was a coincidence.

The wedding co-ordinator emerged from the kitchen, carrying a tray with a place setting.

"Now," he said. "The chef has said that everything can be split between the three of you. How lovely, doing this as a family."

CHAPTER THIRTY

Sadie and Phipps walked in silence along the quiet streets, occasionally passing a solitary walker coming the other way. Phipps was a fast walker, but Sadie had no problem keeping up. She swam weekly and worked out when she had time, and she prided herself on her fitness.

Besides, she was at least thirty years his junior.

At last they came to a pub, the William Walker. Phipps stopped, gestured towards it with a nod of the head, and headed inside. She followed.

At the bar, he ordered a pint of bitter shandy and asked her what she was drinking.

"It's OK," she said. "I'll get this."

"No way," he told her. "I'm not having any hint that you're paying me for information."

"It's just a drink."

"What are you drinking?"

"Diet Coke."

He turned to the barmaid, who was waiting with a

bemused expression. "Pint of bitter shandy and a Diet Coke coming up."

He grunted, paid with cash, and tapped his fingers on the bar as they waited.

"I'll go and find a table," she said.

"Knock yourself out."

She left him at the bar and walked to a quiet corner of the room. It seemed a nice pub, smart, with gastropub vibes. Not what she'd been expecting.

Here they would be tucked in next to the inglenook fireplace, and difficult to overhear from the neighbouring tables.

He approached the table, drinks in both hands and a knowing look on his face. "You picked the most secluded table."

"Did I?"

"You know you did. I'm a copper, remember?"

Were a copper, she thought. She gave him a smile and took the Diet Coke.

"So," he said. "I don't want to keep you here any longer than I have to. A couple of fellas I know might be popping by in half an hour."

She suspected that was a lie, but half an hour was more than enough time. And she preferred to get to the point.

"Fine," she said. "Can you tell me why the investigation into DCI Mackie's death was suspended?"

"It wasn't suspended."

"It was opened, then it ground to a halt. That sounds like suspended to me."

He took a pull from his pint then wiped his upper lip and twitched his nose. "I took early retirement before the case was concluded. I wasn't made aware of the case being formally closed. But that's Dorset's business. Not mine."

"Can you tell me what you did find?"

He watched her for a moment. He took another drink from his pint, his eyes not leaving hers.

She held his gaze.

At last he put his pint down and looked down at the table. His hands lay flat on the wood. She noticed that his fingernails were chewed. There was no wedding ring.

"Officially, DCI Mackie's death was a suicide," she said. "But I don't believe that, and I don't think any of his colleagues do either."

"Who've you been talking to?"

"I'm not about to divulge my sources."

He took another drink, staring at her again. It was unnerving, but she wasn't about to let him rattle her.

"Why are you doing this?" he asked.

"If DCI Mackie was murdered, then it's in the public interest for there to be an investigation into that crime. Just as it is for any murder."

"Especially the murder of a senior police officer," he told her.

A retired police officer, she thought. A realisation came to her.

"It took me months to track you down," she said. "Are you scared for your safety?"

He looked back at her but said nothing.

"Did you uncover something that could put you in danger? Is that why you went back to Hampshire and retired?"

"It takes more than a case to scare me, Miss Dawes. I took retirement because it was offered to me and I wanted to relax."

But then you came and hid here.

"What was DCI Mackie investigating, before he died? Was there a case he hadn't dropped, after his retirement?"

Phipps took another drink. He put the glass down and leaned across the table.

"I'm not telling you what he was investigating. But I am telling you that it might be worth your while taking an interest in Dorset's newest murder investigation."

"Arthur Kelvin."

His expression was impassive.

"You think Mackie was investigating Arthur Kelvin," she said, "and he was killed because of it?"

"All I'm saying is speak to his lawyer."

"Whose lawyer?"

"Kelvin's. Or rather, the lawyer who worked for him at the time. Elsa Short. Speak to her."

CHAPTER THIRTY-ONE

"LET's start by welcoming our new team members," Lesley said. There were seven of them in her office, some sitting, most standing. It was cramped. But she didn't want to do this in the outer office in case anyone came in.

"Thanks," said DI Varney. "We're happy to help."

"Anything to solve Arthur Kelvin's murder,' added DC Young. Her eyes shone.

Lesley smiled at her. This was a big case, and local CID would be only too happy to get involved. She could have asked every detective in Dorset to join in, and none of them would have said no.

"Right," she said. "So here's where we're at. Arthur Kelvin was found early yesterday morning by a young couple taking a walk at the Blue Pool."

"They're not suspects?" asked DC Young.

"No," said Lesley. "Just unlucky. He's now at the morgue, and the PM was carried out yesterday afternoon."

"That was quick," said DI Varney.

"If you don't mind," she said. "I'd like to bring you up to speed quickly so we can move on to allocating roles."

"Sorry, Ma'am."

"And don't call me Ma'am. I prefer boss."

"No problem. Boss." He smiled.

Lesley sniffed. She didn't like having to get used to a new team. It had been hard enough with Dennis and the others when she'd joined. What were this lot like? And could she trust them?

She'd just have to have some faith in Dennis's judgement.

"Cause of death was a stab wound," she continued, pointing at the relevant photo on the board. "Pathology say he was dead around twenty-four hours before we found him. He died offsite and was brought to the Blue Pool overnight."

"How?" asked DC Young. She was as young as her name, with a wide face and ruddy cheeks.

"We don't know that yet. CSI and Uniform are back out there already, continuing their search. We can't find any sign of gates being forced, but it's a big site with fencing around it. Fencing that isn't exactly high-tech."

"So it wouldn't have been hard to bring him in," said DI Varney.

"No." Lesley bit down her irritation. *Shut up and let me finish.* "There are some other minor wounds around the one that killed him. Practice wounds. Except, they're not. We believed they were faked, to make us believe the killing was done by an amateur."

DC Young opened her mouth, spotted Lesley's expression, and quickly closed it again.

"I've spoken to the widow, and I have no reason to suspect her right now," Lesley said.

"Err..." Mike raised his hand, slowly.

"It's not school, Mike. Have you got new information?"

"Tina and I were doing some online research last night."

"You got your wife helping you?" asked Stanley.

Mike glared at him. "She's a member of this team. And she thought of something I don't believe any of us did." He looked at Lesley. "With respect, boss."

"No offence taken. Glad to have Tina on the team, even if only vicariously. What did you find?"

"Kelvin filed for a divorce a week ago."

DI Varney let out a low whistle. Dennis coughed.

"OK," said Lesley. "So we need to find out what that meant, legally." She closed her eyes. "That means talking to his solicitor."

"Aurelia Cross," Dennis muttered.

"Yes."

"You want me to go?"

She considered.

"Yes please, Dennis. I think that would be best. Anything else on Kelvin's marital woes, Mike?"

"No. Sorry, boss."

"Don't apologise. It could be a useful lead. But don't let it fool you into assuming we have a definite suspect. We need evidence before we can come to that kind of conclusion."

She thought of the call from Gail last night. The scarf. It would come out soon enough.

"Forensics have also found some physical evidence. A scarf. It could have been left by a member of the public—"

"The site was open on Sunday night," Dennis said.

"It was." She eyed him. She didn't want DI Varney and his team knowing about the connection. She'd talk to Dennis about it, in private.

"Are they checking it for DNA?" DC Young asked.

My, but you're keen, Lesley thought.

"No," she said. "There's no reason right now to think it's pertinent, so we're keeping it as evidence but holding off on expensive analysis."

"I thought money was no object," Stanley said.

"Up to a point," she told him. She could sense herself losing control of this briefing.

"How did you get on with the social media manager?" she asked Stanley.

"I wouldn't call her that. She's just a young woman helping her dad out."

"Did she have any video that might be useful to us?"

"She's got footage of the Sunday night. But nothing past eight pm when they closed."

"Is she sending it over? You never know."

"She is."

"Good. You work through that, will you? DC Vedra can work with you."

"I thought DC Vedra was going to work with me on the stab wound?" Mike said.

DC Vedra looked from Stanley to Mike, and then to her DI.

"I'd appreciate it if my team's roles can be allocated via me," DI Varney said.

"OK," Lesley told him. "I'll pass work to you, and you can put your team on it as you see fit. But I reserve the right to assign tasks to your team in your absence, or if it's urgent."

"Of course. I have worked major investigations before."

"Good. In that case, I have two jobs for this morning. One is helping Stanley trawl through the video. The other is to work with Mike to identify exactly how Kelvin was stabbed."

Varney nodded. "Katie, you work with Stanley. Meera, you can go with Mike."

"Boss," the two women muttered in unison. Lesley noted that he'd allocated them in exactly the way she'd intended to.

She sighed. She hoped the acquisition of extra team members wouldn't prove to be a futile exercise in office politics.

"OK," she said. "I'm heading to the morgue. The victim's mother and widow are scheduled to come for a viewing, and I'd like to have a chat with them both." *And see what their relationship is like.*

"What about the crime scene?" asked Dennis. "Do we need to check if there's any news on the knife, or on an entry point?"

"Gail can inform us of any progress by phone," she told him.

"Yes, boss."

"You go see Aurelia Cross. Find out what you can about Kelvin's legal situation. Had he changed his will? Were there any cases that might have resulted in someone wanting him dead?"

"Boss."

DI Varney cleared his throat. "I can go to the crime scene. Have a chat with the CSIs. See if I can direct their work."

"You don't need to direct Gail Hansford. She knows what she's doing."

"Well. With respect, Uniform might need some overseeing."

Lesley eyed him. The team of uniformed officers was

already being overseen by PS Dillick. She doubted they needed the DI's help.

"No," she said. "I want you to do some background work. Find out what you can about Kelvin's current business dealings. Look online, and talk to your colleagues in Bournemouth and Poole. They'll have had their ears to the ground."

Organised Crime weren't telling them anything, and with good reason. But Kelvin had run a string of businesses in the east of the county, and CID and Uniform in that area would know about it.

"No problem, boss." He gave her an insincere smile.

Lesley sighed.

Yesterday she'd felt like they'd have plenty of lines of enquiry to follow, what with Kelvin having so many potential would-be killers. But now, having decided to focus on the evidence and not on the cast of characters, she felt as if they were dragging their heels.

And now she had Varney and his team to deal with.

But the longer they went without an arrest, the higher the chances of a revenge killing.

"OK, everyone," she said. "Get to work. I want everyone reporting back to me in an hour."

CHAPTER THIRTY-TWO

Dennis sat in Aurelia Cross's office, tapping his heel against his knee. It made a pleasant change to be brought in here to wait: on previous visits, he'd been forced to sit outside in the gloomy reception area. Sometimes for half an hour or more.

He looked around the office. It was a blank, modern space, with floor to ceiling windows overlooking a shopping street. But Aurelia Cross had done her best to make it her own. There was a heavy chest of drawers against one wall, a vast mahogany desk, and plants on every surface.

The door opened behind him and he rose from his chair.

"Oh, do sit down, Detective. I can't be doing with formality. What do you need me for? I'm due in court in half an hour."

She hurried round the table and slumped into her chair, her eyes roaming over the desk as if she were looking for something specific. She hadn't been like this before, but now she was the sole partner in the firm. That would be hard work for anyone, and Aurelia Cross wasn't a young woman.

"You'll have heard about Arthur Kelvin's death," he said.

"Indeed I have." She sat back in her chair, her hands in her lap. "And I was wondering how long it would be before you came knocking on my door."

"Why's that?"

"Oh, Detective. Don't behave like a fool. And don't you dare take me for one, either. Arthur Kelvin was represented by this firm. And we both know it."

Dennis nodded. At least she wasn't denying that.

"We do indeed. And I'm sure you'll understand that I'm coming to you for any information that might help us to apprehend his killer."

She raised an eyebrow. "So he was definitely murdered."

"He was found floating in the Blue Pool. I thought you didn't want me to insult your intelligence."

She chuckled. "Touché. But you know as well as anyone about lawyer-client confidentially. I can't tell you anything that Mr Kelvin told me in the course of my work for him."

"I know."

She smiled. Her pale cheeks brightened, just a little. "So what can I do for you, DS Frampton? I know we make good tea here," she glanced down at his empty cup on the desk, "but I'm sure that's not what you came for."

Dennis uncrossed his legs and took a breath. His skin felt clammy, and his collar was tight. He'd talked to the DCI before coming here. There was a plan. But he hadn't expected Aurelia Cross to be quite so... cold.

Think, he told himself. *Focus*. He pulled his glasses off and gave them a wipe with the handkerchief he kept in his pocket.

"Yes," he said. "I know you can't tell me the details of your discussions with your client."

"No." She stood up. "Sorry for you to have made a wasted trip."

"But if I'm not mistaken, I can ask you to confirm whether or not you represent the man."

She scowled. "I've already told you that."

"And your colleagues have to do the same."

"Why would you need them to do that?"

He glanced out towards the open plan office that Aurelia Cross looked onto from her grand desk. The space seemed shabbier than it had been when Harry Nevin had been in charge. But then, Harry Nevin had been killed.

"According to your website, each associate specialises in a specific area of the law. Family law, probate law, criminal law. For example."

She looked hesitant. "I don't see what that has to do with anything."

"You won't mind if I ask each of them if they worked for Mr Kelvin, will you?"

She looked past him, at the associates outside. At least, he assumed they were associates. Truth was, he had no idea who was who. All these lawyers looked the same to him.

"That way, we'll know which aspects of the law your firm represented him for."

Aurelia shrugged. "Why is that relevant?"

"Did, for example, a family lawyer represent him?"

Her gaze went out past Dennis and to his right. He tried to remember who he'd seen there. He couldn't.

"Why do you want to know?" she asked.

"Was one of your family lawyers working for him, on divorce proceedings? One of your probate lawyers, on his will?"

Aurelia smiled. "Clever DCI Clarke."

Dennis felt his face fall. "Pardon?"

"Well, you didn't think of this, did you? Plodding old fool like you. She put you up to it, didn't she?"

He blinked.

She leaned forward, across the desk. "Yes, DS Frampton. If you must know, Lucy over there was representing Mr Kelvin in areas of family law. Geraint was his probate lawyer, not that you'd expect a successful businessman like Arthur Kelvin not to have a will. But of course, it's not my place to tell you any more than that. Now, if you don't mind letting me get on with my day, I'd appreciate it if you left."

CHAPTER THIRTY-THREE

"Dr Bamford."

"DCI Clarke. How's your investigation coming along?"

"Slowly. But the evidence you were able to give us about the practice wounds was helpful. Thank you."

"Only doing my job."

Lesley was in the reception area of the morgue. Bamford had come out to see her after she'd identified herself to the assistant, but there was no sign of Kelvin's widow or mother yet.

"Are you here for the toxicology report?" he asked.

"No," she said. "I'm hoping to speak to his family."

"That's a bit untoward, doing it at the morgue."

"It's the Kelvins. Normal rules don't apply."

He frowned. "I suppose not."

"But the tox report would be useful, if you have it."

"I'm about to finish up now. I'll bring it out to you, if you're still here."

"Thank you."

He disappeared through a door. The door behind her,

immediately opposite it, opened, and an elderly woman entered. She wore a black-trimmed fur coat and a black hat that obscured her eyes. Her low-heeled shoes were also black.

Old school, Lesley thought. Just like her late husband.

She stepped forward. "Mrs Kelvin?"

The woman looked up at her, her eyes full of malice. "You can fuck right off."

Lesley struggled to hold her expression. The woman had just lost her son, but she was still every inch the gangster's wife.

"I was hoping to talk to you. To find out who might have held a grudge against your son."

Lesley knew full well that wasn't going to happen. But she'd wanted a chance to see Vera Kelvin in the flesh. And to witness her with her daughter-in-law.

Where was Amanda, anyway?

Did the two women hate each other so much that they wouldn't even come to identify Arthur's body together?

"Did you not hear me?" Vera said. "I told you to fuck off."

"I don't want to intrude," Lesley said. "But I was expecting to see Amanda here."

Vera jabbed a finger into Lesley's chest. "You're a pretty shitty detective, aren't you?"

"Why d'you say that?"

"Because Amanda's not here, because Amanda's fucking dead."

Lesley blinked. She'd misheard, surely.

"Did you say Amanda's dead?"

"Dead as the fucking dodo. Killed herself, little bitch. Fucking selfish way to go."

"When was this?"

"Don't you talk to your colleagues, you dowdy cow?"

Lesley swallowed. It would take her seconds to find out what had happened. "I'm sorry for your loss, Mrs Kelvin," she lied, and started to walk past the woman.

A hand shot out and grabbed Lesley's wrist. "I thought you wanted to know how she died."

"I do." Lesley didn't turn to look at the woman.

"Slit her wrists. Such melodrama. They found her in the bath this morning. Good riddance, I say."

CHAPTER THIRTY-FOUR

Lesley was driving to Sandbanks from the morgue when her phone rang.

"DCI Clarke."

"DCI Clarke, it's Sadie Dawes."

Lesley felt her heart sink. *Bloody journalist.*

"What do you want?" Lesley turned a bend towards the harbour. The water was on her right, dull in the wintry light.

"I've been talking to Detective Superintendent Phipps."

"Phipps? Why?"

"He was heading up the investigation into DCI Mackie's death."

"I don't need you to tell me that. But I don't see why you're calling me about it. I'm in the middle of a murder enquiry and I really haven't got time f—"

"Arthur Kelvin. I know. I think his death is linked to Mackie's."

"How?"

"Mackie was investigating Kelvin before he died. After

his retirement. I think a member of your team might have been helping him with it."

Dennis.

"You're talking rubbish, Sadie. Now please just let me get on with my job."

"Is that on the record?"

"No, of course it isn't. And you aren't going to use it."

"Maybe not. But you're going to want to help me when you learn what else Phipps said to me."

Lesley rolled her eyes. She checked her rear-view mirror, anxious to focus on the drive and not on this ridiculous call.

"Go on then," she sighed.

"He told me to talk to Kelvin's lawyer."

"Aurelia Cross." Lesley's mind went to the conversation she'd had with Dennis before leaving the office. Aurelia wouldn't be able to tell them anything about her conversations with Kelvin. But Dennis would know by now, she hoped, whether he had filed for divorce through her firm.

"Not Aurelia Cross. His former lawyer. Elsa Short."

Lesley's foot slipped off the accelerator pedal and onto the brake. The car behind flashed its lights in her mirror.

"Sorry," she called, hitting the accelerator again. "Sadie, I don't know what you're talking about."

"I just wanted to give you the chance to tell me anything you might know, before I talk to your fiancée. Or is she your wife now?"

"The wedding's on Saturday." Why had Lesley told the journalist that?

Elsa had represented Kelvin from the time she'd come to Dorset. That had been just weeks before Mackie's death. Surely she would know nothing about that?

Sadie was bluffing.

"You just carry right on with your questions," she told the woman. "I'm busy with this investigation."

She hung up, her hands trembling.

CHAPTER THIRTY-FIVE

A SQUAD CAR was parked on the road outside the Kelvin house but the gates were shut. Lesley parked her car in the same spot she'd used just the previous day and approached the squad car. Two uniformed officers sat in the front.

"Everything OK?" she asked, holding up her ID.

"I'm PC Truscott, Ma'am. We've been told to come here and check the place over," the woman in the driver's seat told her.

"Why?" Vera Kelvin had told her Amanda had committed suicide; no reason for Uniform to be here.

"Neighbours heard an altercation." PC Truscott exchanged a look with her colleague. "Early hours of this morning. Screaming, apparently. Crashing."

"So why aren't you in there?"

"They won't let us."

"Are you aware that a woman died here this morning?"

PC Truscott nodded. "Yes, Ma'am. Ambo – Ambulance I mean, Ma'am – was called at four fifty-five am."

"OK." Lesley looked at the gate. *Suicide, my arse.*

She turned back to the PC. "I don't suppose you know where they took her? Ms Frobisher, the woman who died?"

"The morgue at Poole Hospital, Ma'am. Or so we've been told."

The very place Lesley had just driven from.

"OK." Lesley stood up and looked over the car towards the gate. She had no idea who was in there. Vera Kelvin would be at the morgue still. Amanda Frobisher was there too, albeit in a very different capacity. As was her husband. So who had refused them entry?

The nephew. Kyle had come back from Devon. It had to be.

She strode to the buzzer and held it down.

No answer.

She held it down again. Longer this time.

Still no answer.

Shit.

She went back to the car. "OK," she told the two constables. "You park along the road and I'll call in a response unit. We're going to need to force our way in."

As she straightened up, she heard a noise behind her. The large gate, the one that spanned the entire driveway, was shuddering. Lesley watched as it drew open. A man emerged: early thirties, brown hair with blond highlights, moustache that would have made her laugh out loud if the face sporting it wasn't so sinister.

Kyle Kelvin.

"Mr Kelvin." Lesley approached him with her ID held up. "My name's DCI Clarke. A woman died here this morning, and we have reports of a disturbance. By law you have to allow us access."

He made a sweeping motion with his arm. "By all means,

Detective. I wouldn't dream of preventing you from doing your job."

She turned back to the squad car and motioned for them to enter via the gates.

She turned back to look at the house. Not letting Uniform in had given Kyle Kelvin time. But time to do what?

CHAPTER THIRTY-SIX

Mike made a lunge for Meera, a fake knife in his hand. She stood still, waiting for contact.

"Ow," she said. "Not that hard, eh?"

"Sorry."

"Don't move."

They were in a meeting room on the second floor of Police HQ, experimenting with potential angles for the attack. Mike had set a video camera up in the corner and was recording everything, although to be fair the notes he was taking would probably be of more use.

"That's not it," she said, looking down. "It's too high."

"Sorry." He pulled away and sighed. They'd been doing this for over an hour and they weren't getting anywhere.

"Let's swap again," she said.

He handed her the knife. It was a dummy one, the type whose blade retracts into the hilt as soon as it makes contact. The thing was weighted just like a regular knife, and was a similar size to the murder weapon. Mike had taken care to test it on a table before they'd used it.

"I bet you didn't think you'd be doing this when they assigned you to this case," he said.

She tested the knife's tip with her finger, pushing it in gently. "Bloody convincing, this thing." She looked at him, then passed the knife from hand to hand. "Maybe I should stand on something. Chances are the killer was taller than Kelvin."

Kelvin wasn't a tall man, but he hadn't been tiny. The assumption so far seemed to be that his wife had killed him, but the size difference between Mike and Meera was comparable and when she held the knife, they still hadn't been able to establish an angle that accurately reflected the wound.

"We've tried everything with each of us holding it," he said. "In front, behind, to the side."

"Even lying down." She shook her head. "Shall we get a cuppa? You never know, fresh heads..."

He nodded. She pocketed the knife and they left the room, making for the kitchen. The one on this floor was quieter than the one on Mike's usual floor, with less in the way of supplies.

"No milk," he said.

"I'll have black coffee." Meera was rummaging through cupboards.

"How's life in Bournemouth CID these days?"

She shrugged. "OK. Not as exciting as what you get up to, I imagine."

"Oh, I don't know. You're getting a taste of it right now."

"It's a thrill a minute, clearly." She gave him a shrug.

"What about Jill? She still on maternity leave?"

A nod. Meera pulled two mugs out of a cupboard. Inside they were dark with tannin stains, but would do the job.

"They're letting me take a part of it. The modern police force, even prepared to accept me as a mum."

"And so they should. Suzi's what, five months now?"

"Four and a half. How's little Louis doing? I heard Tina was struggling."

He stopped, his hand on the kettle. "Where did you hear that?"

"Sorry. Should I not have?"

Mike bit down on his bottom lip and switched the kettle on. "No. Yes. It's fine. I know what it's like. All of us coppers, and that."

"Yeah. How is she, anyway?"

"She's helping me with cases. Says it keeps her sane."

Meera chuckled. "Jill's the same."

"But she works in Organised Crime, right?"

"They've been having a reorganisation. She might well be looking for a job when she starts back at work."

"They can't do that, surely."

Meera shrugged. "Oh, she'll be alright. But she'll be looking for a posting, and she's not much looking forward to finding a DI who'll accept a DS who's not only a mum, but a lesbian."

"What about the Major Crimes Team? We've got DCI Clarke, there won't be any problems here."

"You've got no vacancies though, have you?"

Mike poured water over the coffee granules. Gold Blend. It would be barely drinkable, but he needed caffeine.

"Not right now. We don't have enough hands, though. Not with the crimes we have to solve."

"I'll mention it to Jill." She chinked mugs with him. "Cheers, Mike. You're a good mate."

He nodded and held the kitchen door open for them to

return to the meeting room. Meera picked up the knife in her left hand, her coffee in the right. He smiled at her.

"That's it," he said.

"What?"

"We're both right-handed. We haven't tried the left yet. I know the direction of the wound suggests a right-handed attacker, but it's worth a try, isn't it?"

Meera looked down at the knife in her hand. "You're right. OK, let's give it a go."

CHAPTER THIRTY-SEVEN

LESLEY STOOD on the doorstep of Kelvin's house, his nephew in front of her.

"We need access to the entire house, Mr Kelvin."

"Of course, Detective." He looked past her towards the two PCs standing in the vast driveway. "Will it just be the three of you?"

"I'll need to bring colleagues in. A forensics team. It would make our job much easier if you vacated the house while we work."

He smiled and stood back. "Of course. Feel free to have a look around."

"But don't go anywhere," she added, stopping in the hall-way. The doors to Kelvin's office were open, as they had been last time. The other doors were closed.

Even with the man and his wife dead, the house hadn't changed.

"I thought you wanted us to vacate the house?" Kyle said, his tone light.

Don't mock me, you bastard.

"I'd like to talk to you first. And to anyone else who was in the house this morning. Who found Miss Frobisher?"

"The maid. Gerta." He turned away. "Gerta!" He turned back to Lesley. "I wasn't here, however. So I won't have any useful information for you."

"I'd still like to speak with you." She gestured towards the office. "Can you wait in there, please, while I take a look around?"

"Of course." He retreated to the office.

"And please, don't touch anything."

"Certainly not, Detective."

Lesley didn't know what was worse, Vera Kelvin's obnoxiousness or Kyle Kelvin's obsequiousness.

She stepped outside, resisting the urge to prop the front door open in case Kelvin changed his mind, and approached the two uniformed officers.

"You two stay here, please. Log anyone coming in or going out."

"Can we stop people from entering or leaving?" PC Truscott asked.

"Not yet, not legally." This wasn't even a murder enquiry yet. "But keep a log, yes?"

"No problem, Ma'am." The PC pulled a notepad from her pocket and stood to one side.

Lesley went back to her car and grabbed a forensics kit and gloves out of the boot. This was the Kelvin house. She had no idea who might have come through here since Amanda's death. But whatever was in there, she wasn't going to contaminate it and mess up the investigation.

She returned to the house and pulled on her suit at the threshold. She grabbed her phone and dialled Dennis.

"Boss."

"Where are you?"

"I've just left Cross and Associates. I'm on my way back to the office."

"Scrap that. I want you with me at the Kelvin house."

A pause. "Why?"

"Amanda Frobisher is dead. I've got two PCs with me but we need to search this place and identify any evidence before the Kelvins' lawyers find grounds to kick us out."

"She was murdered? At her house?"

"The family are calling it suicide. She was found in the bath."

"Poor woman."

"Obviously, I don't believe a word of it." Lesley looked through to the office.

"I'll be there in fifteen minutes, boss." Dennis hung up.

Lesley kept hold of her phone. She wanted to capture this search as she carried it out, to make sure nothing was missed. She switched over to the camera and started recording video.

"Kelvin house, Sandbanks, Poole. I'm the first officer on the scene following the reported suicide of Amanda Frobisher and an altercation reported by neighbours in the early hours." She made a mental note to get someone to interview the neighbours, if it hadn't already been done. "I'm in the foyer of the house, about to go upstairs and examine the room where the death occurred."

She climbed the stairs slowly, listening. Just like last time, she could hear children's voices.

Who let children stay in a house where a woman had died? And who was looking after them?

A nanny, she imagined. The Kelvins had enough money for one.

She'd find the nanny and suggest that the children be taken away.

But first, the bathroom.

At the top of the stairs, the layout was similar to below. Six doors, all closed. And a set of double doors opposite a tall window that looked out on the driveway. The double doors would lead to a room over that office, with views of the harbour.

The master bedroom, she guessed. There would be an ensuite in there.

She turned the handle and pushed open the doors. Sure enough, a broad window in front of her afforded a breathtaking view of the harbour. To the side was a rumpled bed, as wide as it was long. She resisted the urge to stop and look at the view, instead checking the room for more doors.

There were two, one to each side. She tried the one on the right, which opened into a walk-in wardrobe with no further doors off. She went back to the left-hand door and opened it.

Beyond the door was a vast bathroom. A freestanding tub sat in the centre, with a double-sized shower beyond it and two huge marble sinks.

Ostentatious. Exactly what she'd expect of Kelvin.

She approached the bath. It was clean. She bent over, examining it for traces of blood.

Nothing.

She crouched down and scanned the floor. Again, no sign of blood. There wasn't even a scrap of dust.

"I'm in the master bathroom," she said into the phone. "I'm assuming this was where Amanda died, but it's clean. Too clean."

She used the camera to scan the room. The place smelled of bleach: it had recently been cleaned. Scrubbed, more like.

She had a thought. The Kelvins were getting a divorce. Maybe Amanda was no longer sleeping in this bedroom.

She retreated through the bedroom and went back to the landing. She opened one door at a time. The first gave onto a double bedroom, with a neatly made-up bed and no doors off.

The second opened into a playroom. Two children sat on the floor, piles of Lego surrounding them. A young woman stood in the far corner, arranging books on a shelf.

She turned. "Oh. Who are you?" She had an accent. Italian?

Lesley stopped the video and held up her ID. "DCI Clarke, Dorset Police. This house is a crime scene. I suggest you take the children somewhere more appropriate. Speak to your employer, I'm sure they'll have an alternative location you can go to."

The Kelvins were loaded. They'd have houses in every town along this stretch of coast.

"Of course." The woman went to the children, her steps hurried. "Josie, Bailey. Let's go downstairs."

"Not just downstairs," Lesley told her. "And I'll need your phone number, so we can take a statement from you."

The woman's gaze flicked towards the door. "My number?"

"Please. Unless," Lesley looked at the children then back at the woman, "unless you'd prefer to talk to me now."

"No." The woman rattled off a phone number. "But I will need to speak to Mr Kelvin."

Lesley nodded and the woman hurried past her, holding each of the children's hands. The boy looked to be about ten and the girl eight. Lesley gave them each a reassuring smile as they passed, wondering how much they'd seen.

They might have seen Amanda die, or be taken away. And as members of the Kelvin family, they could have witnessed plenty more.

She checked the room for more doors off and found one, leading to a small toilet. It too was clean.

Back at the landing, she checked each of the doors in turn. There were three more bedrooms, two of them ensuite, and a family bathroom. All were clean. No blood, no dirt, no nothing.

Shit.

The time during which Uniform had been sitting outside had been enough for the Kelvins to clean up.

Lesley grabbed her phone and dialled Gail. No answer.

"Gail, I'm at the Kelvin house. Amanda Frobisher was found dead here this morning and we'll need to establish a crime scene. It's been cleaned but I'm hoping you can get past that. Give me a call."

She pocketed her phone and hurried down the stairs. She went into the office at the back of the house.

It was empty.

She returned to the hall. "Mr Kelvin?"

No response.

She approached the stairs. "Mr Kelvin!"

A door opened, and the woman who'd answered the front door to her the previous day appeared. "Please, you don't need to shout. How can I help you?"

Lesley looked the woman up and down. She wore rubber gloves and held a can of cleaning spray.

Lesley grabbed the can off her. "You can stop with your cleaning right now."

The woman reached for the can but Lesley held tight. "What do you think you're doing?"

"Don't you know? Amanda Frobisher died here this morning. We need to examine the house, and you've cleaned it."

The woman shook her head. "Amanda slit her wrists." She looked down. "Sad business, but all her own fault. I didn't want the smell of blood for the children."

"Where are the children?"

"Mr Kelvin took them."

"Kyle Kelvin?"

The woman looked up. "Of course."

Lesley ran to the front door. The two PCs were still on the driveway.

"PC Truscott!" she called.

"Ma'am?"

"Has anyone come out of the house?"

The PC nodded. "A man came out, with two children. He told me you'd given strict instructions for the children to be taken away."

"Did he give you his name?"

"Of course, Ma'am. Kyle Kelvin."

Shit. Lesley punched the wall.

"Thanks, PC Truscott. You were only doing your job."

CHAPTER THIRTY-EIGHT

"Where was it, again?"

Gail was following a uniformed officer to a spot where he said he'd seen tyre marks, to the east of the site.

He pointed. "Over there."

She squinted. They were separated from the track he was indicating by a thicket of hedges and a fair amount of mud.

"And there's prints in the mud, right there." He indicated the ground beneath the hedges.

"Good work, PC...?"

"PC Laurence, Ma'am."

"You don't have to call me that, I'm a civilian."

He shrugged and walked away.

She eyed the prints in the mud, and the track beyond. She could just about make out the tyre tracks.

It might be nothing. It might be a farm vehicle.

"PC Laurence?" she called back.

He turned back to her. "Yes?"

"That track. You don't happen to know where it leads, do you?"

"I think it loops back round to the road. It doesn't go anywhere, really."

Perfect.

"Thanks. But how do we access it? Does it go past the entrance?"

A shrug. "I guess it comes out of the car park, but I'm not sure."

"Great. Thanks again."

Gail took some photos, then texted Gav and headed back to the pool. Gav was on the other side of the site, helping the police finish their search there. Gail strode to the tea room and the exit, hoping Gav would catch her up.

He was already waiting for her in the car park. "What's up? I was grabbing my lunch."

She smiled. "You and your packed lunches." She checked her watch. "Blimey, half one already. Where did the morning go?"

He shrugged. "What have you found?"

"There's a track running around the eastern side of the site. Uniform found tyre tracks, and boot prints leading to it."

"They did?"

"It could be the way the killer brought the body in."

"It could indeed." Gavin turned away from her. "Let's take a look."

"Hold on a minute." Gail pulled out her phone. "We don't know where we're going yet."

"Ah. Well, I assumed—"

"Let's not assume. Let's pretend we know what we're doing, and use a map."

"Sorry."

She gave him a glancing punch on the arm. "I'm toying with you." She examined the Ordnance Survey maps app on her phone. "There's a line here, an unfinished track. That'll be it."

"Lead the way."

"I shall." Gail strode away from the cars, making for a gap in the hedge.

"Watch the ground for tyre marks," she said as she walked.

"I'm recording this. But the ground's dry. I can't see anything. You sure Uniform found tracks?"

"There's some boggy ground round there, apparently it forms a lake at the top when it's wet enough."

"And that's enough for prints and tracks to be left."

"Exactly. Presumably whoever left them didn't realise."

She continued walking. The track turned to the right, following the edge of the site. A fence ran between them and the woods, and on their left were open fields.

"It's quite an anomaly, this place," Gav said.

Gail continued scanning the ground as she walked. "How so?"

"This area's all gorse and deciduous trees. Here it's conifers. I wonder why."

"Perhaps the owners have cultivated it, over the years."

"It feels older than that."

"Could have had any number of owners." She held up her hand. "Stop." She pointed. "There it is."

The two of them stopped next to each other and observed the track. About ten metres ahead of them were tyre tracks. Off to the right, leading into the trees, were boot prints.

"Fucking bingo," she breathed. "At last, some physical evidence."

"Might not be." Gav scratched his nose. "Could have been anyone."

Gail pointed. "Look, the fence has been cut. Right there. Whoever came down here wanted access to the site, but not via the official route. I'd say that was suspicious, wouldn't you?"

"What's that?" Gavin indicated a shape on the ground under the spot where the fence had been cut.

Gail took a few steps forward. She wasn't at the muddy patch yet, so wouldn't be disturbing the tyre tracks.

"No," she said.

"What?" Gav asked her.

Gail squatted down to get a better angle. The object was dirty, conical. She laughed. "It's a chip cone."

"What, from a chip shop?"

"Yup."

"What's a chip cone doing out here?"

Gail turned to Gav. She grinned. "God knows, but here's hoping it's got prints on it. Or maybe even DNA."

CHAPTER THIRTY-NINE

DENNIS'S CAR drew up outside while Lesley was in the driveway talking to PC Truscott. He turned into the driveway and stopped with his car half in, half out.

He wound down the window. "Alright to park on here, boss? Only there's enough of us on the double yellow lines as it is."

Lesley scanned the block paved driveway. Might there be forensics hidden here somewhere?

She doubted it.

"Just park where you are, Dennis." He'd already disturbed the spot he was on, anyway.

"I'm half on the road."

She sighed. "OK. Pull in enough to get your tail out of the way of the traffic. That good enough for you?"

He gave her a look. "You OK, boss?"

"Fine. Sorry. I shouldn't have snapped at you."

Dennis had pulled his handbrake but the car wasn't moving. He looked round, frowning. "That's the radio in the squad car."

Lesley looked past him into the road. "Is it?" Dennis had better hearing than she did.

She turned to see PC Truscott on her personal radio. The young woman nodded and approached Lesley. "I've had an update, Ma'am."

"Yes?"

"Kyle Kelvin's car's been seen on the Sandbanks ferry. He's over the other side, heading towards Swanage."

"Good." The man didn't have many options, going in that direction. She wondered why he hadn't headed towards Bournemouth, where it would be much easier to get lost.

But there was more CCTV in Bournemouth. More people around to spot him.

Dennis was getting out of his car.

"Dennis," Lesley said. "I need you to go to Swanage."

"OK. Why?"

"We need to speak to Kyle Kelvin, before he disappears."

"He's in Swanage? I thought he was in Plymouth."

"He was here this morning. I spoke to him. And his car's been spotted on the ferry, heading that way."

"You let him go."

"I didn't..." She stopped herself. She was right. She hadn't been sufficiently precise in her instructions to PC Truscott, and she'd let Kyle go.

"Yes, Dennis. I let him go. Now I'm going to get Uniform to stop him, and I'd like you to have a chat with him. He isn't a suspect yet, so you can't caution him or bring him in. But he knows we need to interview him in relation to his aunt's death." She wondered what the age gap was between Kyle and Amanda: probably not much more than five years.

"Anything in particular you need me to ask him?"

"I want to know if he was in the house when Amanda

died. What he saw. He says he wasn't, but press him on that. Carefully. And ask him why they decided to clean the place before we got here."

"I'll see if I can find out how long he's been in the county, too."

"Thanks, Dennis. Let me know how you get on. And—"

"What else?"

She put a hand on his shoulder. "Be careful, Dennis. He's a Kelvin. He might not be alone. Stay with Uniform, and don't let him do anything stupid."

CHAPTER FORTY

ELSA STARED at herself in the mirror. Her makeup was in place but not excessive, her clothes professional.

She hadn't had much opportunity to wear her suits lately. It felt good to do it again, to be heading out to meet a client.

Potential client.

She just hoped this client would hire her. And that she'd turn out to be lucrative. Amanda Frobisher, if she *was* a suspect in her husband's murder, might have a significant sum of money. Assuming he hadn't revoked access to it, after filing for divorce.

Be positive, she thought. *Don't put the dampeners on it before it's even started.*

She fumbled in her bag for her makeup bag and applied lipstick. She smacked her lips together a couple of times then stood back to examine herself for a final time.

You'll do.

She reached for her best coat, the cashmere one she rarely wore because it hated the rain. It was still cold out. Where the hell was her scarf? She hadn't been able to find it yesterday. The blouse she'd picked out was emerald green, and her green paisley scarf would offset it perfectly.

She went into the bedroom and opened the chest of drawers on her side of the bed. She rifled through it. No scarf.

Where are you?

She went to the wardrobe and pulled out the basket she kept spare scarves in. There was a burgundy one in there that might work.

But the green one would be best. She'd worn it to client meetings since before she'd moved to Dorset. It made her feel lucky.

She upended the basket on the bed and rummaged through its contents.

Thank God.

The scarf was in there, in amongst three black scarves and a navy one that had been obscuring it.

Good.

She tossed the scarves back in the basket, leaving it on the bed for later, and wound the green one round her neck.

Now she could go to her meeting feeling confident.

CHAPTER FORTY-ONE

How LONG HAD Lesley been at the house, waiting?

There'd been no word from Dennis, and no sign of Gail or her team. And she didn't want to do anything until Gail had secured the scene.

She'd taken the housekeeper into the kitchen and asked her about Amanda Frobisher's death, but the woman claimed not to have arrived at the house until after the ambulance had left. She also claimed not to have found blood when she'd cleaned the bathroom that morning.

Lesley didn't believe a word of it. But the woman had her story straight and was sticking to it.

She was in Kelvin's office, staring out at the harbour. She didn't like being in the house, potentially contaminating a crime scene, but she had a feeling Amanda wouldn't have come in here after her husband's death. Probably not before either, based on the kind of man Lesley knew Arthur Kelvin was.

Amanda, did you really kill yourself? Or did someone get rid of you before you could claim all your husband's money?

Or before you could tell the police or your solicitor something they didn't want you to?

She was disturbed by her phone ringing: Gail.

"Gail, where are you? We really need to get this crime scene established before—"

"I'm sorry, Lesley, but we've got new evidence up at the Blue Pool."

"What kind of evidence?"

"Tyre tracks, leading to a spot in the fence that's been cut. Boot prints, and a discarded chip cone."

"What's a chip cone?"

"A cone they put a portion of chips in. They do them at the Chipperies in Wareham."

"Can you tell how long it's been there?"

"It's intact, so not too long. I'm hoping the forensic gods are smiling on me and I'll find prints or DNA on it."

"Good luck with that," said Lesley. "So can you leave that with your team and get over here?"

"I'm sending Gav to you. I want to finish up casting the moulds for the tyre prints and the boot. If we can identify the vehicle that came down here, it'll be a big help."

"It certainly will. How long will Gavin be?"

"He's already left, so half an hour maybe?"

"OK. Let me know when you've got more on the prints and the cone, yes?"

"Of course."

Lesley dropped her phone onto the desk and strode over to the window. Today was dull, the harbour choppy, but she could still appreciate the pull of the view. Properties like this went for sums of money that were never advertised in the local estate agents. But she'd hazard a guess that this house was worth at least ten million pounds.

How did you earn that money, Mr Kelvin?

He ran a string of assorted businesses across the county, none of them that lucrative. Unless you counted the money they most likely laundered.

She leaned against the desk and checked the clock on the wall beside it. Twenty-five minutes until Gavin would arrive. Uniform were still outside, making sure no one came in or out now, and the housekeeper was in the kitchen. Lesley should be keeping an eye on her, but didn't relish spending the next half an hour under the woman's harsh stare.

She picked up her phone. This wasn't the only case on her mind. She didn't like that Sadie Dawes was sniffing around the Mackie case again. She'd wanted to investigate it further herself, when she'd arrived here. But if it was going to be investigated, it should be done by the police, not by the local news.

Sadie believed Dennis was connected. She was also asking questions about Elsa.

Lesley sighed.

She didn't want to involve her team in this. They'd been members of CID. Dennis and Mike here in the Major Crimes Investigation Team, before she'd started. Tina had been one of the uniformed officers most closely involved with the MCIT. They'd worked with him.

Most of them.

But there was one member of her team who'd never worked for the man.

CHAPTER FORTY-TWO

STANLEY PUT DOWN HIS PHONE.

"Everything OK?" Brett asked him. The two of them were in the office at the Forensics lab in Dorchester.

"Fine." He swallowed, his mouth dry. "So you said you'll be looking for prints on this chip cone?"

Brett nodded. "Gail's sent photos, but that won't be much help. The thing needs to be thoroughly dusted once it gets here. And tested for DNA."

"The boss reckons the killer might have been his wife, or maybe a nephew. Do you have their prints on file?"

Brett scrolled through the fingerprint database on his screen. "We've got the nephews. Darren Kelvin's in prison, so that's a no-brainer. Then there's Kyle, looks like Devon charged him with drunk driving a year ago."

"That's a bit careless, given his line of business."

A snort. "You could say that. Anyway. We'll see if we can get a match, and if that doesn't give us anything... well, it'll be up to your DCI."

Stanley eyed the pile of evidence bags on the bench along from Brett. "Those from this case?"

"Yeah."

"I can put them away for you, if you'd like."

Brett looked up at him. "You know how the evidence store is organised?"

"Course I do."

Brett smiled. "OK. Thanks, mate. There's already a few boxes in there for this case, labelled with the case reference. Right hand side, near the front."

"Sure thing."

Stanley picked up the evidence bags, trying to keep his walk casual.

On the phone just before, the boss had said the evidence from the Mackie case had been kept here. That the two cases were linked.

He wasn't sure why this had to be done without the CSIs knowing. But the boss knew what she was doing.

He opened the door to the evidence store and quickly found the boxes for the Kelvin case. It didn't take him more than a minute to store the bags.

He looked back at the closed door. He had to be quick. The boss had told him exactly where to look.

The evidence from the Mackie case wasn't as far back as it might have been, given how long ago it had taken place. He supposed it had been brought forward when Phipps reopened the investigation. His heart racing, Stanley pulled the first box down and rifled through it.

There wasn't much. A jacket, boots and hat, all bagged up. More bags with a phone, some papers, and samples taken from the scene. Only problem was, they'd been taken from the scene months after the man had died.

The boss had told him to ignore the phone. He supposed she'd already looked at it. She'd instructed him not to remove anything. Instead, he was to note what was there, take photos, and send them to her.

He did so, his hand shaking so much he was forced to fire off multiple shots of each item to get just one that was clear.

He sent the images attached to a text to the boss.

Her reply came back almost instantly: *Thanks. Now get back to work.*

He frowned and pushed the box back onto its shelf.

The door to the evidence store opened: Brett.

"Stanley? Everything OK?"

"Yeah." Stanley was quickly by the CSI's side. "Just making sure it was all labelled."

Brett gave him an odd look. "Fair enough." He shivered. "I don't like it in here. Paranoid I'll get locked in. Come on. Let's get out."

CHAPTER FORTY-THREE

"AT LAST," Lesley said, as the CSI van pulled up outside the house. "I thought you'd never get here."

"I came as soon as I heard," Gavin replied. He walked to the back of the van and started unloading kit. "Now, where's the primary scene?"

"One of the bathrooms. I'm guessing it's the ensuite of the master bedroom but it might have been another one."

He slammed the doors to the van. "You haven't found anything in any of them?"

"You go in and smell the place. Stinks of bleach."

He laughed. "Oldest trick there is. Don't worry, a little bit of chlorine won't stop us finding traces." He patted the pilot case in his hand.

"Good." She followed him into the house. "How long will it take you to get initial samples from the bath?"

"Half an hour. Maybe an hour. Depends if I get lucky and pick the right bathroom first. I need to wait for the reactions, but I can run them all concurrently."

She looked outside.

It was starting to rain, droplets darkening her jacket sleeves.

She was no good to anyone hanging about here. Dennis was tracking down Kyle Kelvin, but where the hell was Vera? And...

She remembered something. The children. Bailey and Josie.

She thought back to the conversation with Amanda the previous day. Finn and Lottie, she'd said. Darren's children.

So whose children were these?

She needed Tina. Tina would have got to the bottom of this hours ago. She'd have produced a full list of every member of the Kelvin family, with relationships, criminal records and current whereabouts. What they'd had for breakfast too, knowing Tina.

She'd speak to the team. Find out who had capacity, and who had information for her.

She went back into Kelvin's office, took out her phone, and started to dial.

Five minutes later, she had the whole team in a conference call. All except Dennis, who still wasn't picking up.

Dennis, where are you?

She'd have to call Uniform at this rate, check he hadn't got into trouble.

"Right," she said. "I hope I'm not interrupting you all. But we've had a number of developments, and I wanted to make sure we're all up to date."

"Appreciated, boss," said DI Varney. Is there any reason DS Frampton isn't in on this call?"

"He's busy tracking down someone we want to interview. Kyle Kelvin, Arthur's nephew."

"I thought he was in Devon."

"Not any more. He was at Kelvin's house this morning, but... but he left."

"Why do you want to speak to him?" DC Young asked.

Lesley clutched her phone. "Right. This is confusing enough as it is with six of us on a call. Everyone stop talking while I run through what we've got."

Silence.

Thank God for that.

"So," she said. "Amanda Frobisher died this morning. She's currently at the morgue in Poole, or so I'm told. Her mother-in-law says it was suicide, but I'm not buying that. We have to treat her death as suspicious. I'm at the Kelvin house, where she died, and I've got Forensics in there now looking for evidence."

"Slit wrists. There'll be blood everywhere," Mike said.

"What did I say?" Lesley asked.

"Sorry."

"There isn't any blood, but there's a hell of a lot of bleach. And there were two children here when I arrived. Kyle has them with him. The thing is, they aren't Darren's kids, like we thought. They were here yesterday, if it's the same voices I heard. I'm thinking they must be Kyle's kids." She hesitated. "Does he have kids?"

Silence.

"Anyone?"

"I can look into it," said DC Young.

"Thank you. If Kyle's kids were here yesterday, then he's lying to me about when he arrived at the house. And he might have been in the county when Arthur died."

"I'll look into it as soon as we're off this call," DC Young said.

"Thanks. Katie, isn't it?"

"Yes, Ma—, boss."

"Call me as soon as you have confirmation."

"With respect, boss," Varney said, "just because Kyle's kids are here doesn't mean *he* was."

"Katie," Lesley ignored the interruption. "Find out if there's a mum on the scene. And if so, where she is. I want everything you can get on Kyle's kids, and Darren's kids too."

"No problem."

"Good."

Where was she?

She pulled in a breath. "We've also got more forensics from the Blue Pool site. Tyre tracks, a boot print and a chip cone."

She waited for someone to ask what a chip cone was.

"That's a cone used for chips," she said, when no one spoke.

"We know that, boss," Stanley said. "They do them at the Chipperies."

"What is this, a bloody advert for the Chipperies?" she asked. "Surely it's not the only chippy that does cones."

"Only one nearby that I've heard of," said Mike. "You think it's relevant?"

"It might be nothing, but the CSIs are looking at it."

"That's where I am," said Stanley. "They've also established a definite match between the knife we found, and the wounds on Kelvin."

"Good. Mike and Meera, how are you getting on with that?"

"It took a bit of doing," said Mike, "but we've managed to work out the angle of entry. The killer would have been standing behind Kelvin and slightly to the left."

"And," added Meera, "they're probably left-handed."

"A lot of people are left-handed," Lesley told her.

"Yes." She sounded chastened.

"But that's good work, you two. We had thought the wound was inflicted by a right-handed attacker, so this definitely helps. So you reckon both people were standing when the wound was inflicted?"

"I spoke to the pathologist," said Mike. "Apparently if he'd been lying down, there would have been less blood lost, on account of his heart being level with the wound."

"But the wound's to his abdomen. Not far from his heart."

"It makes enough difference," Mike replied. "Apparently."

"OK. So the killer was standing up, behind Kelvin and to the left, and he or she was left-handed. Which means they took Kelvin by surprise."

"Domestic killings are normally face-to-face," said Meera. "Especially when committed by women. It's more likely to be a heat of the moment thing. She grabs a knife, she plunges it into him."

"Less of the melodrama," Lesley said. "None of that rules out Amanda Frobisher getting someone else to do her dirty work for her."

"But she's been killed too," DC Young pointed out.

"Not necessarily by the same person," said Lesley. "It might have been in revenge. If Kelvin's nephews believed Amanda killed the head of the family, they might have wanted her out of the way."

She wished Dennis was here. He would have more hypotheses. More knowledge of the Kelvins and how they worked.

Dennis, where are you?

"OK," she said. "We need to find out where Kelvin was when he was stabbed. Let's find out his movements, working backwards from the day he died. Anything we can get from CCTV, his lawyers, his business associates. I want to know when he disappeared."

"The pathologist said he hadn't been dead more than twenty-four hours," said Mike.

"Which means he was probably killed on Saturday night. So why did no one miss him on Sunday?"

His widow, she thought. Even if they were separating, Amanda would have noted his absence. But it was too late to talk to her now.

"I'm going to speak to his mother," she said. "She lives here, she'll have known."

"Good luck with that," said Varney.

Lesley thought back to the conversation at the morgue. If she had to caution Vera Kelvin and bring her into the station, she would. There had to be a way.

"Thanks, Will. Have you been able to talk to any of your colleagues about Kelvin's businesses?"

"I have," Varney replied. "He wound five businesses up the week before his death."

"Was that normal? He was the kind of man who opened and closed businesses all the time, wasn't he?"

"They're all the same kind of business. Nail salons."

"Classic fronts for money laundering," said Stanley.

Lesley nodded. She leaned back in Kelvin's chair, stretching out her neck. If someone had told her three days ago that she'd be sitting here in Arthur Kelvin's chair, looking out at the man's view of the harbour and conferring with her team on his murder, she'd have accused them of being mad.

"OK," she said. "Did he have any other nail salons?"

"He opened three more last week, too."

"Turnover," she mused. "OK, Will. Find out what more you can about those businesses for me, please. I need to make a call."

"Boss." It was Stanley.

"Yes, Stanley?"

"I had a thought."

"Go on."

"Is there CCTV, by the ferry?"

"I imagine so. Why?"

"It's just that given where Kelvin's house is, if he went out, good chance he'd have gone past the ferry. Even to get back to the mainland, you have to go round via the one-way system."

Lesley tried to picture the road leading to the ferry slip-way. There was a hotel there, and businesses. There had to be cameras.

"Nice one, Stanley."

"Except if he cut through Brownsea Road," Meera said.

"Sorry?" Lesley asked.

"There are roads through the centre of the peninsula. Someone who knew what they were doing and didn't want to be seen by CCTV might go that way."

"But they're all mansions," said Stanley. "Or posh flats. They'll have CCTV too."

Lesley wasn't sure how willing the residents of Sand-banks would be to hand over CCTV footage. But it was worth a try.

"Thanks, Stanley. I want you to stay with Gail. See how they get on with the new evidence. Mike and Meera, you move to the CCTV. Speak to the council, see if there's any public CCTV. The Haven Hotel, and the homeowners along there too."

"Got it," said Mike.

"Good. We'll check in at the end of the day. Everyone back at base at six pm, OK?"

Muttered agreement.

"Thanks, folks."

Lesley closed down the conference call and dropped her phone on the desk.

CHAPTER FORTY-FOUR

XAVIER HAD TOLD Elsa to drive to the Sandbanks Hotel to meet Amanda. Apparently he'd reserved a room, so they could meet in private.

She pulled up in the hotel car park and turned back to look at the harbour. The sun was setting, framed by the hotel's sign. Brownsea Island was a red-shrouded shadow across the water.

Elsa didn't stop often enough to appreciate where she lived. She spent so much time in and around Bournemouth that she rarely got out to enjoy the countryside. Maybe she'd suggest a trip over to the island with Lesley, when they got back from honeymoon.

But then, the last time Lesley had been over there, it had been to investigate a murder. She might not want to go back.

She turned back towards the hotel. She needed to focus. If she was going to win over this client, she had to travel back in time to a year ago, when she had been a successful lawyer. Before things had started to go wrong at the firm.

When had that been? When Harry died. She'd been

inclined to pin all the problems on the discovery of the bodies of Sidney Fogarty and Catherine Lawson in Lyme Regis. But the truth was, the firm had never been the same after losing its founder.

She strode into the reception area.

"I'm here to see Ms Frobisher, please." She'd been surprised Amanda had used her real name. But then, the name that was notorious was Kelvin.

"Certainly," said the receptionist. "One moment." He picked up his phone. After a moment he gave her a smile. "The Brownsea Suite."

She looked past him towards the restaurant and the view over the beach. "Where will I find that?"

"Sorry. Turn right and go through the function room. It's on the ground floor three doors along."

"Thank you."

She followed his directions, walking through a deserted function room with a large dance floor and views over the sand. She knocked on the door of the suite.

The door flew open. Xavier Robson stood in front of her, his face full of expectation. It fell when he recognised her.

"Oh. You."

"Yes, me," she said. "Why are you here? I was expecting Amanda."

"I can't get hold of her," he replied. "Her mobile's dead, and she's not returning my calls."

Elsa checked her watch. "I'm a few minutes early. Maybe she's just running late."

"She was supposed to be here an hour ago." He drew back and fell into a chair by the window. Another view of the beach. The waves were choppy, the sea grey.

"An hour?"

"We had a pre-meeting. I've been calling her all that time." He looked up at her. "I'm sorry, Elsa. But it looks like she won't be requiring your services."

CHAPTER FORTY-FIVE

LESLEY HAD SPENT the last two hours securing the home of Dorset's most notorious criminal. She had Dennis and Uniform out looking for his nephew, who she imagined Devon would be interested in, too, and she was commissioning expensive tests.

She needed to speak to Carpenter.

Lesley knew as well as anyone that seeking forgiveness was often easier than asking for permission. But in this case, she needed to do a bit of both.

She dialled his number and got his PA.

"Hi, Carla, it's DCI Clarke."

"He wants to talk to you. I'll put you through."

Lesley stopped, her mouth open. She'd been about to ask for him.

This didn't bode well.

A few seconds later, the line clicked and Carpenter started shouting.

"Where the fuck have you been?"

"Er..."

"I've got Organised Crime onto me saying we've ballsed up one of their most sensitive operations. I've got the Assistant Chief Constable of the Devon force chewing my ear about your team sniffing around Kyle Kelvin. I've—"

"Sir. I feel I should update you on the latest developments in the Kelvin case."

"Update me? Yes, you should bloody well update me. Before all the relationships this force has spent years building up are torn to shreds in one day by you and your bloody team. Since when did DI Varney work for you, anyway?"

"Sir, you said I could take on extra resource. With PC Abbott on maternity leave, we're short of a team member, and you made it clear that—"

"Tell me, Lesley. Tell me this is getting results. Or I'm going to hand the investigation over to Organised Crime, like DCI Pilton is asking me to."

Shit. Lesley hadn't met Samantha Pilton but knew of her reputation for being a political animal. Could Organised Crime take over a murder case?

When it involved a man they'd probably been following for years, most likely they could.

"Sir, you may be aware that Arthur Kelvin's widow has also died. She—"

"Yes, I know that Amanda Kelvin has died. I'm not entirely clueless, you know."

"Amanda Frobisher."

"What?"

"Her name. She didn't use Kelvin."

A snort. "Well, who can bloody blame her. Although she did choose to marry the man, after all."

"She died this morning, Sir. The family are saying it's suicide, but I don't believe them."

"I should think not, too. And what are you doing about it, except pissing everyone off?"

"I've closed off the house. Forensics are here examining it. I've asked the housekeeper not to go anywhere. I spoke to Kyle Kelvin briefly and I've now got Uniform looking for him."

"You mean you had Kyle Kelvin standing in front of you and you let him go?"

"Sir, he's not under immediate suspicion. I had no reason to detain him."

Silence.

"Sir?"

What were the Devon force doing, that she wasn't aware of?

"Is there an operation relating to Kyle Kelvin, that I should know about?"

"You don't need to worry about that sort of thing. Are you any closer to working out who killed Arthur Kelvin?"

"We have some physical evidence. Tyre tracks, and a chip cone."

"A chip cone! Jesus Christ, if I'm not heading up a team of utter morons."

"The CSIs are examining it for prints and possible DNA."

"Blue Pool is a public site, DCI Clarke. I imagine people drop bloody chip cones there all the time. Why haven't you got a suspect yet?"

"Arthur Kelvin had filed for divorce. We were working on his wife as a potential suspect, but then—"

"Then she ups and dies. I know. You still think she might have done it?"

"I've got no idea, Sir. But we're trying to piece together Kelvin's movements in the hours before his death."

"Kelvin? Which Kelvin?"

There's only one dead Kelvin. "Arthur Kelvin, Sir."

"Tell me you've got a reliable way of doing that. And that it isn't going to cost me any more money."

Lesley placed her hand on the surface of Kelvin's desk and pushed against the wood. The housekeeper would be able to overhear her. Carpenter too, if her ears were any good.

"Sir, I'm in the Kelvin house right now. I'm not alone. I think it would be wise if you—"

"Don't."

"Sorry?"

"Don't tell me what to do, Lesley. Just solve this bloody case, and come back to me when it's all over."

He hung up. Lesley sat motionless, not moving her phone from her ear.

CHAPTER FORTY-SIX

Dennis sat in his car, his hands gripping the steering wheel.

He was in a lay-by outside Swanage, his motor idling and the car angled in a way he'd have condemned any other motorist for.

He didn't know what had come over him.

He leaned forward, touching his forehead to the steering wheel. The plastic felt cool. Soothing.

Get a grip, man.

He'd been to see a psychologist, the one provided by the police. He'd had a dozen sessions, and the man had pronounced him fit.

So what was he doing here?

A lorry sped past, making the car shake. Dennis whimpered.

"Nothing is going to happen to you," he told himself. He pulled down the visor, looking at his reflected eyes. "Just calm down and do your job, man."

But Mackie had believed nothing would happen to him.

Mackie had retired, he'd made plans to go on a cruise with his delightful wife. And then he'd died.

On Ballard Down. Not more than quarter of a mile from where Dennis's car had ground to a halt in the lay-by.

He'd never noticed it before. He'd driven this route hundreds of times, from Swanage over to Poole on the ferry and back again. But today was the first time he'd seen the wooden waymarker.

Ballard Down.

For some reason, it had been too much.

It wasn't as if he hadn't heard the words a dozen times since Mackie had died. It wasn't as if he hadn't said them himself.

But there was something about seeing them in a place that was simultaneously old and new, that had made him unable to drive.

He lifted his forehead from the steering wheel. A car passed. His own car shook, less violently this time.

You've got a job to do, he thought. *An important one.*

What if Kyle Kelvin disappeared because of him? What if they never solved the Kelvin murders?

Kelvin was mixed up in Mackie's death. He knew it. He just hadn't been able to prove it.

And he wasn't sure he wanted to. His fragile mind couldn't deal with thinking about that day again.

It had been bad enough when they'd reopened the case. The day Detective Superintendent Phipps had returned to Hampshire, Dennis had gone home to Pam with a smile on his face for the first time in weeks.

His phone rang. It had rung three times while he'd been sitting here.

He picked it up, trying to think of a convincing lie.

"Boss."

"Dennis, where are you? I've been trying to get hold of you." She sounded harassed.

"I'm in Swanage. Sorry."

"Are you with Kelvin? Have you spoken to him?"

"Not yet. I'll let you know when I have." His voice was flat.

Silence. He waited.

"Dennis, are you OK?"

There it was. The concern. He couldn't cope with her concern. He'd preferred the police back when it was unheard of for senior officers to ask after their subordinates' welfare.

He closed his eyes.

"I'm fine, boss. Just impatient to find the man. I'll call you when I've spoken to him."

He hung up. He was being rude. But the alternative was to tell her the truth.

And he wasn't about to do that.

CHAPTER FORTY-SEVEN

LESLEY STARED at her phone for a moment.

Dennis, what's wrong with you?

He'd been signed off by the psychologist six months ago. He was supposed to be fine. And for five and a half months, he had been.

But two weeks ago, he'd started going off sick again. She didn't believe the migraine story any more than she believed Amanda Frobisher had slit her own wrists.

She punched the desk. She didn't need this. They were working the biggest case this team had seen in years, and she couldn't lose her best detective to mental health problems.

She shook her head, resolving to deal with the Dennis situation after the case was solved, and dialled the morgue. If Vera Kelvin was still there, she wanted to know.

"You."

She looked up to see the woman standing in the doorway.

"What the fuck are you doing in my son's chair?"

Lesley stood up. Any other murder victim, she would never have sat at their desk. It was insensitive.

But Arthur Kelvin...

Sensitivity didn't come into it.

"I'm sorry, Mrs Kelvin. How are you?"

"Like you care." The woman turned away. "Follow me."

Lesley grabbed her phone, switching on the recording function, and followed the old woman into the same sitting room where she'd spoken to Amanda the previous day.

"Sit down." Vera stood by the window, glaring at Lesley.

Lesley didn't like being ordered around, but she did want to get into Vera's good books, or at least try to climb out of the bad ones. She took the nearest sofa.

"Ha!" The laugh was spat out. "You don't say boo to a goose, do you?"

"Mrs Kelvin, I've got some questions I'd like to ask you about your son's—"

"Shut up."

Lesley balled her fist on her lap. She wasn't letting this happen. "When was the last time you saw Arthur?"

Vera crossed the room and stood in front of her. For a woman in her eighties who had been limping at the hospital, she could move fast.

"Don't you dare," she hissed.

"I'm trying to establish where your son went in the hours before his death, and who he saw. That will help us determine who saw him last, and who might have killed him."

"Butt out."

Lesley sighed. "Surely you want us to find your son's killer."

"Of course I fucking don't."

Lesley sat straighter. "You don't?"

Vera stamped her foot on the carpet, just once, then

walked back to the window. She moved more slowly this time, remembering to limp.

"No." She looked out of the window and put her hands behind her back, her fingers entwined.

"Why not?"

"We sort out our own messes in this family."

"If you're talking about vigilante justice—"

The woman raised a hand to stop her. "I'm talking about what's right. We no more want your lot poking your noses into our business that we wanted poor, dear Arthur to die."

Poor, dear Arthur. That was the first time Lesley had heard anything even closely resembling grief from the woman.

And it wasn't that close a resemblance.

"It's our job to bring your son's killer to justice, Mrs Kelvin. And we will do that. If you help us, we can do it more quickly. And leave you alone."

Vera turned. "Oh, I'm not worried about that."

"With respect, Mrs Kelvin. By law we are entitled to be in your house to search for evidence and to question anyone we—"

The door opened and the housekeeper entered. She dipped slightly as she saw the old lady.

Lesley stifled a laugh. Who did she think Vera was, the queen?

"Mrs Kelvin," the woman said. "A phone call. For the DCI."

Vera's face brightened. She gestured towards Lesley.

"Well, you can see her. Hand the phone over."

"It's on the landline. In the kitchen." The housekeeper gave Lesley an embarrassed look. "If you'll follow me?"

Vera laughed. "Go on then. Don't dawdle."

Lesley stood up. She eyed the old woman. "Please don't go anywhere."

"It's my house."

"I still have questions for you."

"I'm sure you do." She made a shooing gesture.

Lesley bit down her anger and followed the housekeeper into the kitchen. She'd been in here earlier, before Gavin had arrived. It was smaller than she'd expected. The domain of the staff, she imagined. Not the family.

A phone receiver sat on a worktop. Gerta gestured towards it. Lesley picked it up.

"DCI Clarke."

"Lesley."

"Sir?"

It was Carpenter.

"Yes. I need you to stand down."

"Sorry? Sir, if you needed to talk to me, why didn't you call my mobile?"

"You weren't answering."

That was a lie.

"What do you mean, stand down?"

"The Chief Constable has requested that we leave the Kelvins alone. Just until we've regrouped. I need you to leave the Kelvin house. And take any Forensics people you have with you."

CHAPTER FORTY-EIGHT

"Got it," Brett said. Stanley was standing behind him, watching the man's screen. He imagined it was irritating, but the boss had told him to stay here and keep an eye on the forensics as they came in.

"Got what?"

"Those tyres. We took an impression from them and I've got a match."

"Great."

Brett turned as the door opened. He smiled. "Sunil. What can we do for you?"

"Hang on a minute," Stanley said. "Those tyre tracks..."

Sunil was a digital forensics specialist who sometimes did crime scenes when they needed extra people. Stanley knew he'd worked on the Lyme Regis case. "I've got some unusual transactions going out of Arthur Kelvin's bank account," he said.

"You've got access to Kelvin's bank accounts?" Stanley asked.

Sunil nodded at him. "Only a couple of savings

accounts. The family swooped in and revoked access, then transferred all the business ones into other family members' names. But there were two they didn't seem to know about."

Stanley turned back towards Brett's screen. "We've just found out what kind of car brought Kelvin to the spot where he died."

"Oh." Sunil placed a sheet of paper on the desk and slumped into a chair at the next desk. "Don't let me interrupt you."

Brett raised an eyebrow at him.

"I need a screen break anyway," Sunil said. "You carry on."

Brett frowned then turned back to the screen. "OK. This won't take a minute. The tyres that left those tracks are Pirellis. They're the kind you get on the top of range Land Rover Discovery."

"That's a heavy vehicle, to be driving down a track like that." Stanley had seen the photos Gail had sent through.

"Common vehicle for organised criminals, though," said Sunil. "It's not just on TV they drive around in those things."

Stanley nodded. "Yeah, but there'll be gazillions of them around the county."

Brett shrugged. "Still worth a punt. Try a PNC check."

"Yeah." Stanley stood up. "Can you write down the model for me?"

Brett tore a post-it off a pad, wrote on it and handed it to Stanley.

"I'll need to go back to the office, run that check."

"You can access the PNC database from here," Sunil said.

Stanley nodded. "OK. Where?"

"My computer. Do I get to tell you about the bank account now?"

"Sorry." Stanley glanced down at the sheet of paper on the desk.

"Right." Sunil grabbed it. "So we've got a regular monthly sum going out to a savings account held at the Skipton Building Society in Dorchester. To a Jacob Frampton."

"That's your DS's name," Brett said.

Stanley felt his mouth dry up. "There's a few Framptons in Dorset."

"Yeah," said Sunil. "Local name. Like mine." He grinned.

Stanley put a hand out towards the sheet. He felt like it was on fire. "Can I take that?"

"Course."

"Thanks." Stanley tried not to lunge for it. "I think I will go back to the office to run that PNC check. The boss needs someone to hold the fort."

"You sure?" asked Sunil.

"Sure," replied Stanley.

CHAPTER FORTY-NINE

THE TREES SURROUNDING the Kelvin property made it feel like night had already descended as Lesley and Gavin walked to his van.

"I'm sorry," she said. "If it was up to me..."

He shrugged. "It's fine."

"Did you get anything?"

Gavin looked up at the house, then eyed her. "I did."

She felt relief wash through her. "Thank God. What?"

"We'll need to analyse what we have. But there were remnants of blood under the freestanding bath in the ensuite. Whoever cleaned up didn't do round the back properly."

"Thank God for that," Lesley said.

He cocked his head. "You seem stressed."

"You don't need to worry about me, Gavin. What's Gail doing now?"

He checked his watch. "She'll have finished at Blue Pool. It's too dark now. If she's got any sense she'll be heading straight home. Her boy's got a party to go to tonight, I think."

Lesley nodded. "Good for her. I'll catch up with you both

in the morning. Let me know when you've worked out whose blood that is."

She needed to go back to the morgue, find out if a post-mortem had been carried out on Amanda. They'd be going home soon. In all the pressure to track down the Kelvins, she'd forgotten to call Dr Bamford.

Not to mention Dennis. Where was he?

"You didn't let me finish," Gavin said.

"No?"

He grinned. "There wasn't just blood. I found fragments of skin too. They look like they were clawed off in a struggle."

Lesley reached out a hand, then withdrew it. "I could hug you."

"Save your affection until we've identified who it all belongs to. Could be nothing. And don't forget that whoever killed her might have had a legitimate reason to be in that bathroom anyway."

"It's an ensuite off the main bedroom. I'd say anyone other than her, her husband and the cleaner would have a bit of explaining to do."

Gavin slammed the van door shut. "Let's hope so."

CHAPTER FIFTY

Meera was enjoying working with the Major Crimes Investigation Team. So far she'd messed around with that toy knife, which had been fun but which, she hoped, had provided the DCI with useful information. And now she was walking the leafy roads of Sandbanks, looking for houses with CCTV and speaking to business owners to find out if they could help.

It beat sitting in living rooms taking statements on car thefts and burglaries that would never be solved.

She'd spoken to the owner of the café by the ferry slip road. She'd been in to speak to the manager at the Haven Hotel. It had cameras, but they didn't cover the road. And the café's CCTV from Saturday hadn't been saved.

Typical.

She hoped Mike was having more joy knocking on doors in the roads running through the middle of the Sandbanks peninsula. Few of the occupants would be in, but she hoped there was at least someone with a sense of civic responsibility.

She stood outside the hotel, sniffing the harbour air and looking across the water. The ferry's lights shone against the darkness of the Isle of Purbeck beyond, piercing the descending dusk. The ferry chugged towards Shell Bay on the opposite shore, veering on its chains as the current tried to drag it out to sea. She'd been using that ferry since she was a girl, heading over to the beach at Studland. Her mum's favourite.

She slumped down on a bench. It was almost five pm. She was no stranger to odd hours, and expected to be working for a good while yet. They had a murder to solve, after all. And the boss was getting married on Saturday.

Good for her. Meera liked the idea of working for another woman who understood what it was like to be queer and in the police.

The ferry paused on the other side, unloading cars and letting more drive on. Headlights moved in the distance. She watched as it made its way back across the narrow channel separating the Isle of Purbeck from Sandbanks.

As the ferry approached, Meera narrowed her eyes.

Of course.

She stood up, approaching the slipway as the ferry ground to a halt against the tarmac. She looked up at the bulkhead, nodding to herself.

The ferry had CCTV, and it pointed right at the road.

She pulled her coat tighter and walked towards the pedestrian gates as they swung open to let people off.

CHAPTER FIFTY-ONE

"DI Gough, sorry to bother you." Will Varney was on the phone in his car, parked in the car park of Dorset Police HQ at Winfrith. He didn't like using the MCIT office; he still felt like he didn't quite belong there. "We've had some developments in the Kelvin murder and I was hoping to have a chat with you about Kyle Kelvin. I know it's sensitive but—"

"I'm sorry, Will. I can't help you."

"But you—"

Gough sounded clipped. "Not my decision, mate. But my bosses are bloody pissed off with your lot."

"Sorry? Why?"

"Look, I can't tell you much. But there's an operation. A big one. And you've thrown a grenade into the middle of it."

"What kind of operation?"

"Inter-force. That's all I'm saying. But now you've got DCI Clarke and the bloody CSIs sitting in the Kelvin house. Everything's had to stop."

"We're investigating a murder, mate."

"I know, the murder of the man who was the biggest fish in Dorset crime circles."

"Was?"

A pause. Gough cleared his throat. "He's dead, isn't he? Someone will have already stepped in. And that... well let's just say it's not panning out the way we expected it to."

"I'm not going to apologise," said Will. "Two people have died. It's our job to find their killer. Or killers."

"Yeah. I know that. Just think about everyone else doing their job too, eh? And the fact that more people than two might die as a result of what you've done."

CHAPTER FIFTY-TWO

GAVIN DROVE OFF, heading for Shore Road and the A35 back to the lab in Winchester. Lesley had other priorities.

She checked her watch: five fifty. She dialled a number.

"Poole Morgue, can I help you?"

"It's DCI Clarke, Dorset Police. Is Dr Bamford there?"

"Sorry. He's left for the day."

Damn. "Do you know if he's done the post-mortem on Amanda Frobisher yet?"

"Hang on a minute."

Lesley hurried to her car. She slid into the driver's seat and turned the key, ready to move as soon as she knew it would be worth it.

"Hello? Sorry for the wait."

"It's fine. Has he done the PM?"

"Not yet, no. It's scheduled for the morning."

"Fine." That was a trip she didn't need to make then. "Can you tell him a member of my team will be in attendance?"

"Will do. Anything else I can help you with?"

"No thanks."

She hung up.

Where now?

Back to the office. She wanted to wrap things up with the team, check on progress. They were scattered across the county, Mike and Meera in Sandbanks looking for CCTV, Stanley at the lab in Dorchester, Dennis in Swanage.

Dennis. He'd seemed distant on the phone earlier, like he'd just woken up. She hoped he would be OK.

Maybe she should let him go home for the evening, after he'd spoken to Kyle Kelvin, assuming they ever got hold of the man. It wasn't as if they were going to be making any arrests today. Not until they had the post-mortem report and the results from the tests on the blood and skin that Gavin had found.

She started her engine and made for Bournemouth. It would be nice to spend some time with Elsa, just the two of them. Sharon was out for the evening with college friends and as far as Lesley was aware, there wasn't any wedding prep to do. Maybe they could go out for a quiet meal together. Their last as single women.

She smiled as she rounded the headland near the ferry. There was no sign of Mike or Meera. Should she stop and speak to them?

They were experienced detectives.

But still...

She didn't want to abandon her team, when she was probably just yards from them.

She pulled into the car park outside the Haven Hotel and scanned for Mike's car. No sign. Maybe he'd parked in one of the streets he was combing for CCTV.

She dialled his number.

"Boss."

"Mike, how are you getting on?"

"OK. I haven't managed to find anyone who's both in and has working CCTV. But Meera had a brainwave."

"What kind of brainwave?"

"The CCTV on the ferry covers the road. If he came past when the ferry was in, it'll have caught him."

"Not that much of a brainwave," Lesley said. "It's on the water or over the other side most of the time."

"S'pose so. Anyway, turns out it *was* a brainwave."

"Go on."

"Arthur Kelvin took the ferry across on Saturday evening, around 7pm."

"It was definitely him?"

"I did a check for his car reg. He got on the ferry at 7.12. He had his window down, so there's a perfect shot of his face."

"It would have been cold."

"Looks like he was smoking, boss."

Lesley thumped the steering wheel. "Brilliant. Now we just need to track where he went after that."

"There aren't many cameras in Purbeck, boss. But we can have a chat with the CCTV operators in Swanage and Wareham. See if he was spotted."

"Do that. Please."

"Meera already tried. They can't access archives till the morning."

Of course they can't.

"OK. Where are you right now?"

"In my car, about to head back to the office."

"You go home now," she told him. "Go see that baby of yours."

"I'll need to give Meera a lift first."

"OK. I'll see you in the morning, Mike."

"Cheers, boss."

Lesley sighed as she hung up. They had the blood and skin fragments. Kelvin travelling across to Purbeck on Saturday night, which meant he was still alive then. And there were the tyre tracks and the chip cone.

She was about to call Stanley when she spotted a familiar figure sitting on a bench in front of her, gazing out towards the ferry.

She put down the phone and got out of the car.

"Elsa? What are you doing here?"

CHAPTER FIFTY-THREE

DENNIS'S PHONE RANG. Again.

He was still sitting in the lay-by, staring ahead.

He took a long, shaky breath, and picked up the phone. He didn't bother with hands-free; he wasn't driving and he hated the thing anyway.

"DS Frampton."

"DS Frampton, it's PS Wright from Response."

Dennis straightened in his seat. "How can I help you?"

"We've found Kyle Kelvin. He's in a house up towards Durlston right now. I've got a squad car stationed at the end of the road but we haven't got too close as we were told not to make ourselves obvious."

Dennis swallowed.

"Thank you. You've done the right thing."

"So are your lot coming down here? We'd quite like it if the man was arrested before he spots our car."

Dennis clenched his fist. He wouldn't be arresting Kyle Kelvin. But knowing where he was... at least he could question the man.

"Thanks, Sergeant Wright. I'll be right there."

CHAPTER FIFTY-FOUR

"Elsa? Everything OK?"

Lesley closed her car door and made for the bench. Elsa turned, flinching as she saw her.

She hurried to the bench and sat next to her fiancée.

Elsa gazed out to sea. "I don't know what to do."

"Do? About what?"

Elsa turned to her. "That new client I told you about?"

Lesley felt her stomach dip. "The one you had the meeting with? How did it go?" She could predict the answer.

Elsa shook her head. "Amanda didn't even show up. I was pinning all my hopes on her, then she didn't bloody turn up."

"Amanda?"

Elsa drew back. "Amanda Kelvin. Her divorce lawyer reckoned she'd be needing a criminal lawyer very soon, what with her husband dying just days after filing for divorce—"

"Hang on." Lesley put a hand on Elsa's arm. "Are you telling me you spoke to Amanda's divorce lawyer?"

"Xavier Robson. Yes."

"And Kelvin filed for divorce last week?"

Elsa blanched. "I can't tell you. Client confidentially."

Lesley leaned in. "But she's not your client. You just told me she didn't turn up."

"But I don't know anything. I didn't even get a chance to meet the woman."

Lesley grabbed Elsa's hand. Her gaze snagged on something.

"Your scarf," she said. "You're wearing your green scarf."

Elsa fingered it. "Oh. Yes, I thought I'd lost it." Her voice dropped. "I wanted to look professional." She slumped in the bench. "I'm toast, love. I don't see how I'm ever going to get this damn practice off the ground."

"Come and sit with me in the car, sweetie." Lesley eyed the scarf again. If Gail had put the scarf she'd found into evidence, there was no way it could have been Elsa's.

Thank God.

"Come on." Lesley stood up and pulled at Elsa's arm.

"OK." Elsa stood, her movements jerky, and followed her.

In the car, Lesley turned the heating up to full blast. "Tell me what happened."

"Nothing, really. I got a call from this Xavier Robson and he told me his client needed a criminal lawyer. When he told me who she was and what had happened, well, I considered talking to you about it." She clutched the fabric of her trousers. "But we've faced each other across an interview table plenty of times before. If you'd had to interview her in connection with her husband's death, we wouldn't exactly be breaking new ground."

"That's true, I suppose," replied Lesley. She wasn't comfortable with the idea of Elsa representing her suspects, and she never would be, but it was something they'd got through before and she had no doubt they'd have to get through it again. Not on this case, though.

Elsa turned, quickly. "Is that it? Have you arrested her?"

Lesley shook her head. "She's dead."

Elsa screwed up her face. "What?"

"She died this morning. The family are saying it was suicide but I don't believe a word of it."

Elsa held her open hand against her face. "That explains it, at least. Poor woman. You think Kelvin killed her?"

"She was alive after his death. So no."

"He might have got one of his goons to do it."

"You used to represent the man," Lesley said. "You have much dealing with these 'goons'?"

"No. And I shouldn't be talking to you about him. I'm not myself."

Lesley grabbed Elsa's hand. "I don't blame you, love. But it will get better. He can't warn people off working with you now."

"Can't he?" Elsa pulled her hand away and jabbed her forehead with her fingertips.

Lesley put a hand up to stop her. "Don't do that. We can't have you scarred for the wedding, can we?"

Elsa's hand stopped moving. "No. Sorry."

"You don't have to apologise. But it will get easier, I'm sure. Just... just try not to take on any clients I'm planning on arresting, yeah?"

Elsa laughed. It was a small laugh, but a laugh none-theless. "That might be tricky, given your reputation."

Lesley smiled. "I know. And I don't mean it. I'm sorry about your client. I love you."

Elsa looked at her. Her eyes shone in the streetlight from outside. "I love you too."

CHAPTER FIFTY-FIVE

THE OFFICE WAS quiet when Stanley arrived, no one in. He wondered if they'd all gone home for the day or if everyone was out following leads.

Still, it didn't do any harm to have no one breathing over his shoulder, given what he was about to do.

He draped his coat over the back of his chair, cursing when it caught in the wheels as he pulled it out, and sat down. He was gasping for a coffee, but he wanted to get this done before anyone else appeared.

He put the sheet of paper Sunil had given him on the desk. It was a printout of Kelvin's statement from a savings account, one with payments going out to a Jacob Frampton.

He'd heard Dennis mention his son in the past. His name was Jacob.

But if he remembered right, Dennis's son lived in London. Why would Kelvin be sending him money?

He clicked his fingers as he waited for his screen to boot up, then yawned. He needed to get to bed earlier tonight, not stay up late playing *Settlers of Catan* online with a bunch of strangers.

OK.

What should he look at first? The car, or the bank account?

The bank account. Get it done.

He smoothed the sheet of paper out on the desk. £500 a month, to Jacob Frampton.

It was nothing. If you were going to accept money from a man like Arthur Kelvin then surely it made sense to take him for more than that?

The sarge was risking his career, his pension, and possibly his safety by doing this. All for just £500 a month?

He'd start by checking the name. Jacob Frampton. Maybe there were more than one of them.

He googled the name and got four hits. One in London: that was Dennis's son. Two of them in Dorset. The fourth was in Canada. Almost certainly unconnected

It was a local name, alright. So maybe this was nothing to do with Dennis at all. Maybe there was another Jacob Frampton who was mixed up with Kelvin.

The only way to know for sure was to contact the bank.

Stanley needed to take this to the DCI.

Or maybe to the sarge.

He needed to give it some thought first.

He took a breath, feeling the cold air in the unoccupied office sting his nostrils, then turned to his computer.

He'd run that PNC check. Find out what car Kelvin drove.

His phone rang: Mike.

"Alright, mate?"

"Hiya," Mike replied. "I was just calling about that drink we were supposed to be going for tomorrow night."

"You're cancelling it cos of the case."

"Not that. It's just, I'm still down at Sandbanks finishing up with the CCTV and I feel bad that I'm getting home to Tina so late. I don't want to leave her on her own tomorrow night as well."

"We can do it another time. Maybe Tina can come too?"

"Yeah. She'd like that. Cheers."

"Mike?"

"Yeah?"

Stanley stood up from his desk. He glanced at the door then walked to the window. There were a few cars in the car park, none of which he recognised.

"If you're doing the CCTV, does that mean you've got details of Kelvin's car? Arthur Kelvin?"

"I have. Kyle Kelvin's too, if you want it. I'll send them over."

"Cheers. What did Arthur drive?"

"A Land Rover Discovery. Black."

"Which model?"

"Hang on." A pause. "A Metropolitan."

Stanley put a hand on the window. *Yes.*

"It matches," he said.

"The tyre prints at the site?"

"Yeah."

"And me and Meera have got CCTV of him heading over to Purbeck on the ferry on Saturday night."

"So whoever killed him took him to Blue Pool in his own car," said Stanley. "Cheeky bastard."

"Makes sense," Mike said. "Use your own car, if something goes wrong it might be traced back to you. Plus it's got your DNA all over it. Use the victim's car, and all you've got to do is wear a protective suit and you're clean."

"You think the Kelvins would have access to forensic suits?"

"You can buy them on Amazon. Of course they do."

"Yeah." Stanley turned at the sound of the door opening. "Hang on, someone's here."

It was Katie Young. Stanley gave her a wave then turned away towards the window.

"Gotta go."

"The boss has told us to knock off for the day," Mike said.

"I've got a couple of things to finish up here, then I'll do the same. See you tomorrow. Say hi to Tina."

"Will do." Mike hung up.

Stanley turned to see Katie standing next to his desk. His gaze went to the bank printout.

He hurried to his chair and plunged himself into it, covering the sheet of paper with his sleeve.

"You alright?" he asked.

She gave him an odd look. "I'm great."

"Great?"

"I managed to get the names of all the Kelvin kiddies."

"Oh?"

"Yeah. Darren, he's the one that's in prison—"

"I do know that. I was there when he was arrested."

"Oh. Sorry." She gave him a shrug and a smile. She had a wide face and large blue eyes. She was, what, twenty-four? Keen as toast, too.

"So, who are the other kiddies?" He folded up the printout and put it in his desk drawer.

"Darren's got Finn and Lottie. Kyle has got Bailey and Josie."

"Cute names. You'd never know the kind of family they come from."

"No."

"They got mums?"

"Oh. Yeah." She pulled out her notepad. "Darren's wife is called Becca. The kids are living with her in Southampton."

"Not at Arthur Kelvin's house?"

"Nope. Kyle's girlfriend is called Charlene. I haven't managed to track her down yet."

"But it sounds like her kids were in the house the first time the DCI visited. Before Amanda died."

"Which means it's likely he was in the county." Katie's eyes shone.

"It does. You told the DCI?"

"Not yet. Gonna talk to my DI first."

Stanley frowned. The DCI hadn't said that was how it worked.

Still. *He* knew now. He'd tell the DCI in the morning. After he'd talked to her about the bank statement.

Or to the sarge. He still had to decide.

CHAPTER FIFTY-SIX

TINA WAS in front of the TV when Mike got home. The living room was tidy and the house quiet. He could smell cooking.

"Wow," he said, plonking himself down on the sofa next to her. "You've been busy."

She raised an eyebrow. "Don't be so sure. That's a Chinese takeaway you can smell, keeping warm in the oven. Where have you been?"

"Can we afford all these takeaways?"

Her face clouded over. "If you want to eat home-cooked food, Mike Legg, you can bloody well get home earlier and cook it yourself."

"Sorry." He attempted to kiss her but she pulled away. "I'm sorry," he repeated.

She humphed.

"So is he upstairs?" Mike asked. "I was hoping to give him his bath."

"He had his bath half an hour ago. Peed on my favourite jeans again."

Mike stifled a laugh. She hit his leg.

"It's not funny."

"Sorry."

"Anyway. You stink. Get changed."

He sniffed himself. "Do I?"

"What you been doing, running a marathon?"

"Walking around Sandbanks. Trying to get hold of some CCTV."

Tina turned to him, tucking her legs under her. Her face brightened. "Go on then. Give me the latest."

He cupped her face in his hand. "Can't we eat first?"

"Not until you give me my daily fix of adulthood. What's been happening?"

He leaned back. "OK. So, we've got CCTV of Kelvin on the ferry last Saturday, which means—"

"He was still alive then."

"Yeah. And – oh, I nearly forgot the most important bit – his wife died. Slit wrists in the bath, early hours of this morning."

Her eyes widened. "He was divorcing her."

"He was."

"So does the boss reckon she killed him and one of his blokes got to her? Surely she can't have topped herself out of grief at losing Arthur Kelvin?"

"The boss doesn't reckon anything, yet. But we've got forensics that might help."

"Like what?"

"Tyre tracks at Blue Pool. A discarded chip cone, too."

"A match?"

"The tracks match Kelvin's car. His nephew's turned up, too. I think the sarge is talking to him."

"Darren?" She shook her head. "No. We arrested him. Kyle?"

Mike laughed. "How come you remember all this stuff?"

"Because it keeps me sane, remember. Where's the chip cone from?"

"Chipperies in Wareham."

Tina stood up. "That decides it, then."

"Decides what?"

"The Chinese can wait another night. I'm sure it'll microwave."

Mike stood up and grabbed her hands. "So you *are* cooking?"

"Don't be daft. No, we're getting fish and chips again."

"But we did that last night."

"There wasn't new evidence last night."

Mike dropped her hands. "T, I don't think this is a good idea. I'm not going there off duty and—"

"Not just you. I'm coming too."

"What about Louis?"

"He's got a car seat, hasn't he?" She was at the living room door, her body full of energy.

"T, he's asleep." Mike followed Tina into the hallway. She'd pulled her coat off its peg and was rummaging in a bag for Louis' blanket. "Don't you think we should—"

"Mike. Humour me. I'm going insane, stuck here on my own. Take me to the Chipperies. Mind Louis while I talk to them."

"You're on maternity leave, love, you—"

She raised an eyebrow at him. "Who was it found out the Kelvins were getting divorced?"

He raised his hands in supplication. "OK. You want to get him out of his Moses basket, or should I?"

CHAPTER FIFTY-SEVEN

DENNIS PULLED up at the town centre end of Durlston Road, next to the squad car. He wound down the passenger window.

"I'm DS Frampton. Can you tell me which house he's in?"

The constable in the driver's seat pointed ahead of them. "Number 136. Right at the far end. You can't see it from here, we didn't want to be spotted."

"Sensible. Leave it with me."

"You want us to go?"

"No. If you don't mind, stay here." It didn't do any harm to be cautious, especially where the Kelvins were concerned. There was every chance one or more of the cars around them had Kelvin's men in them, spying on the spies.

"Will do, Sarge." The window went back up.

Dennis flexed his fingers against the steering wheel and surveyed the surrounding cars. There were just four parked on the road, and they all looked empty.

Still, that didn't say anything.

Too late to worry now. He was here, and the DCI had told him what to do.

He drove to the end of the road and parked outside number 136. A black SUV was in front of him, the shape of a man in the driver's seat.

He looked at the house. It was a blank modern affair, generously proportioned. The front curtains were drawn and there was no sign of movement.

Should he knock on the door, or wait?

Wait.

The driver of the car in front would already have told Kyle about Dennis's arrival. So if the man was going to leave by the back, he'd have done so already.

The front door to the house opened and two men stood silhouetted in the light from the hallway. Dennis held his breath.

After a moment, the men embraced. One of them turned to walk along the neat path towards the street.

Dennis went to open his door. He wasn't going to give Kyle the chance to get into his car and drive away.

As he was putting his foot out, the passenger door opened and a man got in.

Dennis froze, his driver's door still open.

"Close the door, DS Frampton. No point in pretending I don't know who you are."

Dennis clamped his lips together, brought his foot back in and closed his door.

The man shut the passenger door behind him and grunted. Dennis glanced over to see Kyle Kelvin wincing and rubbing his hands together.

"Mr Kelvin," he said.

Kelvin lifted one hand and sucked at it, briefly. He

lowered the passenger side visor and checked his face in the mirror. "That's me. Now, why are you lot following me, when I'm grieving for my poor dear uncle and aunt?"

Dennis glanced across at the man. He was slight, with short blond hair. His clothes were expensive.

This was a man who hired others to do his dirty work.

"My boss wanted to speak to you about this morning," Dennis said. "But you left before she had the chance."

"I had a meeting to get to."

"I can tell."

"So she sent you along in her place. Why couldn't she come herself?"

Dennis realised he didn't know what time Amanda Kelvin had died. Had the post-mortem been done yet?

"Mr Kelvin, where were you between five am and nine am this morning? Were you in the house when your aunt was found dead?"

"Aunt. She's young enough to be my sister."

"Were you there?"

Kyle leaned in towards Dennis. "No. I wasn't there. I live in Plymouth, but I'm sure you know that."

"So when did you arrive at the house?"

"Ten o'clock. The housekeeper rang me and told me what had happened. I came straight over, of course."

"You came over for your aunt's death, but not your uncle's?"

A sniff. "I did."

"Did you and Arthur not get along?"

Kyle's jacket rustled against the seat. "None of your business, Sergeant."

"Were you at your home in Plymouth over the weekend, too?"

"What do you think?"

"I have no idea." Dennis stared ahead at the SUV, trying to ignore the fact that his heart was racing.

Was Kyle carrying a weapon?

It was OK. Uniform were at the other end of the road.

Where they couldn't be seen.

Which meant they couldn't see him, either.

He swallowed down a wave of nausea.

"Can you tell me where you were between Saturday evening and Monday morning?"

"Let me see. What times?"

Dennis thought.

"From seven pm on Saturday to eight am on Monday."

Kyle shook his head. He pursed his lips. "Shall I get my calendar out, check?" He reached for his inside pocket.

Dennis put out a hand.

"You alright, DS Frampton? You seem a little nervous."

"I'm fine."

"Only I'd hate for you to have a heart attack sitting here next to me. That wouldn't be pleasant at all. And I'm sure your mates would take the opportunity to pin it on me, too."

"Just take a look at your calendar please, Mr Kelvin." Dennis blinked. His vision was blurring.

"Very well." Kyle took a phone out of his pocket and unlocked it. "So... Let's see..."

He rapped the phone's screen with a fingernail. "Here we are. Three to five pm on Sunday. My son was at a party in Plymouth. His little friend, Vincent. That's nice, isn't it?"

"You went with him?"

"I did. Thought I'd give Charlene the afternoon off."

"Will there be people who can vouch for you?"

"It was a party. In a fucking Wacky Warehouse. Yes, there'll be people who can vouch for me."

"And what about the times outside that slot?"

"Ah well, that's where you're going to have to trust my word."

"Your word for what?"

"Saturday night I was in a bed in Exeter. Shagging my girlfriend, if you must know."

"But you live in Plymouth."

A laugh. "Different town, different girlfriend, mate. And yes, she'll vouch for me. Lola Raymond. Look her up."

He shot a hand out and grabbed Dennis by the wrist.

Dennis gasped. For a small man, Kyle was strong.

Kyle dropped Dennis's hand, flinging it away like it was a rotten piece of meat. "Now if you don't mind, I need to get back to visit my poor old nan. She's grieving, you know."

He opened the passenger door and swung his body out, all in one smooth motion. Dennis sat motionless, focused on his breathing.

Kyle strode to the SUV and jumped up into the back seat. Dennis gulped for air.

He needed to get hold of himself, if he was to continue in this job.

CHAPTER FIFTY-EIGHT

Lesley leaned back in her chair as Elsa walked to the restaurant toilet.

Would things be OK, from now on? Did Arthur Kelvin's death mean Elsa was finally safe?

And that scarf...

Had she really thought her future wife capable of murder?

She placed her palm on the table and pushed against the wood.

It was a ridiculous thought. Elsa had been scared of Kelvin. He'd wrecked her business. And yes, she might have wished him dead...

But Elsa, a killer?

The scarf was on the back of Elsa's chair, draped over it like just another item of clothing. Not an object which had made her doubt her own fiancée.

She needed to stop thinking about it. And she needed to trust Elsa.

She brought out her phone. She hadn't got round to

looking at the photos Stanley had sent her. The evidence store, from the Mackie murder.

The old DCI's phone she knew about. She'd gone through the text messages herself. Dennis had been in contact with the man on the day of his death, about an old case Mackie insisted on pursuing.

An old case that related to Arthur Kelvin.

Lesley flicked through the rest of the photos.

The soil and vegetation samples were new. They'd been taken when the case was reopened. No use at all, given how much time had passed.

Then there was the paperwork. Lesley glanced towards the toilets: still no sign of Elsa.

When Gail had taken her to the evidence store, there'd just been the one sheet of paper: Mackie's handwritten suicide note.

But now there was a small stack of items. Stanley had taken hurried photos of them and the text was grainy.

It looked like there were bank statements, a letter from the Inland Revenue and a receipt from a holiday company.

Where had they come from? Were they from Mackie's home? And if so, would there be more scanned into the case file?

"Hey." Elsa was behind her chair. "You OK?"

Lesley looked up. She put her phone on the table, face down. "Of course. You want pudding?"

Elsa's eyes brightened. "I've had my final dress fitting and it's too late to make a difference now. So yes."

"Good." Lesley picked up the menu. She had a wedding and honeymoon to think about. Not to mention a double murder case.

DCI Mackie could wait.

CHAPTER FIFTY-NINE

"COME ON, THEN." Tina swung the baby carrier out of the back of the car and looped her arm around the handle. "I'm starving."

They'd parked in the car park on St John's Hill, as close to the Chipperies as they could get. As they'd passed the chip shop, Mike had noticed a queue outside.

"Wait," he said, running round to the back and closing the door. Tina had hurried off without closing it after lifting Louis out.

He pressed the button on his keyfob to lock the car and watched as the indicators blinked, then turned to see her disappear into the alleyway leading to South Street.

He needed to pay for the parking.

But he didn't have time.

OK, he told himself. *You're police. It's fine.*

He raced to catch her up and barrelled into two women coming the other way as he rounded the corner into South Street.

"Sorry," he muttered. They frowned at him and carried on walking.

"T!" he shouted.

She was up ahead, the baby carrier in her arms.

How could she move so fast, with all that weight? And how was she not waking Louis?

Truth was, Louis had a knack of sleeping like the dead when he was in that carrier. Mike had often considered bringing it up to the bedroom when he wouldn't go back to sleep in his Moses basket at night.

Tina had reached the queue now.

"Tina!" He was right behind her. But instead of stopping at the back of the queue, she went straight inside.

The queue parted to let her through, mutters of *Look where you're going* quickly replaced by *Look at the little guy* and *Isn't he cute?*

Mike finally caught up with his wife inside the shop. The baby carrier was on the floor by her feet, their son miraculously still asleep.

She was holding up her police ID.

"Tina," he hissed.

She shook her head, not turning to look at him. She was smiling at the woman behind the counter.

"So on Saturday night it would have been turned on, then?" she asked.

"What are you doing?" Mike muttered.

"*Your* job," she replied, her voice low. She put a hand on the counter. "Any chance you could let us take a look at it?"

The woman sighed. "Sorry, love. It's only accessible from the office, and Dan's not working tonight. He's got the only key."

"Someone must be able to access your office. What if there's an emergency?"

The woman blushed. "Well, it's not the office, you see. It's the computer. I don't like to touch it."

Mike stepped in next to Tina. He was aware of Louis on the floor between them. *Don't wake up, kiddo.*

"Sorry about this," he said.

"Who are you?"

He hesitated.

"DC Legg."

"I have to say, this seems very strange, bringing a baby on a police investigation. Don't they let you put him in a crèche or something, love?"

"It's OK," said Mike.

"I wasn't asking you." The woman looked from him to Tina.

"It's OK, though," he replied. "We're off—"

Tina stepped on his foot. "Don't worry about Louis," she said to the woman. "But can you tell me when Dan will be in, so we can take a look at that CCTV?"

"Half seven tomorrow, love. I suggest you take that baby home. He'll catch his death."

"We will, thanks. Can we get a large cod and chips and a cone of chips, while we're here?"

There was muttering behind them.

"T, we've pushed in," Mike said.

She looked at him. "You want me to stand outside with Louis and wait for the queue to go down?"

"No, but..."

"It's fine," the woman said. She handed over a packet. "Here, it's on the house. Come back in the morning, and let me get on with clearing this queue."

CHAPTER SIXTY

DENNIS WAS in his pyjamas when his mobile rang. He frowned, picked up his specs and stood up.

"Don't answer it, love," Pam said. She was in bed, sitting up reading a library book.

"It could be urgent," he said.

"You're CID," she reminded him, her eyes raised over her reading glasses. "Not Uniform anymore. What can be so urgent that you're getting a call this late?"

"I won't be long. Besides, I was going to go down for a glass of water."

"No, you weren't."

He said nothing, instead closing the bedroom door and padding down the stairs in his slippers. The hall was dark, the only light the dim shard from a streetlight beyond the front door.

His phone was in its usual spot, next to the charger on the kitchen worktop. He'd charged it in the evening, as usual, then unplugged it before bed, also as usual.

Dennis checked the clock over the stove: nine thirty.

He checked the display: the DCI. He slumped.

He could go back up to bed, pretend he hadn't heard it.

But then he'd never sleep.

Scratching his neck, he picked up the phone.

"Boss."

"Dennis, I do hope I haven't disturbed you."

"I was just going to bed."

"What? At nine thirty?"

"Early start in the morning."

"Oh. Yes, I suppose so. Anyway, I wanted to check in on you."

"You want an update on Kyle Kelvin?"

"No. Yes. How did you get on?"

"He was as unpleasant as you'd expect. Didn't give anything away, apart from providing an alibi for Sunday afternoon. A children's party in Plymouth."

"Sunday afternoon."

"Yes."

"Not Saturday evening or even Sunday evening?"

"He said he was with a woman on Saturday evening. I doubt that she'll corroborate it."

"No. Well, thanks. I hope he wasn't too difficult."

"It was fine, boss. Is that all?"

"No. Look, I'm sorry to call so late, Dennis. But I've just got back from an evening out and I can't stop worrying about you. You sure you're up to this case?"

"Why shouldn't I be?"

"I know it's been a few months since you got signed off as fit to work again. But I have been watching you, you know."

"I don't need watching, boss."

"Yeah well. That doesn't stop me worrying about you. You'll tell me if it all gets a bit much, won't you?"

"I will." He hesitated. "Boss?"

"Yes?" She yawned. "Sorry. What is it?"

"Was there a specific reason for this call?"

A pause. "No, Dennis. No specific reason. You get a good night's sleep. I'll see you in the morning. Briefing at eight."

"See you in the morning."

CHAPTER SIXTY-ONE

Elsa was woken by her phone ringing beside the bed. She reached out a hand, feeling for it on the bedside table.

"Wha's that?" Lesley turned over next to her. "Your alarm?"

"Go back to sleep," Elsa told her.

"Hmmm." Lesley wriggled back down under the duvet.

At last Elsa found her phone. She fumbled for it, almost knocking it onto the floor. She grabbed it and held it in front of her.

Number withheld.

She squinted at the display. It wasn't even six o'clock.

Who calls before six o'clock in the morning?

She sat up. Her mum was coming to the wedding. Elsa had been trying not to think about it.

But she'd been calling at odd hours. Bothering Elsa with complaints about her health.

Elsa opened the call. "Hello?"

"Elsa Short?" It was a man's voice.

"That's me. Is it my mother? Is she OK?"

"Your mother? No. It's not your mother."

Lesley snored next to her. Elsa sat up higher, propping herself against the pillows. She lowered her voice.

"If you're trying to sell something, it's only—"

"I'm not trying to sell anything. But *you* might be able to sell *me* something."

"Oh?"

Elsa swung her legs out of the bed, careful not to disturb Lesley. She went to the bedroom door, grabbed her dressing gown and tugged it on, managing to keep the phone to her ear by passing it from one hand to the other.

"Who are you?" she asked as she closed the bedroom door behind her. Sharon was asleep in the next room; she hadn't got home until after one am. Elsa had woken at the sound of the door closing, but Lesley had slept though. Elsa wasn't sure if she should speak to Sharon about that, or Lesley.

"You used to represent my uncle," the man said.

Elsa eased herself down onto the sofa. She stretched out the muscles of her face and rubbed her cheek with her free hand. "You'll have to be more specific. Have you been arrested?"

"No. But I want a good local brief, just in case."

She sat up straight and puffed out her chest. "Then I'm your woman."

A laugh. "Don't delude yourself, darling. I just happen to know you don't have much in the way of principles, is all."

"I don't know what you're talking about."

"OK. Let's not beat around the bush. My name's Kyle Kelvin. You might have heard of me. You used to work for my poor deceased uncle."

Her skin prickled. "I haven't worked for your uncle for almost a year."

"That's not what I heard."

"Mr Kelvin, have you been arrested? Do you need someone to come to the station and represent you? Because I don't normally get calls at this time of day unless it's an emergency."

"It's not an emergency."

Elsa heard movement behind her. She turned to see Lesley standing in the doorway, her face drawn.

"What are you doing?" Lesley asked.

"Nothing. Go back to bed."

Lesley shook her head. She grabbed the phone from Elsa's hand.

Elsa's grip on the phone was loose and it fell to the floor.

Lesley kicked it away.

Elsa stood up. "What the—"

"I heard. That was Kyle Kelvin, wasn't it?"

"Why did you—"

"He wants a lawyer, because we're onto him."

"Onto him for what?" Elsa glanced at her phone. "Lesley—"

"Don't Lesley me. Not when you're about to make the second most stupid decision of your life."

Elsa eyed the phone, still on the floor. Could Kelvin hear this? "What's the first?"

"Working for his uncle."

"I didn't have much choice."

Lesley bent over and picked the phone up. She switched it off.

"Well, you do have a choice now. And if you choose to represent that man, you'll regret it for a very long time."

CHAPTER SIXTY-TWO

"STANLEY, is this about that drink tonight? I'm sorry, but—"

"It's not that, mate. Have I woken you?"

Mike laughed. He was standing in Louis's room, which was only used for night-time pacing and nappy changing, given that the baby slept with him and Tina.

"No. That job was done by my son over an hour again."

"Ouch."

"It's OK. What's up?"

"Nah. It's nothing. I'll see you in the office later."

"Stan. You've called me at quarter to seven in the morning. Something's up. What is it?"

Stanley inhaled. "OK. Don't tell anyone I talked to you about this, please."

"OK." Mike was worried now. "You're not leaving, are you?" He frowned, remembering his former colleague, Johnny Chiles. "Don't tell me the bloody Kelvins have got to you too."

"What? No. Although it's to do with them."

Louis stirred on his shoulder. He'd given the boy a bottle

of milk, something he'd started doing lately so that Tina could have a lie-in. The milk coma had lasted about twenty minutes and was already starting to wear off.

"Spit it out. I'm going to have to change a nappy in a minute, judging by the smell in here."

"Ew. OK. It's about the sarge."

"The sarge? What's he done?"

"I don't know," said Stanley. "He might not have done anything. It's just... Have you ever met his son?"

"Jacob? He lives in London. I spoke to him on the phone once, when I had to call the sarge on Easter Sunday. Not doing that again in a hurry. But no, I've never met him."

"OK."

"What about him, Stan?"

"Look, I shouldn't be telling you this. I should probably tell the DCI instead."

"What's up? What's all this about Jacob?"

"Forensics found something. Bank statements. Of Kelvin's."

"I thought the family had revoked access."

"There were a couple of savings accounts they missed."

"So what about these bank statements? Hang on a minute."

Louis was awake. Mike sat in the armchair Tina used for feeds, jiggling the baby. He smiled, burped and farted.

"I haven't got long, Stanley. Can you just get to the point?"

"OK. Kelvin was putting money in Jacob's account. Five hundred quid a month."

"Jacob Frampton? You sure it's the same one?"

"There's only four of them, according to Google."

"Oh, and Google knows everything."

"Mike, what are the chances of Kelvin sending money to someone who just happens to have the exact same name as the sarge's son?"

Stanley had a point.

Louis started to cry.

"Look, mate," Mike sighed. "I've got to go. Can we talk about this later? I'll be in the office in half an hour."

"OK. See you in a bit."

"Oh, and before you go..."

"Yeah?"

"We went to the Chipperies last night. Long story, don't ask. They've got CCTV. So we can head over there this morning and see if any of the Kelvins were there on Saturday night."

"That's a coincidence, you getting chips just when we had that chip cone as evidence."

"Yeah, well you try cooking with a three-month-old baby in the house. I've got to go. Louis's just puked half his milk down my t-shirt."

"Rather you than me, mate. I'll let you get off."

CHAPTER SIXTY-THREE

LESLEY PULLED into the car park at seven thirty. She switched off the ignition and sat back in her seat, rubbing the skin between her eyes.

She and Elsa had had a lovely evening last night. They'd gone to the Arbor in Bournemouth and bought a bottle of fizz to celebrate their wedding in advance. Elsa had been playful and sexy and it had reminded Lesley of their early months together.

She was regretting it now. Half a bottle of Prosecco coupled with an early morning *something* she refused to label as an argument, not to mention the near certainty that she would have to deal with the Kelvins again today. It all made for one hell of a hangover.

She leaned over and reached into the glove compartment. She pulled out a pack of paracetamol, swigged down two with the water in the cup holder, and grimaced at the thought that the bottle had probably been there for a week. She took a few deep breaths, willing herself to keep it down.

Three days. Lesley had three days before her wedding, and she needed to wrap this case up.

Hopefully the forensics would give them what they needed. And hopefully Carpenter would let her do her job.

She checked her reflection in the rear-view mirror, rubbed the mascara under her eyes, and got out of the car. She rolled her shoulders as she walked, desperate to pump blood into her body.

Wake up, woman.

"Morning, Tony," she said as she entered the reception area.

"Morning, Ma'am," replied the duty sergeant.

Almost two years she'd been here, and still he insisted on calling her Ma'am.

"You're getting married in three days, aren't you, Ma'am?"

Lesley stopped and turned back to him. "How did you know?"

He tapped the side of his nose. "I keep my nose to the ground. Anyway, I've been given a message for you. Detective Superintendent Carpenter wants to see you."

Lesley felt all the energy she'd pumped into her body drain away in an instant.

"Now?"

A shrug. "You know the Super."

Lesley gave him a curt nod and headed for the lift. The stairs were too much.

Two minutes later she was outside Carpenter's office, knocking on the door.

"Who is it?"

"DCI Clarke, Sir."

"Come in."

She pushed open the door to find the Super on the corner sofa, DCI Pilton from Organised Crime in the chair at right angles to him.

"Sir," she said. "And Samantha, good to see you."

"Hmmm," the DCI replied.

"What can I do for you, Sir?"

"Come and sit down." Carpenter patted the sofa next to him. Lesley resisted a grimace and dragged a chair over from near the desk. He raised his eyebrows as she sat down, a disapproving look on his face.

"Sir," she said. "I'm assuming that as DCI Pilton is here this is related to the Kelvin case."

"Can I be frank with you, Lesley?" DCI Pilton asked.

"I think you're going to be, whatever I say."

"Touché. In that case, you should know that the Super has managed to find a way to smooth over what might have been some very choppy waters."

Enough with the metaphors. "And what choppy waters might those be, Samantha?"

"I think you're aware that your murder investigation has interfered with a major operation of ours."

Lesley glanced at Carpenter. "I have been made aware, yes. But you'll understand that—"

"The Super is prepared to let it slide, this time."

Oh is he? Lesley looked at Carpenter. He was twirling his fingers together on his knee, gazing at them like they were the most interesting thing in the room.

Bastard. Getting a DCI to do his dirty work.

"If you'll help us with something," Pilton continued.

Lesley looked at her. Her head hurt. "That depends what it is."

"I thought you might say that." Pilton leaned back. "This mustn't leave this room. No telling your team."

"Especially not DS Frampton," Carpenter interjected.

Lesley looked at him. Why the specific reference to Dennis?

"OK," she said. "Confidential." Inter-departmental plans and discussions were often kept from more junior officers. It was nothing new.

"In that case, I want you to leave Kyle Kelvin alone." DCI Pilton uncrossed and recrossed her legs and cocked her head, giving Lesley a piercing stare.

"You do?"

"I do."

"Are you going to tell me why?"

Lesley glanced at Carpenter, who licked his lips.

"Lesley," Carpenter said. "I mentioned an operation to you yesterday. I can't divulge full details, but suffice to say it involves DCI Pilton's unit and their opposite numbers in the Devon force."

"You've been observing Kyle Kelvin. Building a case so you can arrest him for his county lines operation."

Carpenter frowned but said nothing. It didn't take a genius to know Lesley was correct.

Carpenter gave her a thin smile. "I'm sure you'll understand, Lesley, that an operation like this. It's delicate, fragile. It takes months to prepare—"

"Years," said Pilton.

Carpenter's right eye twitched. "It takes years to prepare. I can't have the whole thing falling apart because you have your eye on Mr Kelvin."

"For murder," Lesley said. "Possibly more than one."

"People will die if we don't take this man in," Pilton said.

"People who matter. Not other members of the Kelvin family."

Lesley looked at her. "Since when were murder victims ranked?"

"Don't be naïve, Lesley."

Carpenter cleared his throat. "The reality is, DCI Clarke, that I'm giving you an order. And I expect you to carry it out."

"Sir. I will come to you before I or my team make an arrest. Is that good enough?"

"It's not," said Pilton.

Carpenter frowned at her. "You come to me if there are any major developments," he told Lesley.

"I will. Is that everything?"

"Yes," Pilton said. Carpenter's eye twitched again. Lesley looked between the two of them.

"You can leave," Carpenter said.

Lesley stood up, smoothed her hands on her skirt, and made for the door. She was sweating.

As she put her hand on the doorknob, Carpenter spoke.

"How's DS Frampton, Lesley?"

She turned. "Why do you ask?"

A smile. "Just concerned for his welfare."

I bet. "He's been certified as fit to work again. He's making a valuable contribution."

"Good. Glad to hear it."

CHAPTER SIXTY-FOUR

THE TEAM WERE ASSEMBLED in Lesley's office as she reached the team room. DI Varney and his two DCs were huddled in one corner, standing together. Dennis, Stanley and Mike were gathered around the desk. The six of them waited in silence.

Lesley pushed open the door to her office. "Did I say you could all come in here?"

Dennis stood up. "Sorry, boss. I did—"

DI Varney stepped forward. "We didn't want to waste your time making you wait for us to come in, boss."

Lesley looked at him, then at Dennis. She gave Dennis a questioning look and he shook his head.

Great. Now the two teams were engaged in some kind of standoff.

Well, she knew how to deal with that.

"OK everyone." She approached the board. "Where are we? Mike and Meera, how are you getting on with the CCTV?"

Mike and Meera exchanged glances. Meera smiled.

At least someone's on speaking terms, Lesley thought.

"We got CCTV from the Sandbanks ferry," Mike said.

"Arthur Kelvin got the ferry across from Sandbanks to Studland at 7.12pm on Saturday." Meera had her notebook open.

"And did he come back?"

Meera looked up. "We checked the footage for the rest of Saturday evening. Nothing."

"That doesn't mean he couldn't have come back via the land route," Lesley pointed out.

"It means he was alive on Saturday night, though," Mike said. "And I reckon the CCTV at the Chipperies'll show him there."

"What CCTV?" Lesley asked.

He flushed. "Me and Tina went there last night. Didn't have time to cook, what with the baby and that. Tina asked them if they've got CCTV, and they have."

"Tina did?"

"Er. Yeah."

"OK. And did you get a chance to look at this CCTV?"

He shook his head. "The manager wasn't there. They said to come back tomorrow. Today."

"OK. That'll be a priority. Dennis, I want you on that."

"I can—" said Mike.

"It's OK. Dennis, you alright with that?"

"Of course."

"Good."

Katie Young was muttering with Varney.

"You got something to add?" Lesley asked them.

Varney looked up. "Sorry, boss. Katie was volunteering to go with Dennis."

"She was?"

"There might be more than one camera," Katie said. "Two of us can go through the footage quicker than one."

And you're thinking your younger eyes will be better suited to the work. "Very well," said Lesley. "Dennis and Katie, you're on the Chipperies CCTV. Have we got any forensics from that chip cone yet, Stanley?"

"Not yet, boss. I'll give them a call as soon as we're done here."

Lesley shook her head. "I want you and Meera looking into Kyle Kelvin's movements on Saturday and Sunday. He claims to have an alibi. Dennis?"

"He says he was at a kids' party in Plymouth on Sunday afternoon. And that he was with a woman called Lola Raymond in Exeter on Saturday night."

Katie raised her hand.

"You don't need to do that, DC Young," Lesley said. "What is it?"

"The kids. Amanda told you that Darren's kids were in the house on Monday. But they were in Southampton all along, with their mum. It was Kyle's kids who were there."

Lesley gave the board a rap. "Good work. So we know Kyle was lying when he said he'd only arrived at the house yesterday morning."

"Not necessarily, "Dennis told her. "Just because his kids were here, doesn't—"

"You're right." Lesley gave the board another rap. "But they've been lying to us, which means they're hiding something."

"You want us to talk to the woman he says he was with?" Meera asked.

"I doubt you'll find her. And even if you do, she'll only

say what Kyle has told her to. No, I want you and Stanley to talk to Traffic. Get camera footage from Saturday and Sunday. What roads are we talking about?"

"A38 and A35 are most likely to have cameras," said Meera.

"Right. We know what Kyle drives, don't we?"

"He was in a Honda SUV last night, boss," said Dennis. "Not driving himself, though."

"Doesn't matter who was driving. If he brought that vehicle up from Plymouth in the hours before Arthur's death, then we know he was in the county."

"Are you sure it was Kyle?" asked Varney.

Lesley sighed. "I'm not really sure of anything. But Kyle has been lying to us, and so have the rest of the family. I think that's as good a starting point as any. I'm going to head over to the forensics lab."

"Are you sure?"

Lesley eyed him. "Yes, DI Varney. I'm sure. And can you and I have a chat?"

"Of course."

"Get to it, then." Lesley looked around the room.

Meera gave Mike a smile as she approached Stanley and left the room with him. Dennis motioned for Katie to follow him. She looked at Varney, who nodded, then followed Dennis out of the room.

What the hell's going on there?

"Mike," Lesley said.

"You haven't given me a job, boss."

"No. I want to speak to you about something. You wait at your desk, while I talk with DI Varney."

"I can help Stan and Meera with the CCTV while I wait."

"You do that."

Mike waited for a moment, then realised he was dismissed and stood up.

Lesley turned to Varney. "OK, Will," she said. "What's your problem?"

CHAPTER SIXTY-FIVE

GAIL WAS RELIEVED to have a day in the warmth of the lab. Two days out in the biting cold at the Blue Pool had given her a nasty cough, and she was glad to be in the warm and dry, all but mainlining tea.

She returned from the kitchen with a tray of four mugs. One for Gav, one for Brett, and two for her. She was hoping hot drinks would shift this cold. There was no way she was missing Lesley and Elsa's wedding on Saturday.

"What you working on?" she asked Gav as she placed a mug on his workbench.

"I've dusted the chip cone, now I'm running what we have against the database."

Gail nodded and slurped her tea. "I thought you were working on the blood and skin you found yesterday at the Kelvin house."

"That's over there," he said.

"I'm keeping an eye on it," said Brett. "Waiting for a Plex-S test to run."

Gail smiled. She went to her desk and sat down, briefly closing her eyes. Would anyone notice if she took a little nap?

She was disturbed by Gavin's voice.

"Gail, come and see this."

Gail opened her eyes. Had she fallen asleep?

She stood up, rubbing her eyes and hoping she hadn't been snoring. She walked to his desk, her footsteps uneven.

"What is it?" She shook herself out. *Wake up.*

"The prints, on the chip cone. I've got a match."

"Nice one." Brett was on the other side of the room, stooped over a monitor.

Brett had been at his work bench when Gail sat down. When had he moved?

"Who to?" she asked, rubbing the bridge of her nose and stifling a cough.

Gavin looked over his bench at her. "Arthur Kelvin."

She smiled. "Really?"

"Really." He indicated the image on his screen. "Here, there's a pattern."

Gail rounded the bench and joined him, looking at the screen.

"You're right," she said.

The image showed a definite pattern of prints.

"It's what you'd expect if he was holding it," Gavin said. He picked up a cardboard cone from his desk.

"What's that?" she asked.

He grinned. "I went to the Chipperies last night and asked for a cone. I've been holding it in different ways, comparing it to the one we found."

"And it checks out?"

"It does," he said.

"OK," she said. "But please tell me you've found more

prints on it. I mean, we know Arthur Kelvin was near the chip cone."

Gavin curled his lip. "Sorry. Just the one set."

She sighed. "Ah well. At least we know one thing for sure, and that's where Arthur Kelvin went in the hours before he died."

CHAPTER SIXTY-SIX

"WILL," Lesley said. DI Varney had said nothing so far.
"What's this about?"

Will Varney looked through the partition wall separating
them from the team room, and back at her. "Is there any way
we can get more privacy in here?"

"You think we need it?"

"I don't want the team seeing tension between us."

"I didn't know there was any, DI Varney. You think
there is?"

He sat down in the chair opposite her desk. "I'm worried
about DS Frampton."

"Oh you are, are you?" Lesley lowered herself into her
chair. The headache was receding but it wasn't gone yet.

"He was off sick last year, with mental health issues,
wasn't he?"

"Dennis's health is his business."

"Have you seen how he's behaving?"

Lesley resisted the urge to look out into the team room.
She knew that Dennis would be gathering his things,

checking he had everything he needed, taking his coat down from his peg and smoothing it over his arm before carrying it out to the car.

But none of that indicated mental health problems. Dennis was a fastidious man, and always had been.

"Will, I think you need to be careful how you talk to me. I'm your senior officer and I'm in charge of this investigation. I don't know what you're used to in Bournemouth—"

"I don't mean to undermine you, boss."

She raised an eyebrow. "Doesn't look that way to me."

He placed his palms on his knees. "OK. Do you mind if I make a suggestion?"

"You go right ahead."

"I think we're uncoordinated. We have a range of leads, and people are just running out to follow them up without any sense of oversight."

"Will, I..."

Lesley stopped herself. She considered.

She didn't need to justify herself to this man. Of course they were following up leads as they came in. And there was no way to know what evidence they'd find, until they found it.

"If you have a problem with the way I run an investigation, you can always request an immediate return to CID."

He blanched. "That's not what I—"

Lesley stood up. "No. I'm sure it isn't."

This morning she'd had to put up with DCI Pilton criticising her methods and telling her what to do. She'd sat through that because Carpenter had been right there and she'd had no choice.

But she wasn't having this.

"Will, you have a choice. We don't have time for debate on how this investigation proceeds—"

"I know you're under pressure because you're getting married."

Lesley felt blood rush to her head. She fought an urge to put her fingers to the main point of pain.

"How dare you."

He shrank back. "I didn't mean to—"

Lesley gestured for him to stand up. "DI Varney, if you prefer not to be a part of this investigation, you're free to return to your full time posting. You're also free to lodge a formal complaint, if you think that'll get you anywhere."

He said nothing, not meeting her eye.

Coward.

"But in the meantime," she said, "I suggest you focus on contributing to taking down whoever killed Arthur Kelvin and Amanda Frobisher."

"Boss."

"Good. Now there's a post-mortem being carried out on Amanda Frobisher's remains any minute now, and I promised them an officer. Get over to Poole Hospital and report back to me when it's done."

CHAPTER SIXTY-SEVEN

Dennis sat two cars back from the level crossing at Wool station. Surely it didn't normally take this long, from the barriers going down to the train coming through?

Beside him, DC Young pecked away at her phone. All he could hear was the clicking noise it made every time she tapped a key.

It was annoying.

"DC Young," he said.

"You can call me Katie, Sarge."

"Katie."

She put her phone in her lap. "Yes?"

"Nothing."

The train came through and Dennis felt himself relax. Katie tapped her foot in the passenger footwell.

"Are you alright, Katie?"

"Yes, Sarge." The tapping continued. "Are you?"

He flashed her a look, then turned back to the road. The car ahead edged forward as the barriers came up. "Pardon?"

"You seem quiet."

Dennis felt his chest clench. "I'm quite alright, thank you, DC Young."

"Katie."

"I'm quite alright, thank you." They drove over the crossing, Dennis feeling the familiar dread he experienced every time he drove over one of these things. "Are you familiar with the Isle of Purbeck?"

She shook her head. "I live in Blandford Forum. Never had reason to come down here." She yawned.

He gripped the wheel tighter. "In that case, let me do the talking, when we arrive at the chip shop."

"OK."

"Good."

"I don't mind taking over, if you'd rather I did."

Dennis checked his rear-view mirror. There was nothing behind, and nothing ahead except a lay-by.

He pulled over and stopped the car. He turned to her, tugging at his seatbelt when it dragged on his neck.

"DC Young," he said.

She opened her mouth to correct him, then, seeing the look on his face, closed it again. He raised his eyebrows.

"Sarge," she said.

"Do you have some reason for thinking I'm not capable?"

The DC drew back. "Er. No."

"Has someone told you something about me?"

"Who? No. Well... No."

"You're not very good at lying, DC Young. You'll have to get better at it, if you're ever going to make Sergeant."

She straightened in her seat. Ambitious, no doubt.

Heaven save us from ambitious young women.

"Now," he said, adjusting his seatbelt, checking his mirror and starting the car up again. "When we arrive at the Chipperies, I shall speak to them. You can help with the CCTV analysis. I'm sure you understand."

CHAPTER SIXTY-EIGHT

LESLEY LEANED out of the doorway to her office as Varney hurried out of the team room door.

"Mike," she said. "You got a minute?"

He looked up from his screen. "Course, boss."

She retreated into her office, stood at the board and waited for him. A moment later he was in the room, closing the door behind him. He looked from her to the board.

"Everything OK, boss? Something you want me to do?" He stepped forward. "Was it something you didn't want the new team in on?"

Lesley thought for a moment. There was plenty around this case that she'd rather not bring Will Varney in on. But she knew better than to keep secrets.

And Carpenter had made it clear that he knew everything about her and her team. Which made any attempts at privacy pointless.

"No, Mike. It's not that."

His expression dropped. "OK. What can I help you with, then?"

She smiled. "I know you meant well."

"Sorry?"

"The CCTV. Going to the chip shop with Tina."

"Well. We wanted chips. Louis keeps us so busy it's impossible to find time to cook. T fancied a Chinese but I thought fish and chips would be easier. So we went to the chip shop, it's our nearest one. And it seemed to make sense to—"

"Mike. You can stop now."

"Sorry."

"Tell me – honestly – whose idea was it?"

He blinked back at her. "Whose idea was it to get chips?"

Lesley shook her head. "Don't insult me, Mike. Was it Tina's idea? I know what she's like with witnesses. It was her who spoke to them in the chip shop, wasn't it?"

"Well... Yes. She got there before I did. She had Louis, but she carted him along in his car seat. I never knew she could go that fast, I—"

"Again. Stop. You're garbling."

"Am I?"

"You are. And that's because you know what I'm about to say to you."

"Do I?"

Lesley smiled. "Tina's missing the job. She's at home with a baby, and she's bored. Knackered too, I should imagine." She took a step towards him. "I'm a mum too. I remember what it's like. Bloody nightmare."

Mike let out a nervous laugh. "She loves Louis."

"Just cos she loves him, doesn't mean she has to enjoy every second with him."

"No. It's bloody hard work, boss. He shits everywhere."

"Haven't you heard of nappies?"

"That's not what I mean, I—"

"I'm joking, Mike. I know what you mean."

"I don't understand. Is it a problem that Tina spoke to them at the chip shop?"

"She's on maternity leave, Mike. By law she's not allowed to undertake police duties."

"Oh."

"Strictly speaking, you shouldn't be discussing cases with her."

Mike looked crestfallen.

"But I'm not naive enough to think I can expect you not to do that."

"Oh. Thanks."

"Look," she said. "You can talk about cases with Tina. You can even come back to the office with her insights, if she has them. But I want to know when something is her idea and not yours. It's not fair on her otherwise."

"It was Tina who worked out about the Kelvin divorce."

"You already told me that."

"Oh. Did I?"

"You did, Mike. But here's the important thing. Tina can't get herself actively involved in a case. She can't talk to witnesses, she can't access police records. She can't do anything that wouldn't be possible if she was just another member of the public."

"I get it. Because she *is* a member of the public, right now."

Lesley winced. "Well, I wouldn't go that far. And I certainly wouldn't repeat that to her if I were you. But yes. Just make sure she doesn't do anything that might put her at risk."

"All she was doing was chatting to the chip shop woma—"

"Did she tell the woman she was a DC?"

He reddened. "She might have."

Lesley gave him a look. "I'm not going to ask you if she showed her ID."

He looked down.

Shit. "Do I need to revoke her ID while she's off?"

"No. I'll have a word." There was a look on his face that said *she won't like it.*

And she wouldn't. Lesley hadn't. But it wouldn't last forever.

"Here," she said. "I've got an idea. How about you share the leave with her?"

"Huh?"

"You're both in the same unit, so it doesn't affect staffing. Now her first two weeks are up—"

"More than up."

"Now her first two weeks are up, she can elect to transfer the rest of her leave to you. Or some of it."

"But she's got up to eight months."

"Is she planning on taking all of that?" Lesley held up a hand. "I'm not supposed to ask you that, sorry."

"She's not."

"OK. You have a chat with her. See if you can work something out between you. I'll talk to HR, if you need me too."

Mike scratched his chin. There was stubble; when had he last shaved?

"Boss?"

"Yes?"

"Are you saying you'd rather have Tina here than me?"

"I'm not going to dignify that question with an answer, Mike. Now I need you to go to the post-mortem with DI Varney."

"Do you?"

"Yes." She didn't tell him she wanted him keeping an eye on the DI. She went to the window and looked out. Varney was on his phone in his car. Again.

"Hurry now and you'll catch him in the car park."

"Oh. OK. I'm on it, boss."

CHAPTER SIXTY-NINE

Watching Mike dash out of the office, Lesley went to her chair and slumped into it. She took in a few breaths, then reached into her handbag and pulled out the packet of paracetamol.

When had she taken the previous ones?

Less than an hour ago.

She put the packet back in her bag, stood up and walked to the door to the team room. Stanley was at his desk, deep in concentration. Meera was at the bank of desks over by the far window. She looked up.

"Can I help you, boss?"

Lesley approached the woman. "I don't suppose you've got any ibuprofen, have you?"

"Er... yeah. I reckon I have."

Meera took her coat off the back of her chair and rummaged in the inside pockets. At last she drew out a packet, a look of triumph on her face.

"Have it. You look like you need it."

Lesley raised an eyebrow. "That bad?"

Meera's face fell. "Sorry, boss. I didn't mean to…"

"It's OK. Thanks for the pills." She waved the packet and went back to her office.

"Do you need some water to wash them down with?"

Lesley turned back to see Meera holding up a bottle of water.

"It's fine."

"It's a new bottle." Meera tugged at the cap. "See? Never opened."

Lesley walked to her and took the bottle. "Thanks." She went back to her office, gulped down the pills and downed half the bottle of water.

Maybe that was all she needed: hydration.

She needed to look after herself if she was going to be on form for the wedding on Saturday. Part of her was aching to have it over and done with and be in Scotland, enjoying some peace and quiet with her wife.

Wife. Lesley still couldn't get used to it. She'd been one for eighteen years. Then she hadn't. And now, not only was she was going to be one again, she was going to have one of her own.

She rubbed the necklace Elsa had given her after their engagement and picked up her phone. She dialled Gail.

"Lesley. I was about to call you."

"Good news, I hope."

"Very good. Gav's been able to match the prints on the chip cone to Arthur Kelvin, and they're in a pattern that indicates he was eating from it."

"So he ate chips, not knowing he'd be dead within hours."

"I'd say poor bloke, but…" replied Gail.

"Indeed." Lesley stood up. "Look, I don't like asking you

this, but can you keep this to yourself, for now? I'm having some political difficulties."

"OK." Gail's voice dropped. "You alright?"

"I'm fine. Thanks. Have you got the samples from the Kelvin house? Gavin had skin and blood, he told me."

"Brett's running tests on them now. We should have a DNA profile by the end of the day."

"That quick?"

"It's the Kelvins. We're as keen as you are to get this done."

"Good. I'm coming over."

"You really don't need to."

"The only way we're going to get Kyle Kelvin is with physical evidence," Lesley said. *And that's the only way I'll be able to convince Carpenter to get me an arrest warrant.* "I want to be there when you get what we need."

"OK. I don't suppose you can bring some Lemsip with you?"

"You got a cold?"

"Yeah. I won't sneeze on you, though. Promise."

"That wouldn't be good, catching a cold before my wedding day."

"No. Lemsip, though?"

"I haven't got Lemsip, but I have got plenty of paracetamol and ibuprofen."

"You're a life saver. See you in a bit."

"I'll be about twenty minutes. Can you wait that long?"

"I'll have to, won't I?" Gail replied. "Oh, I almost forgot. Sunil sent me an email about some bank statements. Apparently he passed them to Stanley. Have you got them?"

"Bank statements?"

"Arthur Kelvin's savings accounts. There were two that

the family didn't manage to transfer to another name before we had a chance to speak to the bank."

"I don't know anything about any bank statements." Lesley looked through the glass partition at Stanley. "Can you send them over?"

"I'll forward you the email."

"Thanks." Lesley didn't take her eyes off Stanley. "I'll see you shortly."

CHAPTER SEVENTY

DENNIS PEERED through the chip shop window and knocked on the door for the third time. The door rattled.

"Maybe they're not in, Sarge." DC Young leaned against the wall beside him, looking bored.

"I spoke to Mike. He was in here last night and they told him there'd be someone in at 9am." He checked his watch. "It's 9.15 now."

"Not everyone's as punctual as... as the police."

He frowned at her. She blushed.

At least she's got the decency to look ashamed of her insubordination.

Dennis sighed and stepped back, looking up at the first-floor windows. He wasn't about to shout up there. There weren't many people about on South Street in Wareham on a Wednesday morning, but Dennis wasn't about to go broadcasting his business to anyone who did happen to be passing.

The DC had her phone to her ear.

"Who are you calling?"

She held up a finger. "It's DC Young, Dorset Police. One

of my colleagues spoke to your team last night... Yeah... We're outside right now, is it possible to let us in?"

She put her phone away and gave Dennis a smile. "Got the number off their website."

He hesitated. "Good work. But let me do the talking."

A shadow appeared on the other side of the door, and a moment later it opened. A large man wearing a t-shirt and jogging bottoms yawned at them.

"What time is it?" he asked.

"Quarter past nine," Dennis replied. "We were told you opened at nine."

The man shrugged. "It's not a precise art, running a chippy." He looked at Katie and his face perked up. "You police, you say? What's happened?"

DC Young opened her mouth, but Dennis put a hand out to stop her. "We're investigating an incident in the local area, and have reason to think your CCTV might have picked up something that could help us with our enquiries."

The DC turned away, but not before Dennis caught her rolling her eyes.

"CCTV?" The man yawned again. "Yeah. Come on through."

He stood back to let Dennis and Katie past, then locked the door behind them.

"You not open yet?" DC Young asked.

"Not for a few hours yet. Nine am's when I start getting the place set up. There's a lot of prep. Battering fish, peeling and slicing potatoes—"

"If you don't mind," said Dennis, "we are in a bit of a hurry. If you could point us in the direction of the CCTV, I'd be grateful."

The man sniffed. "Fair enough. Here." He unlocked a

door and ushered them in. Beyond it was a tiny office with space for nothing more than a desk and an uncomfortable looking chair.

"You can tell I don't have an office job," he said. "Although I spend more time than I'd like to in front of that computer."

He reached in and turned it on. Dennis noted that the man was able to switch the computer on without even stepping inside the minuscule room.

"How do we access the CCTV images?" he asked.

DC Young was already in the chair, clicking the mouse and typing.

"It's alright, Sarge. I've got it."

The man pointed. "There. Well done. You OK for me to leave you?"

"Thank you." Dennis shuffled into the room and stood behind Katie. She shifted in her chair, and he moved back a little.

"Start from seven pm on Saturday evening. When Arthur Kelvin came over from Sandbanks."

Katie stared at the screen. "It'll have taken him ten minutes to get across on the ferry and then another twenty to get to Wareham, at least. I'll start at half past."

"I think—" Dennis began.

But she was right. He put his hands in his pockets, hoping this wouldn't take too long. If there were two sets of videos, there was no way of watching more than one of them at a time.

"Right," she said. "I've downloaded everything between seven thirty on Saturday and midnight on Sunday. There are four recordings. I've sent two of them to your email."

"Sorry?"

"I said, I've sent two of them to your email. The other two have gone to mine. We can find somewhere more comfortable to sit and go through them there."

"Oh. Very well then. Can you send all four to the team inbox, please. And then delete the history so the chip shop doesn't have access to our email."

"I sent it from their email account. And yes, I've deleted the sent message and any record of where it went to." She tapped her forehead. "Don't worry, Sarge."

"Good. Thanks."

"OK. Where shall we watch it, then?"

"Let's go back to the car."

"I was hoping for a cuppa, Sarge."

He raised his eyebrows. Come to think of it, he *was* thirsty.

"Come on," she said. "Nellie Crumb's open, and it's right next door. I'm buying."

CHAPTER SEVENTY-ONE

LESLEY POKED her head out of her office door. Again. At some point, she might actually get out of here.

"Stanley, can I speak to you a minute?"

At the other side of the room, Meera looked up. She exchanged glances with Stanley then looked at Lesley.

"How's your head?"

"Getting there. Thanks for the painkillers."

Lesley closed the door behind Stanley and motioned for him to take a seat. She sat down opposite him.

"I've just had a call from Gail," she said.

"They done an analysis on the blood yet?"

She shook her head. "Working on it. But it wasn't that."

"The skin. You said there were fragments of it—"

"Stanley. Did Sunil Chaudary give you a printout of some bank statements to bring back here?"

Stanley's mouth fell open. He fished inside his jacket pocket and brought out a folded-up sheet of paper. Swallowing, he unfolded it and placed it on the desk between them.

"I didn't know what to do with it."

Lesley had already checked her emails and knew what was in the document. She also had no idea whether the name Jacob Frampton was a coincidence or not, but she intended to find out.

"Stanley, you do know this would have caught up with me eventually, don't you?"

"I do."

'So why did you hide it?"

"I did tell Mike."

"You...?" Lesley rested her head in her hand. "You told Mike," she muttered. She looked up. "Why?"

"I'm not sure. I wanted to talk to someone, work out what to do."

"When you've got a piece of evidence that might implicate a colleague, then the person you talk to is your senior officer."

"Or PSD."

"Or Professional Standards," she agreed. "You didn't talk to Professional Standards, did you?"

"No. I was going to talk to you next."

"Good. That's what you should have done to start with." She drew the sheet of paper across the table and stuffed it into a drawer.

"What are you going to do with it?" Stanley asked.

"It's evidence in a murder enquiry. I'm going to look into it."

He stared at her. He didn't ask what that meant.

"Thanks, Stanley. And next time something like this happens—"

"I'll talk to you first, boss." He stood up.

"Good. How are you getting on with the traffic cameras?"

"We're going to have to go to their ops centre, I reckon. Meera's talking to someone there now."

"Is she?" Lesley looked out of the window. "She's good."

"Yeah."

"OK," said Lesley. "I'm heading over to the forensics lab. Let me know how you get on at traffic ops."

CHAPTER SEVENTY-TWO

MIKE TRIED to ignore the awkward silence in DI Varney's car as they drove to the morgue. He'd caught up with the DI in the car park, knocking on his window and explaining that the DCI had asked him to accompany him. Stumbling over his own words, he'd told Varney it was part of his professional development, that he needed to observe more post-mortems.

Both men knew he was lying. But Varney, after peering up at the office windows for a while, had shrugged and let Mike into the car.

Now they were on the outskirts of Poole, moments away from the hospital.

Mike stared out of the passenger window, wondering if he should attempt conversation. But the DI hadn't bothered to speak to him, and he was the senior officer.

Besides, Mike hated polite conversation.

At the hospital, Varney gestured towards the pay-and-display machine. Mike walked over to it, searching his pockets for change but hoping it took cards. It didn't. He put in enough for two hours and walked back to the car.

"Thanks." Varney placed the ticket on the dashboard.

They walked to the morgue, Varney's pace determined but not rushed. Still he didn't speak. Mike was relieved when they arrived at the post-mortem room and the pathologist broke the silence.

"I wasn't expecting two of you."

"It's an important post-mortem," Varney replied.

Dr Bamford looked between the two men. Mike gave him a sheepish smile.

"I suppose so," the doctor said. "Come on, then."

Mike stood by the far wall, just as he had for the woman's husband the day before. Varney stood a couple of feet in front of him and to the side, where he had a better view.

Rather you than me, mate.

Should he step forward? The DCI had sent him here for a reason. Maybe she wanted him reporting back, rather than Varney.

He shook his head. If he was going to retain the contents of his stomach, then he'd need to stay where he was.

"Before I open her up," the pathologist said, "I'm going to perform an external examination."

Mike took a breath. At least that would delay the gruesome bit.

He stepped forward, glad to be able to do what he suspected the DCI wanted him to. The DI turned to him as he moved in beside the pathologist's assistant.

Was Varney about to step even closer?

Well, Mike wasn't following him. There were limits.

Varney rocked on his heels for a few beats but stayed where he was. Mike breathed a sigh of relief.

"I'm taking swabs from under her fingernails," said the pathologist.

"Why wasn't that done by the CSIs?" asked Varney.

"The death was originally reported as a suicide. She was brought here before the police were called."

Varney nodded. Mike allowed himself a glance at the body.

She was pale, paler than he remembered Kelvin being. But then, she'd bled out through her wrists. He'd been stabbed. A quicker death.

Poor woman. Did you really do that to yourself, or did the same person who killed your husband have it in for you?

He hoped the DCI would get to the bottom of it.

"There's skin under her fingernails. This one's broken." Dr Bamford held up the woman's right hand. "Evidence of a struggle." Working carefully, he took a few moments to remove what he had found, then looked up at the two detectives. "This was not a suicide."

Mike swallowed. He wanted to step back, to cower against the wall. But there was no way he was letting Varney see his reaction.

"There's bruising on her right elbow, too. Consistent with someone grabbing her. Maybe restraining her. And finger marks on her buttock." He bent to look at the woman's side and indicated for his assistant to take photos.

"Do you want us to get that to Forensics?" Mike asked, pointing at the Petri dish Bamford had placed on the instrument table beside Amanda Frobisher's body. He put a hand to his mouth. *Please, say yes.*

Bamford looked over at him. "If you think that's a priority."

"It's a priority."

Mike held out his hand, keeping his position by the wall.

Dr Bamford smiled. "I know it's not easy." He placed the

Petri dish, now inside an evidence bag, in Mike's hand. "You go and sort that out. I'm sure DI Varney can report back to your DCI."

Mike frowned. Was he doing the right thing?

But he could feel nausea pushing at his throat. If he stayed in here, he'd defile the place.

"Thanks," he said. And rushed out.

CHAPTER SEVENTY-THREE

LESLEY STARED AT THE ROAD, cursing a headache that wouldn't leave her and listening to the ring tone on hands-free.

"Elsa, where are you?" she muttered.

She hadn't spoken to Elsa since their argument about Kyle Kelvin this morning, and she was regretting it. They were getting married in three days, for God's sake. Yes, she didn't want Elsa working for the Kelvins. But Elsa was a grown woman and had to make her own decisions. Lesley couldn't boss her around.

"She's not a member of your team," she muttered.

She reached the CSI office in Dorchester and went straight in, following the route through the building on autopilot. Ten minutes later, she was in the lab, following Gail to her workbench.

"Have you managed to analyse the skin and blood yet?"

"We've got a blood type. AB positive."

"Amanda was AB positive."

Gail nodded. "Arthur was O negative, so there's a good

chance other family members were, too. And there's no sign of his markers in this blood sample."

"But that doesn't tell us anything," Lesley said. "Amanda slit her wrists, or had them slit for her. Her blood would be all over that bathroom."

"We saw the paramedics' report," Gail said. "They took her from the bathroom. The place was a mess."

"So someone cleaned up after they'd taken her away," Lesley replied. She looked over towards a workbench where one of Gail's team was working.

"What about the skin fragments?" she asked.

"We've run a bunch of tests on those. The skin belongs to an IC1 male, blond hair, green eyes."

"How d'you know that from a skin sample?"

"The FDP test."

"Impressive."

Gail flashed her a *haven't you been paying attention?* look.

"What about a DNA profile?" Lesley asked.

"That's next. Based on the hair colour, we can say that it's not Arthur Kelvin's skin. But the DNA might tell us whose it is."

"Only if you've got a sample to compare it with."

"Yeah."

Lesley sighed. "Are we going to have to ask everyone with access to the house for cell samples?"

"I don't know yet, Lesley. It depends on what we get. If we're lucky, it might match someone already on the database."

"If we're lucky."

CHAPTER SEVENTY-FOUR

NELLIE CRUMB WAS EMPTY, the only occupant a young woman standing behind the counter and arranging bread in a basket.

She straightened up as Dennis and Katie entered.

"Oh," she said. "Can I help you?"

The DC gave her a smile. "A cup of tea for me please." She looked at Dennis.

"Me, too."

"Two cups of tea. Sorry, I thought you were police."

Dennis looked down at himself. He wore his tweed jacket under a grey Mac. Was it that obvious?

He eyed the display between him and the woman. "I'll have a toasted teacake too, please."

"Hungry?" Katie asked.

"It's hungry work. Don't worry, I'll pay for it."

She smiled. "I can afford it."

Dennis raised an eyebrow. He knew what young DCs earned, and it wasn't all that much. But she was offering, and he wasn't planning to insult her.

"Thank you," he said, and walked away to find a table. He picked the one furthest from the counter.

The tables were round, made of pine, with the kind of farmhouse chairs that made Dennis feel right at home. He wondered if this place had changed in twenty years.

He approved.

Katie approached the table holding a tray with a large pot of tea, a milk jug and two cups.

Even better.

"Your teacake's on its way," she said. "I decided to join you."

"So," he said. "This CCTV. You're expecting us to work through it on our phones?"

"I know the monitor in the chip shop's bigger. But did you see how low resolution it was?"

Dennis hadn't noticed.

"I'll get a better picture on my phone," she said. "Assuming the source is decent."

Dennis shrugged. The young woman came over carrying two plates with steaming teacakes and a bowl of butter, and placed them on the table.

"Anything else I can get you?"

"No, thank you." Dennis watched her return to the counter.

He dipped his head and kept his voice low as he spread butter on his teacake.

"Alright then," he said. "Let's see what we've got."

Katie had her phone on the table. "We've got two videos each. My first one starts at seven thirty on Saturday."

"Can you scan it? We don't want to watch the whole thing on normal speed."

"I can." She prodded her phone and bent over it.

Dennis took a bite from his teacake. He reached into his pocket for his phone. They needed to be efficient.

"Hang on," Katie said. She pushed her phone across the table.

Dennis squinted at it. He picked it up and brought it closer to his face.

"Is that—?" he said.

"It is."

The image showed the queue outside the chip shop. There were ten, perhaps twelve people in it.

And right at the back, having just joined, were three he clearly recognised.

CHAPTER SEVENTY-FIVE

LESLEY WAS SITTING NEXT to Gail, watching her run through screens of data, when her phone rang.

"Boss, it's Dennis."

"Have you managed to access the CCTV?"

"We've done better than that. DC Young has copied it and sent it to the team inbox."

"Good for her. Is there a lot of it?"

"There is. But luckily, what we wanted was right at the beginning. Seven forty three pm time stamp."

"When you say 'what we wanted'..."

"We've got both of them on camera. Arthur and Kyle. Standing in the queue outside the Chipperies."

"So now we know that Kyle wasn't just in Dorset, he was with Arthur not long before he died."

"And buying the chips that were dropped at the crime scene."

"That's great work, Dennis." She considered. "I want you to see if there are any other sources of video footage along there. Outside the pubs on the quay, maybe. Can we track them travelling to Blue Pool?"

"Katie's already walking along South Street asking businesses if they can help."

"Good for her." Maybe Katie's keenness was a good thing. "How did they look? In the video? Could you see their faces?"

"Back of Arthur's head, top of Kyle's."

"Typical."

Gail put a hand on Lesley's arm. "We've got a DNA profile from the skin samples," she whispered.

"Hang on, Dennis." Lesley put her hand over the receiver and looked at Gail's screen.

"Anyone we know?"

"It's close to Darren Kelvin's but not identical."

"Which means it's very likely to be Kyle."

Gail turned to her. "It's not conclusive."

Lesley could hear Dennis's voice coming through the phone. "Sorry, Dennis. Gail's got a DNA profile on the skin from the bathroom. It's similar to Darren Kelvin's."

"So it's Kyle's."

"Apparently it's not conclusive." She thought of the conversation she'd had with Carpenter. If she was going to get a warrant, she needed this to be watertight.

She sighed. "I need to go, Dennis. Work out how we can—"

"I didn't finish, boss."

"Did you find more CCTV?"

"Not that. But there were three people in that queue outside the Chipperies."

"Three? Did Kyle have one of his goons with him?"

"No. Amanda."

"Sorry?"

"Amanda Frobisher was in the queue with them."

"Hang on. She wasn't in the car with Arthur, when he headed over there."

"No."

"So she must have got there with Kyle."

"Probably."

Lesley stared at Gail. What did it mean?

"Thanks, Dennis. That makes it all the more important that you find us some more CCTV. I want to know how Kyle and Amanda got to Wareham and whether they travelled together."

"We're working on it," Dennis replied. "And that skin sample you were talking about?"

"Yes?"

"I've got an idea."

CHAPTER SEVENTY-SIX

STANLEY AND MEERA stood behind a traffic control officer, watching the bank of screens over her head.

"So this is Saturday morning," she said. She pointed to the top right screen, one of nine ranged in front of them.

Stanley looked from one screen to the next. He was glad he didn't have to do this for a living, it would make his eyes fall out.

"What time?" Meera asked.

"Seven am. That early enough for you?"

She looked at Stanley, her eyebrows raised. He shrugged.

"Good a place to start as any," he said.

His phone buzzed: a message from the Sarge.

He read it.

"Sarge and DC Young have got video of Kyle in Wareham on Saturday evening," he said. "Arthur and Amanda with him, getting chips."

"Amanda too?" Meera asked.

Stanley nodded. He had no idea what this meant. Could Amanda have been involved in her husband's murder?

"Which one of them is it you're looking for?" asked Carla, the traffic officer.

"Kyle Kelvin," he said. He read out the registration number of Kyle's Toyota.

"In that case, we don't need to trawl through the footage," she said. "I'll put his reg in and see if there's a hit."

"You're sure the cameras capture every plate?" Meera asked.

"Each camera doesn't capture all of the plates that pass it. Sometimes they're obscured. But it gets most of them, and if he passed more than one camera, then the chances of him not being picked up are small."

She tapped a keyboard and sat back, waiting.

"There you go," she said.

The moving image on the centre screen was replaced by a darkened image of the motorway, with Kyle's registration plate highlighted in the middle.

"Where was that?" Stanley asked.

"A35 near Winterbourne Abbas. Nine sixteen am."

"So we know he came up to Dorset on Saturday morning," Meera said.

"Not necessarily," replied Stanley. "Carla, have you got any other hits on that reg?"

"Already checking." She hit a key and three more of the screens populated: similar images of darkened roads with the same illuminated number plate at the centre.

"So those are showing him at Buckfastleigh, Bridport and Parkstone."

Stanley turned to Meera. "On his way to Sandbanks."

"But it's Wareham where your sarge saw him on CCTV."

Stanley shrugged. "Maybe he went to Sandbanks first. Did Amanda travel over with Arthur on the Saturday evening, or did she meet up with Kyle?"

Meera turned to look at the screens, her eyes narrowed. "Good question."

CHAPTER SEVENTY-SEVEN

"What's your idea, Dennis?" Lesley asked.

"The skin you found, in the bathroom. It's not Amanda's?"

Lesley put the phone down on Gail's workstation. "I'll put you on speaker, Dennis. I'm with Gail."

"No," said Gail. "The skin isn't Amanda's."

"And it's not Arthur Kelvin's?"

"Nope."

Lesley scratched her nose. "What are you thinking, Dennis?"

"I'm assuming you don't have a sample from Kyle to run a comparison."

"Sadly not," said Gail. "He's never been arrested."

"Yet," Lesley added.

"I might have something you can use," Dennis said.

"Like what?" Lesley asked.

"When we tracked Kyle down in Swanage last night. He spotted me waiting for him and he came and got in my car."

"I know that," said Lesley.

"You're thinking he might have left traces in your car?" Gail asked. "I'd doubt there's enough, from him just sitting in the passenger seat."

"No," said Dennis. "He caught his hand in the car door. He was sucking it when he got in."

"And he might have left skin behind," said Gail.

"Or blood," added Dennis.

"Dennis, you're a bloody miracle worker," said Lesley. "Get over here now, and bring your car."

CHAPTER SEVENTY-EIGHT

Dennis put his phone back in his pocket and pushed the empty plate away. "That was an excellent teacake."

Katie nodded. She had her face in her phone.

"What are you looking for now? We need to get to Dorchester."

She looked up. "Why?"

"I'll tell you in the car. But we need to hurry. Can you do that while we drive?" He stood up.

The waitress approached their table. "Are you finished with these?"

Dennis smiled at her. "We are, thank you. That tea cake was delicious."

"Thanks. Are you here cos of the murder at Blue Pool on Sunday?"

Dennis exchanged glances with Katie. He didn't have time for this. "Well..."

"Only I saw him. The dead guy."

Katie looked up at the waitress, then returned to her phone. Dennis pushed back irritation.

The tearoom was still empty, no one to overhear them.

"Where did you see him?" he asked.

"It was Saturday evening, I'd just got off work. About quarter to eight, I reckon? Yeah, we finish late on a Saturday, there's a lot of cleaning up to do. And I'd been talking to the boss about my shifts for this week."

"Where did you see him?" Dennis asked.

"Down at the quay. I was meeting a mate for a drink at the Old Granary and I almost walked into him as I turned into the car park."

Dennis looked down at Katie, who was still on her phone.

What was so urgent, that it was more important than this?

"You're sure it was him?" Dennis asked the waitress.

"I'm pretty sure. I saw his picture on the news. He muttered something at me and I remember thinking how scary he looked."

Dennis nodded. The girl wasn't wrong.

"Was he alone?" he asked.

"Yeah. Well, yes and no."

"Sorry?"

"He was on his own when I passed him. But then I turned round and I saw him meeting some people."

Katie looked up. "People?"

"A man and a woman. They looked like they were having an argument. They turned away and walked up back this way."

"On their way to the chip shop," Katie muttered.

"Sorry," Dennis said to the waitress. "Who was having the argument?"

"All of them. The two blokes, mainly. The dead guy had

a bit of a go at the woman, and I think the other guy was telling him to back off."

"Thanks," said Dennis. "Would you be happy to make a formal statement relating to this?"

She frowned. "He was a pretty scary bloke. My mum told me he was organised crime or something."

Katie stood up. "He's dead now." She flicked her gaze to the girl's name badge. "Jodie. He can't hurt you."

She looked at Katie. "You sure?"

"Yeah."

A sniff. "OK."

"Thanks," said Dennis. He turned to DC Young. "So Kyle arrived with Amanda, then the three of them went to get chips."

"Why d'you go and have chips, after having a row in the street?"

Dennis shook his head. He found people hard to understand, even after nearly four decades of coppering.

"Anyway," DC Young said as the waitress walked away with their plates. "I've found something else."

"Tell me."

Katie held her phone up. "Amanda's social media. Well, not exactly hers, I can't get at that. But I found one of her friends whose privacy settings are non-existent."

"And?"

She scrolled down to a photo. It showed a man and woman smiling at the camera, their arms around each other. Their eyes shone.

"Amanda and Kyle," Dennis said.

"Looks like they knew each other pretty well," Katie replied.

CHAPTER SEVENTY-NINE

Half an hour later, Lesley's phone rang.

"Boss, we're just outside. There's nowhere to park."

Lesley looked at Gail. "Where should they bring the car?"

Gail gestured for Lesley to hand over her phone.

"Dennis," she said. "Go round the back. Gav'll open the gates. We'll need to bring the car into the garage."

She hung up and looked at Lesley. "Let's get down there."

"In the cold? Surely it'll take ages."

"We've got an indoor area for vehicle analysis. I'm surprised you haven't seen it."

"Never had cause to."

"Follow me."

Lesley followed Gail to a door at the far end of the office, leading to some back stairs. They hurried down to the ground floor and Gail unlocked another door into a large, dimly lit space.

She flicked a switch and fluorescent lights flickered on. It was a large garage, with roller doors at the far end. Gavin was already by them, watching one trundle upwards.

"Welcome to our vehicle analysis facility."

"It's impressive," Lesley told him. "How easy will it be to find traces of Kyle's DNA on Dennis's car?"

"That depends on how much Dennis can remember of where Kyle's hand was when he caught it in the door," Gail said. "But we'll use a UV light, that'll help us pinpoint it, particularly if there's any blood."

Lesley nodded. She hung back as Dennis eased his car through open roller doors and parked it just inside. Gavin hit a lever and the door trundled shut again.

Dennis got out of the car. Katie was in the back seat.

"Why aren't you in the front?" Lesley asked.

"We didn't want to open the passenger door again, disturb any evidence," Dennis explained.

"Good thinking," Gail told him. She approached the car, holding a large light wand. "Can you remember which spot he trapped his hand in?"

"He didn't exactly trap it. At least, that's not how it appeared. But he winced as he got in the car, and sucked his hand."

Gail's eyes widened. "He sucked his hand. Tell me he touched something afterwards. The dashboard."

"He would have touched the inside door handle, to get out. But he also touched the visor, before that. He was looking at himself."

"Perfect. Dennis, your car is a godsend." She crouched to get closer to the inside of the car, Dennis next to her.

As Lesley watched, DC Young approached her. "We've had more evidence come in, Ma'am."

"You can call me boss. What kind of evidence?"

"The waitress in Nellie Crumb said she saw Arthur Kelvin on his own on Saturday evening, before the CCTV caught him in the chip shop queue."

"But he was with Amanda and Kyle."

"She also saw him meet up with them on South Street. She thinks they had an argument."

"So Amanda and Kyle arrived together," Lesley said.

Katie nodded. "I got this, too." She held up her phone.

Lesley looked at the photo. "It's not conclusive. But added to everything else, it makes it very likely—"

"That Kyle and Amanda were having an affair."

Lesley nodded. "Arthur found out, and Kyle killed his uncle before Arthur had a chance to punish him."

"You wouldn't want to get caught having it off with Arthur Kelvin's wife," Katie said.

"Especially not if you're his nephew."

Gail's head appeared over the top of the car. "We've got something," she said.

Lesley nodded at Katie then approached the car. "Skin? Blood?"

"A bit of blood and some skin. Not much, but enough." Gail rounded the car, holding a test tube. "I'm going to run tests on it, see if it matches the skin we found in the bathroom."

Lesley's mouth felt dry. Was this really the evidence they needed to take Kyle Kelvin down?

"I'll come with you," she said.

CHAPTER EIGHTY

"Have you got somewhere private I can make a call?" Lesley asked Gail. She held a printout in her hand. The results of the DNA analysis Gail had performed on the blood and skin from Dennis's car.

"Meeting room, just through there." Gail pointed.

Lesley's phone buzzed: a text. She checked it as she closed the door to the meeting room behind her.

Been observing Kelvin house. Kyle Kelvin returned 9:43am today in taxi. Apols for letting him go. PC Truscott.

Lesley resisted kissing her phone.

PC Truscott, you've redeemed yourself.

She smoothed her hands down her skirt, then ran through everything they had in her head.

The DNA. The photo of Kyle and Amanda. The CCTV. The eyewitness sighting of the three of them meeting up. And the images of Kyle's car approaching Sandbanks. They'd find more, she was sure. She'd have preferred it if they had evidence of the Kelvins being closer to the Blue Pool, and of Kyle meeting Amanda in Sandbanks.

But this was enough. It was enough for her to know they had to take Kyle Kelvin into custody. And it was enough for a warrant.

She brought Carpenter's number up on her screen.

She hesitated.

The more dealings she had with the man, the less she trusted him.

She scrolled through her contacts and dialled.

"Chief Superintendent Price, who's calling?"

"Sir, It's DCI Clarke."

"Lesley. Why are you calling me?"

She closed her eyes. "I tried Superintendent Carpenter and he's unavailable, Sir. It is urgent."

"Very well. What is it you need from me?"

"I have sufficient evidence to make an arrest in the Kelvin and Frobisher murders."

"You do?"

"Yes." She ran through the list. "Do you need me to send anything over to your office, Sir?"

"I know your track record, DCI Clarke. I'm inclined to trust your judgement."

"I appreciate that, Sir."

"Only these are serious people. Are you absolutely sure this won't come back to bite us?"

"I am, Sir."

"And you're aware this is going to cause ructions with other units. Potentially other forces."

"I hope the fact we'll be making an arrest and getting a dangerous man off the streets overrides that."

"Again, I'm inclined to agree." He took a long breath. "Very well. Are you on site now?"

"No, Sir."

"Good. That gives me time to make some calls. But you'll have your arrest warrant. Let your Superintendent know as soon as possible though, yes?"

Lesley crossed her fingers. "I will, Sir."

CHAPTER EIGHTY-ONE

LESLEY HURRIED down to the vehicle facility, where Dennis was watching Gavin work on the car.

"Dennis," she said. "Take my car. It's outside. I want you and DC Young to make the arrest."

"Arrest?" Dennis looked shocked.

She nodded. "We've got a warrant to arrest Kyle Kelvin. I want the two of you to go to Arthur Kelvin's house right now and arrest him."

"But Kyle left the hou—"

She shook her head. "He returned there, less than an hour ago."

"He did?" Dennis looked at her. "So why not you, boss?"

"I need to make some calls. I'll make sure an armed unit's waiting when you arrive. Don't go in without them, or until you've spoken to me."

"No." He looked at Katie. "You OK with this?"

Her eyes gleamed. "Of course I am."

"Good," Lesley said. "Now go, before the Chief Superintendent changes his mind."

Dennis gave her an odd look, but said nothing. She handed him her keys and he and Katie hurried to the doors, which Gavin had opened halfway for them.

"Good luck," Lesley muttered as the DS and DC ducked under the door.

She hurried back up the stairs to the meeting room from where she'd called Price. She made the necessary calls to ensure Dennis had backup at the scene, instructing them to wait until he arrived, then sat back in her chair.

Arthur Kelvin: dead. Darren Kelvin: in prison. And Kyle Kelvin: about to be arrested.

Had she got them?

Was Elsa finally safe?

She picked up her phone.

Elsa picked up on the first ring.

"Hi, love. I'm just having a final fitting for my dress."

Lesley smiled. "I bet you look gorgeous."

"That's what the seamstress says. But then it's her job to flatter me."

Lesley smiled. "I want to tell you something."

"OK." Elsa sounded nervous. "You're not jilting me?"

Lesley barked out a laugh. She felt lighter than she had in weeks, like a weight had lifted.

"No chance, Elsa Short. You're stuck with me."

"Good."

"It's about Kyle Kelvin."

A pause. "Oh."

"This is confidential right now as it hasn't happened yet, but—"

"You're about to arrest him." Elsa lowered her voice. "For his uncle's murder."

"You guessed."

"I'm not stupid."

Lesley licked her lips. "Elsa, can you promise me something?"

"I'm going to be promising you a fair bit, on Saturday."

"This is serious."

"OK," Elsa replied. "What do you want me to promise?"

"Promise me that if he or one of his people call you, you won't take him on as a client."

"You thought I would?"

Lesley ground her fist into the table. "I just wanted to be sure."

"You can be sure, sweetie. I just want to be shot of them. I got a call from a potential client this morning. Someone unconnected to them. And I'm hopeful I won't lose this one."

"That's fantastic news." Lesley wiped under her eye. "I'm so glad."

"I told them I can't do anything for a week, though. I've got a honeymoon to enjoy."

Lesley laughed. "And it's going to be the best honeymoon ever."

CHAPTER EIGHTY-TWO

DENNIS PARKED in the car park by Sandbanks beach, anxious not to be visible from the house.

There was no sign of any other police vehicles in the area. Response and firearms units would be easy to spot; they might not all be marked, but he knew what their vans looked like.

He checked his watch. Forty-five minutes since he'd left Dorchester.

"Where are they?" he muttered.

"They'll be here," Katie said.

He looked at her. She was so young.

"Have you ever been involved in an arrest like this?"

"For murder?"

"Or organised crime."

"No." Her expression was tight.

"It'll be fine," he told her. "We hardly do anything. It's the AFOs who do all the hard work."

"You think the Kelvins'll let us through that gate?"

"I doubt it. But my plan is to drive up there, just us, and

press on the buzzer like it's a routine call. He let the boss in yesterday, he might do the same for us today."

Her eyes widened. "Where will the AFOs be?"

"They'll be further along the road, out of sight. As soon as the gates open, we'll pull back and they'll go in." He caught the tension in her face. "Don't worry. You'll be safe. I'll drive away from the house and park at a safe distance. We'll use radio to communicate with the units until they've secured the house."

"You think there will be guns in there?"

"There's a good chance. But the AFOs will secure them."

"So I don't need to go in at all."

"The AFOs and Response unit will restrain Kelvin, and anyone else they need to. They'll ensure any children inside are safe. Then we'll go in. Make the arrest."

Katie's face had paled. Dennis gave her the best smile he could muster.

"It'll be fine," he told her.

"If you say so."

His phone rang.

"Dennis, it's Lesley. The AFO unit is four minutes away. Are you on the scene?"

"I'm in the car park at the beach."

"I'll make sure they know. There'll be Uniform joining you too, someone to deal with any civilians."

"Children, too," Dennis told her. There'd been at least two of them in there.

Poor little mites.

"Don't worry, Dennis," Lesley told him. "This is Kyle Kelvin. I've got half of Dorset Police heading your way."

Dennis blew out a breath. "Thanks, boss."

"Good luck."

He caught movement in his rear-view mirror: a dark blue van, turning into the car park.

"They're here," he said. He hung up, went to the boot of the boss's car, hoping she had stab vests in there, and pulled two out with relief.

Katie was still in the passenger seat. He slid into the driver's seat and handed one to her. "Put this on."

"You said it would be safe."

"And it will be." He looked at her. Surely she'd received training in making high-risk arrests?

"Do you need me to send you away from the scene? Uniform can take you—"

Her brow furrowed. "No. Definitely not."

"Good." *Well make sure you hold your own, then.* "Wait here."

Dennis approached the van, which had parked two spaces away. Luckily in February the car park was quiet and they hadn't attracted attention. That would soon change.

A woman got out of the driver's seat of the van. "DS Frampton, I'm Donna Turnberry."

"We've met." Dennis remembered her from the Lyme Regis case. Her colleague, Christian Davison, had been set up by the Kelvins.

She nodded. "I've spoken to your DCI and shared images with my team of the man we need to arrest."

"Good. There'll probably be an elderly woman in there, too. Nasty piece of work, but not wanted for anything. And children."

A shadow passed over the AFO's face. "We'll need to wait for a regular unit, then. Children freak out when they see us."

She gestured down at her uniform: bulletproof vest, machine gun, shotgun, helmet. Dennis could see her point.

Another van pulled in, this one marked. A man hopped out and approached them.

"PS Wright, Response. You need assistance?"

"We're here to arrest a known organised criminal for murder. There's likely to be guns in the property, but there'll also be children."

Wright nodded. "We'll follow in once the AFOs have pronounced it safe."

Dennis nodded. He knew this was the best he could do. He could only hope those children wouldn't be too badly traumatised.

Someone would need to be making a call to social services, before long.

He looked past the two sergeants as another blue van pulled in.

"They with you?" he asked.

Turnberry turned round. "That's PS Gates's team. What are they doing here?"

The van parked on the other side of the car park. A grey Mercedes followed it in and parked beside it.

A man got out.

Dennis stared at him.

What on earth was going on?

CHAPTER EIGHTY-THREE

DENNIS FELT his jaw clench as DI Gough strode across the car park.

"Dennis," he said. "I wasn't expecting to see you."

No?

"Sir. Can I ask what you're here for?" Dennis asked.

"I could ask you the same."

Dennis sighed. "We have a warrant to arrest Kyle Kelvin for murder."

"Funny, that. I've got a warrant to arrest him for importation."

Dennis struggled to contain his frustration. "This is murder. I have two units here, and we're ready to go. We don't nee—"

Gough put a hand on Dennis's shoulder. Dennis shrugged it off.

"Look, DS Frampton. We've been watching Kyle Kelvin for months. Working alongside the Devon force. This is one of the biggest inter-force operations the South West has seen in years."

Dennis considered. He wondered what the boss would do.

But he wasn't the boss.

"OK," he said. "We both want him. Between us, we've got two armed units." He turned to Turnberry. "You've worked together on operations like this before, yes?"

"Of course."

"In that case I think we should coordinate our efforts." Dennis watched Gough's face for a reaction. "The two armed units can work together, we have one regular unit, and you and I can discuss which of us makes the arrest."

"I'm sorry, Sergeant. But it'll be me." Gough turned to Turnberry. "OK. Here's what's going to happen."

"With respect, Sir," Turnberry said, "if we don't move quickly, then Kelvin will know we're here. My unit will go in the front of the house. Gates's unit can go along the beach, make sure no one gets out that way. We'll secure the property, make sure Gates's team have got the civilians safe, and then leave either one of you to make the arrest."

Gough stared at her. "Very well."

Thank goodness for that. "Good," Dennis said. He wasn't going to argue about who made the arrest just yet. This would be something for the DCI to sort out. "Kelvin's met me before, he doesn't consider me a threat. He's more likely to open the gate if I'm the one asking him to." He waited a moment, and Gough nodded. "OK. Let's move."

Turnberry withdrew to her van. Dennis rushed back to the DCI's car and jumped in.

"Here we go," he breathed to Katie.

"What's going on? I didn't know there'd be so many of us."

"Don't ask."

He drove towards the Kelvin house and pulled up outside. He gave Katie a final nod, then got out and strode to the intercom.

He hit the buzzer.

"Hello?"

"DS Frampton, Dorset Police. I'd like to speak with Mr Kyle Kelvin, please."

"One moment."

He watched the gate, resisting an urge to tap his foot. *Act calm.*

At last the intercom crackled. "Come in."

Dennis wanted to punch the air. He glanced back at Katie in the car and grabbed his radio.

He turned away from the camera and put it to his lips.

"Pedestrian gate opening."

"Stand back."

Dennis walked away from the gate as it clicked open. As he reached the point where the driveway met the road, the blue van drew up and four AFOs jumped out. They ran to the gate and pushed it open.

Dennis leapt into the car and drove away. He parked a few houses along.

"What now?" Katie asked him.

"We stay put until they've done their job."

He turned in his seat, anxious to know what was happening. His phone rang.

"Boss."

"Dennis, have you got this yet?"

"The AFOs are inside right now. The Kelvins opened the gate, thank God."

"Good."

"There's a problem, though."

"What?"

"Another unit turned up. DI Gough from Organised Crime. He's saying he'll make the arrest, as he outranks me."

"Shit. The interfering bastard." A pause. "He's only done this cos he heard we were going in. Fuck."

Dennis flinched at each swear word. He rubbed his forehead.

"The important thing is we get him, boss."

"It's murder, Dennis. It trumps whatever they have."

"We don't know that."

She sighed. "You've got my car so I can't even join you. Shit."

"I'm sorry, boss. There wasn't much I could—"

"It's OK. I'll deal with it. You just do whatever's needed to make sure Kyle is in custody. We'll sort out the charges later."

"Boss."

She hung up.

"Trouble?" Katie asked.

A voice came from Dennis's radio.

"Yes?" he said.

"House secured. Only one civilian. An elderly woman. She's giving us a right tongue-lashing."

"And Kyle Kelvin?"

"He's right with us. You want to come in and arrest him?"

CHAPTER EIGHTY-FOUR

"Shh, little one. It'll be over soon."

Tina rocked Louis, hoping his cries wouldn't travel to the front of the room. They were in a posh hotel in Bournemouth, right at the back of the wedding guests. Mike had wanted to be sure they could make a hasty exit if it got too much.

She shifted Louis higher up her shoulder and grabbed Mike's hand. "This was us, not all that long ago."

He winked at her. "You had a few more problems with your dress than the boss's new wife did, though."

She pulled a face at him. Yes, it hadn't been easy getting a dress fitted when her stomach wouldn't stop growing. But it had been worth it. She'd wanted to be settled before Louis came along. To get the formal stuff out of the way.

"You wish I'd been slimmer?" she asked him.

He turned to her. "Of course not." He kissed the side of her neck, making her shiver. "You were gorgeous."

Tina shrugged. The size of a house, but she had looked pretty good, even so. Her mum and sister had made sure of it.

"Anyway," Mike said. "Our venue was nicer."

She squeezed his hand tighter. The top floor of a pub overlooking the bay in Lyme Regis, it didn't get much better than that. All her extended family there, Mike's mum travelling over from Poole. And only one sarcastic comment about her 'condition'.

The boss and her wife turned to face the crowd. Their hands were clasped together, their faces bright with happiness.

"Who'd have known, when I met her in the lane down from Corfe Castle over a year ago," Tina said, "that I'd be at her wedding."

"Her wedding to a criminal lawyer, to boot."

Tina raised an eyebrow. "They're not all bad."

Mike had his eye on Elsa. "Hmmm."

She poked the side of his stomach. "What? What d'you know about her?"

"Only who she used to represent."

"He's dead now," she reminded him. "His house has been seized, his nephews both in custody. He's gone."

"Good riddance."

"You've done the interviews?" she asked.

He nodded. "Me and Vick from Organised Crime. The boss delegated it. Skipped the sarge." He shifted from foot to foot. He hadn't passed on to Tina what Stanley had told him; it felt disloyal.

Although now he was being disloyal to his wife. He couldn't win.

"Not sure why," he added, convinced she'd spot the lie.

But Tina was focused on the baby. "Busy planning her wedding," she said, smiling into Louis's face and tickling his tummy.

"Indeed. But what about him?" Mike's gaze went to the DS, two rows in front.

Tina shrugged. The sarge had been acting odd, but she had too much on her plate to worry about it. "But Kyle tried to pin it on Amanda, didn't he?"

Mike turned to her. "Shush."

"No one can hear us."

She was right. The row in front of them was empty; a baby buffer.

Meanwhile, Louis had fallen asleep on her shoulder.

"Bloody heavy, he is," she said. She kissed the top of her son's head.

"He did," Mike said. "My theory is they plotted it together. Not that there's much point in pursuing it, what with her being—"

"Dead," Tina said.

Mike sniffed.

The happy couple turned to the crowd. The registrar said something Tina couldn't make out.

"I've got something to ask you," Mike said, watching the newlyweds as they made their way through the crowd of well-wishers. The two of them – the three of them, Tina reminded herself – would be last.

"You've already asked me to move in with you," she said, "to have your baby and to marry you. What's left?"

"I didn't ask you to have my baby."

"You asked me not to—"

He shook his head. "Let's not talk about that."

"OK. What do you want to ask me?"

He turned to her. "T, would you prefer to share your parental leave with me? The boss suggested it. You can come back to—"

She put a hand on his cheek. "Yes. Yes, Mike. I'll do it."

CHAPTER EIGHTY-FIVE

DENNIS WAS STILL ANNOYED with himself for not being more assertive with DI Gough. Organised Crime had made the arrest, despite his protests. If he'd tried any harder, it would have been embarrassing, what with Kyle Kelvin watching them with that awful smirk on his face. Not to mention the old woman.

He was also annoyed with himself for not persuading his wife Pam to accompany him to the wedding.

She'd never liked police dos, but this wasn't work. It was a wedding. And she'd woken up with one of her heads, the kind that meant she needed to be left alone in a darkened room. If he wasn't going to miss it, he'd have to come alone.

But he wasn't alone, was he? Stanley was here, and Gail with her little boy. Neither of them had spouses to bring along.

He sat back in his chair and sipped at the brandy Gail had bought him. It was good. Strong. Pam would smell it on his breath and be unimpressed.

But he'd earned it.

He felt a hand on the back of his chair and turned.

"Mike," he said. "How's the baby?"

"Settled in his pushchair," Mike replied. "Tina and I are hoping to relax a bit."

Dennis smiled across at Tina, bent over a pushchair in a far corner. It brought back memories.

"You make a lovely family," he said.

"Thanks." Mike looked nervous.

"Everything OK?" Dennis asked him.

Mike tugged on his tie. "Can we have a word in private?"

Dennis glanced at Stanley, deep in conversation with Gail.

"We can." He rose from his chair and followed Mike out of the room. As they passed Tina, Mike grabbed her arm and whispered in her ear.

Outside the function room, Mike stopped and leaned against a wall. Dennis watched him.

"You seem nervous," he said.

"Do I? Oh. Sorry. Yeah." Mike looked back at the doors to the function room. "Tina and I need to ask you if we can share her maternity leave. It was the DCI's idea—"

"Then in that case, there's not much I can do to stop it."

"You're OK with it?"

Dennis inhaled. "You're a more experienced DC than Tina. But you're both valuable members of the team. And I'm sure that whichever of you is in the office, we'll get two for one."

Mike gave him a sheepish smile. "Sorry about that."

"It's fine. She helped us identify the killer."

"Or killers."

"I don't think we'll ever really know the answer to that one."

"No."

Dennis looked at Mike. The DC wasn't meeting his eye.

"Is there something else, Mike?"

Mike kicked the wall lightly. "There is." He still didn't make eye contact.

"A problem?"

"I don't know."

"Just tell me what it is. It's chilly out here."

Mike looked up and rubbed his arm as if only realising that for the first time. "Stanley found some bank statements. Well, the CSIs did, but Stanley told me about them."

Dennis looked back at the doors. "So why are you telling me about it now? Is this evidence, in the Kelvin case?"

"The bank statements showed money going from Kelvin's account. Regular payments."

"To whom?" Dennis felt his skin tighten.

"To... to your son. Or at least, someone with the same name as your son."

"To Jacob?"

Mike nodded, his head down.

Dennis shook his head. "To Jacob? Are you sure?"

Mike looked up. "There aren't a lot of Jacob Framptons around."

"No. But..."

Dennis considered.

Jacob?

It made no sense.

"Leave it with me, Mike," he said.

"Of course."

"And..."

Mike was almost back at the doors. "Yeah?"

"And keep it between you and me, will you? Until we get to the bottom of it?"

Mike blushed. "I'm sorry, Sarge."

Dennis felt his heart pick up pace. "Sorry about what?"

"Well... since we pressed charges against Kyle... you know this is a joint case. Organised Crime are involved."

Dennis closed his eyes. "And they have access to all the evidence."

"Yes."

"It's fine." Dennis brushed a bead of sweat from his brow. "Don't worry."

"No. OK."

Dennis forced a smile. "Let's go back in. See that baby of yours."

CHAPTER EIGHTY-SIX

LESLEY THREW herself into the wedding car and scooted up to let Elsa in beside her. Elsa had tight hold of her hand.

She stared into her wife's eyes, feeling her smile grow.

"We did it," she said.

"We did." Elsa leaned in and kissed her on the lips. Lesley heard a cheer from outside the car.

"Now for Scotland."

"Indeed." Elsa pulled back and met Lesley's gaze, her eyes full of fire. "I can't wait."

There was thumping on the window behind them. Lesley turned to see Sharon mouthing something through the glass.

She put the window down. "What is it, love?"

"You didn't throw the bouquet."

Lesley exchanged glances with Elsa. "Which bouquet?" They both had small bouquets of forget-me-nots and bluebells.

Sharon smiled. "Yours, Mum."

Elsa lifted her hands to reveal they were empty. Empty apart from her new wedding ring, that was.

Lesley looked down at the battered bunch of flowers in her lap. If Sharon hadn't told her, she'd have had no idea which blooms were in it.

She held it out. "Here, you have it."

Sharon grabbed it.

"You got someone in mind?" Elsa asked.

"No way," Sharon replied. "I just think they'd look nice in the flat."

"You're going back there?" Lesley asked. "Your dad didn't—"

"It's fine, Mum. I'll pop back there tonight, dump my stuff and get changed, then I'm staying with Gail before I get the train to Brum."

Lesley grabbed her daughter's hand through the window. "We'll be back in a week. You look after yourself."

"I'll be fine."

"Say hello to your dad for me."

Sharon looked back at her mum. "I will."

Lesley withdrew her hand and grabbed Elsa's. "If that's all?" she asked Sharon.

"It is. Have a wonderful time, both of you."

"We will," Elsa replied.

Lesley closed the window and turned to her wife. "Congratulations, Mrs Clarke."

"Congratulations, Mrs Short."

Lesley laughed. Neither of them had the slightest intention of changing their name. Clarke was Terry's name, but it was Sharon's too. Lesley wanted to preserve that.

Elsa put an arm around her. Someone was drumming on

the roof of the car. People pushed towards them, cameras clicking, smiles on all sides.

"Can you drive?" Lesley called to the driver.

"Of course," the woman replied.

Lesley settled back into her seat.

"I want you to make me a promise," Elsa said as she snaked her arm around Lesley's waist.

Lesley wriggled in next to her. "Go on."

"We're about to have a week in some gorgeous Scottish countryside."

"We are."

"And I know your track record when it comes to beauty spots."

Lesley looked up at her. "I'm not sure what you mean."

Elsa raised an eyebrow and counted them off on her fingers. "Corfe Castle. Brownsea Island. Lyme Bay. Blue Pool."

"Oh. That." Lesley kissed Elsa's hand.

"Just promise me there'll be no murders while we're on honeymoon," Elsa said.

"I promise," Lesley told her.

CHAPTER EIGHTY-SEVEN

"Pam love, I'm home!"

The house was dark. Dennis checked his watch: eight thirty. Was Pam still in bed?

"Pam?" he called.

"In here," she said. Her voice had come from the living room. It sounded strained. At least she was out of bed.

Dennis took a detour via the kitchen to flick the kettle on. He needed something, after that brandy.

It had been a lovely day, but the conversation with Mike had worried him. And he knew it would have been better with Pam there.

He opened the living room door. "I'm sorry, love. You didn't miss much."

"Dennis."

He stopped in his tracks.

Pam was on the sofa, perched at one end. In the armchair, a man he knew.

"DI Gough," Dennis said. "What brings you here, on a Saturday evening?"

Gough stood up. He gave Pam an uneasy look.

"I think it's best if we do this in the kitchen, don't you?"

Dennis looked at him. "I don't understand. Do what?"

Was this about the arrest? Gough had got his way. What could he possibly want with Dennis now?

Gough drew a breath, making a small whistling sound. Dennis watched him.

There was a knock at the door.

Gough took a step towards Dennis.

"Shall I get that?" Pam asked.

Gough smiled at her. "Don't trouble yourself. It's for me."

Dennis frowned at him. "What's going on?" He licked his lips. "Sir."

Gough looked from Dennis to Pam and back again. "I'm sorry to have to do this, DS Frampton."

"Do what?"

Gough took another step forward. Dennis shrank back. Gough grabbed his arm.

Dennis looked down.

What are you doing, man?

He looked into Gough's eyes. The man was no more than a foot away. Dennis could smell cigarettes on his breath.

"Dennis Frampton," Gough said. "I'm arresting you on suspicion of murder. You d—"

Pam gasped. Her hands flew to her face.

"Murder?" Dennis said. "*Murder?*"

"You do not have to say anything," Gough continued, "but it may harm your defence if—"

"I'm sorry," Dennis said. "But you've made a mistake."

"It may harm your defence if you do not mention when

questioned something that you later rely on in Court. Anything you do say may be given in evidence."

Dennis felt Gough's hand tighten around his arm. He should shake it off.

But if this was real, if he was really under arrest... then resisting arrest would make it worse.

He let Gough steer him towards the door. The knock came again.

"Alright, alright," Gough muttered.

As they reached the hallway, Dennis stiffened. Gough stopped moving.

"Frampton," he said. "You don't want to make this any worse for yourself."

"Who? Whose murder is it I'm supposed to have committed?"

Gough gave him a *you don't know?* look. He cleared his throat.

"Tim Mackie," he said. "You're under arrest for the murder of former DCI Tim Mackie."

———

Thanks for reading *The Blue Pool Murders*.

Did Dennis kill DCI Mackie? Can Lesley uncover the truth and ensure justice is done? Find out in The Lighthouse Murders, out in April 2023.

READ A FREE PREQUEL NOVELLA, THE BALLARD DOWN MURDER

How did DCI Mackie die?

DS Dennis Frampton is getting used to life without his old boss DCI Mackie, and managing to hide how much he hates being in charge of Dorset's Major Crimes Investigation Team. Above all, he must ensure no one knows he's still seeking Mackie's advice on cases.

But then Mackie doesn't show up to a meeting, and a body is found below the cliffs a few miles away.

When Dennis discovers the body is his old friend and mentor, his world is thrown upside down. Did Mackie kill himself, or was he pushed? Is Dennis's new boss trying to hush things up? And can Dennis and the CSIs trust the evidence?

Find out by reading *The Ballard Down Murder* for FREE at rachelmclean.com/ballard.

READ THE DORSET CRIME SERIES

Buy now in ebook, paperback or audiobook

ALSO BY RACHEL MCLEAN

Printed in Great Britain
by Amazon

24778967R00199